Dear Reader:

I am proud to introduce a new author, Ruth P. Watson, whose *Blackberry Days of Summer* conjures up images of *The Color Purple*. *Blackberry Days* is a compelling look at African-American life post-World War I, with an interesting and original set of characters. Herman is a womanizer who eventually becomes involved with three women: his wife, Mae Lou; her daughter, Carrie; and a nightclub singer, Pearl. It is about lust, adultery and coming of age; combining romance and suspense.

Against the Southern backdrop of rural Virginia, the novel unravels and leads to a murder, and all become suspects in a complicated web of deceit. It is an intimate look into the world of strangers and their relationships. Ruth plants the seed of a fascinating literary novel as she makes her debut on the author scene.

Thanks also for supporting the dozens of other authors that I publish under Strebor Books. We truly appreciate the love. For more information on our titles, please visit www.zanestore.com and simonandschuster.com, and you can find me on my personal website: www.eroticanoir.com. You can also join my online social network at www.planetzane.org

Blessings,

Zane

Zane
Publisher
Strebor Books
www.simonsays.com/streborbooks

ZANE PRESENTS

BLACKBERRY DAYS OF SUMMER

RUTH P. WATSON

SBI

STREBOR BOOKS

NEW YORK LONDON TORONTO SYDNEY

Strebor Books
P.O. Box 6505
Largo, MD 20792
http://www.streborbooks.com

This book is a work of fiction. Names, characters, places and incidents are products of the author's imagination or are used fictitiously. Any resemblance to actual events or locales or persons, living or dead, is entirely coincidental.

ISBN 978-1-59309-413-3
ISBN 978-1-4516-5564-3 (e-book)
LCCN 2011938327

First Strebor Books trade paperback edition June 2012

Cover design: www.mariondesigns.com
Cover photograph: © Keith Saunders/Marion Designs

10 9 8 7 6 5 4 3 2 1

Manufactured in the United States of America

In memory of my parents, Paige and Mary Virginia,
and the stories shared about a time that is old, yet familiar.
To my grandmothers, I feel your heavenly smiles every day.
For the World War I veterans, and others who saw the need to fight.

ACKNOWLEDGMENTS

For everyone who has dared to dream, I thank you. For it is by faith I have waited for this blessing. I can only say, "To God be the glory for the things he has done."

To my ancestors, who passed the torch of history to me, and to the writers who shared their gift for the written word, I thank you.

Everyone has a story to tell and many people encouraged the one burning deep inside me to flourish into this novel. Thank you everyone for the nudge. To those who said I could write this in the beginning thank you; Andrea Peyton, Andretta Rivers, Cecelia Barksdale, Waple Griffin, Vera Lewis, Sharon Akinsowon, Linda Ashford, Towana White, Celestine Brabble, Lori Weems, Marilyn Brown, Carlisa Lewis, Tiffany Pelton, Betty Walker, Ned Cole, MaiLan Bell and Sardale Jones. It would have been hard to accomplish this without the support of lasting friends, Rhea Bumbrey, Kay Farrow-Smith, Cheryl Jennings-Spence, Sharon Johnson Colemore, Janet Ferguson, Betty Payne, Twyla Banks, Jean Booker, Rosalind Sousa Neal, and Naomi Johnson. Thanks Karen Skinner, Cleo Smith, and Vanessa Lovelace for finding me after all these years.

To my wonderful students, who are artists in their own right, keep doing what you do, and never settle for a no, or a can't, while reaching for your goals.

Thanks to my writer friends for unselfishly sharing bits of what you knew about publishing with me. What you said was valuable. To my first news editor, David Gibson, thanks for the opportunity. To bestselling author Barbara Bretton, and book reviewer, Shica Robinson Bowen, thanks for not hesitating to read my manuscript. To the Southwest Cascade Library Book Club Members, the Cascade United Methodist Church Communications Committee, the Alpharetta-Smyrna Kappa Alpha Psi Silhouettes and The Sisterhood of The Atlanta Alumnae Chapter of Delta Sigma Theta Sorority Inc., thank you for being there.

Thank you so much Sara Camilli for working tirelessly to open this door for me. To Zane of Strebor Books, I am honored to have you as my publisher, and Charmaine Parker, you are the best. To the Simon & Schuster team, wow, and thanks. To the bookclubs and bookstores who continue to uplift authors by reading and promoting our books, I appreciate you.

To my family who are my biggest cheerleaders, I love you. To my husband, and son, you are the reason I do what I do.

To you all, I'm honored.

CHAPTER 1
CARRIE

Mr. Camm barely waited for Papa to be put in the ground. The next day he slithered into our house, mesmerizing Momma with his poison as she lay down with him. That was when all my troubles started.

I vividly remember the awful day when Papa was summoned to die. It was around two o'clock in the afternoon. The thermometer hanging over the kitchen door read ninety-five degrees, and the gray cotton dress I was wearing clung to my back like molasses to a pancake. Momma sat at the kitchen table gazing blankly out the window. The lines in her face were forged by misfortune and her round chestnut-colored eyes were cloudy with sad tears that trickled down her cocoa cheeks. She blotted her eyes with her hanky, but they continued to leak like a river that had long overflowed.

"Y'all come on in and sit down," she mumbled in a voice so muted I hardly recognized it.

My brothers and I each pulled out a chair and sat down. We were not used to seeing her so broken. Usually she was on her feet handing out orders.

"Why are you crying? What's wrong with ya, Momma?" Carl asked, patting her gently on the shoulder.

Her lips trembled as she said softly, "It's your papa. He done took sick. He been complaining of a headache and now his lips are twisted to one side. He can't even stand up. He ain't doing good."

We glanced at each other with puzzled frowns and waited for someone to figure out what to do. But nobody did.

"What can we do?" Carl asked with the same authority my papa would have used if he'd been feeling well.

"Be there for him, he's gonna need you," Momma said.

When I saw Papa lying there in the bed helpless, with his eyes rolled back in his head, tears welled up in my eyes. Papa was a big black man, over six feet five inches tall, and strong as a horse. He never smoked or drank liquor the way most men wished away their troubles, mistresses, or debts. We all believed his mind and his body were solid, too strong to be ravaged by sickness.

Papa had grown up a free man. His daddy had inherited land from his father, given to him by his master, who felt that good service should be rewarded. When the master was fifty years old, dry and nearly dead from pneumonia, he deeded my grandpa some land for all of his hard labor. Yet, even though Papa owned the land, he cut corners every way he could to pay the taxes. Sometimes the profit from his tobacco crop was only enough to break even. He'd help other farmers on Saturday evenings cut down trees or whatever little he could do, all in an effort to make extra cash. He raised pigs, and no matter how many he hung in the smokehouse, our family was only allowed one ham, which was saved and cooked at Christmas.

When I went into his bedroom and saw him lying there, I fell to my knees and began to pray: *Heavenly Father, who's going to take care of us? We need our papa. Please make him well. Amen.*

Momma was both frightened and saddened by Papa's illness. During his sickness, she sat in the rocking chair beside his bed all night and watched him sleep, massaging her temples with the balls of her thumbs and holding her head back while staring at the ceiling, waiting for a sign. Dark circles cast shadows under her big, beautiful eyes. Her hair was frizzled, unattended to, and stuck to one side of her head. Papa was the love of her life even though she never seemed to know how to respond to his affectionate ways, especially the nights when he would stroke her cheeks as they sat close on the porch watching the lightning bugs and counting the stars. She'd ease away from his attention, and he would only shake his head. To see Momma showing her love for Papa now was a clear message to us all: our world was falling apart.

We kept expecting Papa to stand up, stick his big chest out and head right back to the field, anxious to weed the garden, and see if his seeds were sprouting.

Papa moaned and tossed and turned all night, and then when he had enough, he closed his eyes. It was half past four in the afternoon, so hot outside that a drop of water would sizzle if it hit the dry, red dirt. Momma hung her head low and covered her eyes. That's when I knew. I cried until my eyes were swollen almost shut. All I could do was grip her shoulders and hold her tight. A part of me died that day with my papa.

Momma cried out, "I'd seen this day coming. It come to me in my dream the night before it happened; he fell right down in the field, arms pointing east and west, and I couldn't revive him. He was too stubborn to slow down and rest, didn't think anybody could work as hard as he could. I begged him the otha mawnin' to stay inside and he stared me straight in the eyes, put on that ole straw hat and walked out the door. You see, Tuesday was da sun's day. He lay right down in da sun and began to die. Sho nuff did."

Carl drove the two mules down to Aunt Bessie's to pick her up.

We knew that Momma would need the comfort of her sister. I stood in the frame of her bedroom door and watched her take cash out of an old cigar box she kept under her bed. She handed the crumpled money to the rough-looking white man in bib overalls with red dirt glued under his fingernails who'd come from the undertakers. Afterward, he and a field hand put the casket in the front room and left.

Even before the minister arrived to bless Papa's body, Momma and Bessie went in the kitchen and took out some herbs from the cabinet. They went into the bedroom, where Papa was still lying, washed his body from head to toe, and then rubbed the herbs on him. They dressed him in the only black suit he owned—the one he wore to funerals and church on Sundays.

"Bessie, Lord knows that Robert would want us to be strong, but it's hard," Momma said, battling back tears. I knew it was tough because crying was a sign of weakness in her mind.

"He looks like he is just sleeping, Mae Lou," Bessie said, buttoning up Papa's suit jacket and staring down at the corpse.

"He's been struggling all of his life with the mighty sun suffering for a long while, and now God got him, no more fighting." Momma said as she folded Papa's hands across his wide chest. Papa died only a few days after his thirty-eighth birthday.

Bessie sat down in the high-back chair Papa used to sit in, and she stared Momma right in the eyes. "How you gonna run the farm without a man around?"

"I don't know."

"You need a man, Mae Lou."

"Everybody needs a man around, but it ain't right to think about that now."

"Well, it's hard when ya all alone," she said, and began to rock as the thought of being alone lingered in the air.

My papa lay in the front room for two days before I decided to talk to him. After everyone went to bed, I lit a candle and took tiny steps down the shadowed gray hallway to his casket, careful not to knock over anything. The floors creaked and the blackness was all over the country at night. Through the window I noticed only a few stars sprinkled across the midnight sky. I reached the front room without anyone hearing me, and the metal hinge in the casket screeched as I opened it. I wasn't afraid of dead people because Momma and Papa said that the dead couldn't hurt you no way.

An eerie feeling crept over me when I glanced down at Papa's stiff body and leathery skin, sunburned almost black. Tears leaked out the corners of my eyes as I leaned over his corpse and began to speak to him. The candlelight cast my moving shadow on the wall, but I still wasn't afraid. I stood sobbing as droplets of my tears lingered on his burial suit.

"Oh, Papa, I'm going to miss you," I whispered. "I'm sorry you had to die, and I know this house will not be the same." I leaned over and kissed his comatose cheek. "I'm going to be okay, though. I'm going to get away from around here and go to college, like you wanted me to do. I promise, I'm going to make you proud."

I said things to Papa that night that I should have said before he passed. After I finished, I felt relieved. I dried my tears with the back of my hands and went back to my room. Somehow, I knew that he had heard me. I knew that Papa didn't want me to cry for him. Aunt Bessie was right, he looked like he was sleeping, free of all labor and pain, a look of peace permanent on his face.

We grieved for over a week before we buried Papa. If the smell of rotten flesh had not gotten unbearable, he probably would have lain in the front room longer. Members of the New Covenant Baptist Church drove their buggies to our house. Papa was on the board of deacons and everyone respected him. Countless folks brought us fried chicken and ham and potato pies.

The day of the funeral was hard for us. Saying good-bye to my father felt like something I treasured had been ripped away from my arms. The deacons arrived at our house early on that Sunday morning. And like the day he died, the sun stood at attention and peeked at us through the clouds. They loaded Papa's body onto a wagon to take to the church a few miles down the road. When they lifted the casket and slid it onto the wagon, I cried out. I'd felt comforted with his stiff body sleeping in the front room. The deacon with the lazy eye told me to be at peace. I went quiet, but snorted back salty tears all the way to the church.

All during the service, Mr. Camm stood close to Momma as if he knew her and Papa. He even offered her his handkerchief, but she didn't have tears. She looked up at him and he grinned, like a man does with a pretty woman. He reached over and softly touched her on the arm. She didn't flinch.

Papa was buried in the cemetery behind the church, like most of his family. He was buried a few feet from his mother. His daddy was buried in the slave cemetery on the plantation. My brothers fought back tears all through the service, yet Momma still didn't cry. I suppose she had done all her crying at home.

Momma stood at the foot of his grave for ten minutes after the service was complete. We were the last people to leave the graveyard. We even waited until the deacons and the grave attendant had covered Papa's casket with dirt. Then Carl drove us home.

Nobody said a word. Some of the same people who came with us to the church followed us home to celebrate Papa's homegoing.

Mr. Camm came, too, though he shouldn't have been there. I frowned at him, unsettled by his walnut-colored skin and dark, beady eyes set deep in his head. I noticed him peering at me, watching my every move, staring openly without blinking. Words don't do justice to how uncomfortable he made me feel.

He had that effect on a lot of people. It was no wonder that so many people wanted him dead.

CHAPTER 2
PEARL

I watched the new Model T Fords steer around the street cars and horse-driven buggies on Pennsylvania Avenue, as I headed to the LeDroit Park neighborhood, where I performed near Howard University. Folks liked to unwind at the colored restaurants and clubs along "The Colored Broadway." It was a steamy night, and folks with wide grins were delighted to rid themselves of their worries, as if they were shedding their jackets. For two years people had prayed for the safe return of the soldiers fighting in Europe, but this Friday night, in 1919, the spirit was different.

An anxious crowd had been gathering long before the orange sun slid behind the clouds. The nightclub in Northwest D.C. where I performed hadn't seen this much action since Bessie Smith and her big voice packed the joint last summer. As I walked inside, the only lights were candles flickering on each table throwing shadows of heads bouncing across the room. The smooth sound of a blues recording and the jovial laughter of the crowd reverberated throughout the place.

The bartender was busy wiping beads of sweat from his brow with a handkerchief while filling jugs of beer and providing the ever popular setup of liquor and Coke. I took a table in the back that provided me a view of everyone who came through the door. Sitting with my long legs crossed, I watched everyone and everything. I waved to the bartender, Roy, with my red handkerchief.

He always kept his eye on me. I wasn't bothered by him being ten years younger, because he was a tender man who cared for me like I was his woman. He strutted toward me, swinging his thick muscular arms and grinning, showing me all of his beautiful white teeth.

"Can I get someth'n' for ya, Miz Pearl?"

I leaned over the wood table, exposing the cleavage of my heavy breasts. "Sit down for a moment. You know I don't like to sit alone."

He pulled up a chair and eased down in it, gaping at me lustfully. His mysterious large eyes always seemed to be reading people, figuring out things about them.

"I've got to do the bartending, Miz Pearl; can't stay long." His large eyes darted around the room, checking out the traffic. "It's a lot of peoples coming in here."

"I thought we'd have some time, Roy, to catch up on things. How's that girl you had your eyes on the other night?"

"Miz Pearl, I don't know who you are talkin' about. I don't have a girl."

"You sure about this."

"Yes, ma'am," Roy replied without looking her in the eyes, but still scanning the room for new arrivals.

"I've got to go back to the bar, Miz Pearl. Two men are waiting to be served."

I rubbed his shoulder and whispered low and seductive in his ear, "You're right. I need a drink."

"Yes, ma'am." He shivered like a chill had come over his body. I smiled slyly. I had been doing that to young men, and old men too, ever since I was a teenager in the country. My mamma told me that I had grown up with the kind of body that men craved. She said, "Be careful; some of 'em don't mean you no good."

"You're all right, Roy?" I asked.

"Yes, ma'am," he said and cleared his throat.

He sat still for a moment, like he needed to gain his composure, and then asked, "Is there someth'n' else, Miz Pearl?"

"No, baby; some gin and lemon will do fine."

He headed back to the bar, a lot faster than he had come. The room had begun to fill with patrons. People hovered around the bar, anticipating service. The women sat elegantly with their legs crossed and bright red lipstick smeared on their lips, waiting for the men to deliver their drinks. Before Roy waited on them, he rushed back to me carrying a gin and tonic in one hand and a saucer of lemon slices in another.

"Anything else, Miz Pearl?" he asked.

"No, thank you; this is good."

He grinned at me as if I had made his night.

I couldn't believe I had settled in this place. After doing nightclubs and even performing a couple of times as a backup for Ethel Waters in New York City, I was still doing the local scene. When I first came to Washington, D.C. in 1902, I was convinced that after a year or so I would be traveling around the country. I could sing, and everybody felt I was prettier than Ethel. I liked being tall, curvy, caramel, and gorgeous. Men whispered in my ear, begging for my company. I never left the house without a little nutmeg powder and lipstick. I was an elegant colored girl. I could read and made sure I clearly enunciated every word I spoke. Why not? It had gotten me in places other coloreds were not allowed. I had performed twice at the Washington Supper Club for a crowd of white politicians; I was the only colored in the house. One of the blue-eyed darlings wanted to take me home, but as tempting as the proposal was, I had to decline. I couldn't help thinking how the white man had been raping me in some form my entire life.

"Miz Pearl, you all right?"

I looked up to find Roy still standing in front of me. "You're on in twenty minutes," he said.

"All right, thanks," I said, and smiled.

The room was full by now. Heads were bobbing as the tunes spun on the hand-cranked record player. The better places had the new jukeboxes. Soldiers were finally coming home after being gone for a year or two. Most of them had signed up to gain dignity in a country where a colored man had no respect. My Willie would be coming home soon, too, I reflected. That thought didn't fill me with any joy, though. I'd urged him to enlist so I could get rid of him. How in the hell was I going to deal with his ass when he returned?

"Hey, baby."

I glanced up and there stood Herman Camm, a man small in stature, with a dark tan, and sexy beady dark eyes that penetrated like an arrow. Herman was smooth; his voice sharp and cultured. He knew how to dress and he loved women, especially me. So when I saw my reflection bounce back at me from the spit shine on his Stacy Adams shoes, I smiled.

The first time I saw him had been in this same club. He had come in one night wearing a brown suit with a wide collar, and pants with cuffs. On his head was a wide brim Fedora that tilted down over one eye. He was the best dressed man in the place, and everybody took notice. The regulars waved at him as he made his way through the crowd toward the back room where gambling took place.

Later that evening, he stood at the bar watching me sing. When I was done, he came over to my table. "I love what you do," he had said, grinning.

"Thank you. Why don't you have a seat?" I motioned him over

in invitation. The confident way he carried himself was intriguing, and he was friendly, yet often by himself. I had heard mention that he was top dog at the poker table, and one of the best crap shooters around.

He pulled a chair out and sat down. "You are a beautiful woman, and tonight I need a little company," he said, sipping on scotch and water.

"I'm spoken for, I got a man," I commented.

"I don't see anybody around," he said, scanning the room.

"My husband is in the war," I replied.

"Oh yeah? So tell me," he said, and gestured, studying me, "how could a man in his right mind leave a woman like you all alone?"

"Who said I was alone?"

"Where's your man then?"

He was a bold fellow, and his charisma strongly attracted me. I had seen him on many occasions before, flashing fists full of greenbacks. He would buy drinks for a table simply because, and I had a thing for generosity, especially when it came free, no strings attached.

"He's across the sea fighting for his country."

"Well, while he is fighting for the white man, I am going to fight for you," he said.

And from then on, we started spending time together. After a while, I forgot about being married to a World War I soldier, for it seemed like I couldn't get enough of Herman Camm. So as he stood in front of me now, I couldn't help thinking about how he had mesmerized me the first night we met.

"Sit down," I said, and watched the smile light up his face.

Before he sat down, he kissed me lightly on the forehead. From his breath I felt warmth flow from my neck to my shoulders. He instantly grabbed my hand under the table, then he cautiously rubbed my thigh, strumming his fingers up and down my stockings.

"Herman, why do you always do that?" I asked him, enjoying every bit of his inviting touch.

"I don't want you to forget who you're singing for tonight."

I blushed and wondered how this thin man, barely an inch taller than I was, could get next to me and make me want to sing to him.

He tapped me on the thigh. "It's almost time, baby. The crowd wants you."

I sipped on the rest of my gin and tonic to warm up my pipes. As I waited at my corner table, with Herman squeezing my hand, I noticed two women from my past standing at the bar. Both of them were attractive, yet out of place. I pointed them out to Herman.

"I don't know them, Pearl," he answered nervously as if he had something to hide. "Our paths never crossed."

"I know them."

They were dressed as if they had walked into the club mistakenly believing it was a church. The petite one even had on a Sunday hat. They sure stuck out in the crowd. Many nights over the years, Jefferson County, Virginia residents had showed up at the club yearning to hear me sing. Around these parts I was a celebrity, more popular than Bessie or any of the Ma Rainey crew. To the country folks, I was it.

I finished my drink, stood up and brushed the wrinkles out of my dress. The crowd started to clap as soon as they recognized me. Being five feet ten inches tall, I stood out amongst the women of average height; and I wore my red dress with my corset drawn so tight, my waist was twenty-five inches. I loved the noise and accolades. I deliberately placed each step firmly on the hardwood floor as I sashayed to the stage.

A group of men stood up, and as I approached the stage, one shouted, "Girl, you are so beautiful." I turned and smiled at the handsome gentleman that made the remark, and the lady beside him grunted and rolled jealous eyes my way.

The crowd roared as I took the mic and began to sing. Whenever Herman could make it, he sat close to the stage. On some occasions, he would hand me a flower as I performed one of my steamy, seductive blues songs. Most of the seats were taken tonight, except two at the table with the women from my hometown, and I noticed Herman move over to join them. After nearly twenty years, I couldn't remember their names, but I never forgot a face.

Herman started talking and grinning at the two country girls. Seeing him chat with them made me so nervous I almost forgot the lines of the song I was singing. He scooted close to one of the women and stared deep into her eyes. Annoyed, I asked Joseph on the guitar and Max on the drums to play Herman's favorite song.

That got his attention. A smile rippled across his face when he heard me sing "Baby." From that point on, his eyes rested only on me. I seductively licked my ruby red lips and Herman jerked in his seat. His beady eyes had me mesmerized, thinking about the nights when I had crawled into his lean, toned arms and let him take advantage of my body, kissing, licking, and making love to me until I forgot who I was. No man had ever done that to me before. I poured out the last verse of the song, and raised my head in full cry for the applauding crowd as they expressed their appreciation for the powerful crescendo.

As I gazed out over them, my eyes nearly popped out of my head. I had to refocus to see clearly through the smoke circles billowing in the air. In the rear of the club stood Willie Brown, in his soldier's uniform, staring directly at me. I inhaled sharply, and stopped a sudden grimace from overtaking my face. I decided I had better put on a good show.

"Welcome home, Willie," I uttered, and pointed him out in the crowd.

When they turned to see the doughboy all dressed up in uniform, they all started clapping and cheering.

Willie stood straight as an arrow as the folks gathered around him. With his chest inflated and shoulders squared, he stole all the attention. Four other World War I soldiers stood the same way in their turtle shell-colored jackets, pants snug on the legs, and boots to the knee. Men walked up and either patted them on the shoulders or shook their hands. The women stood around grinning shyly and waving. Two nearby women whispered loud enough for me to hear, "He is handsome." Out of the corner of my eye, I noticed Herman peering directly at me from the table he shared with the country women. I turned away quickly; I wasn't going to let Willie in on my secret. Instead, I sashayed over to Willie, right past whispering women, my heart pumping hard. In the midst of all the "Welcome homes," he had been studying my every step with his deep, dark eyes. When I reached him, I threw my arms around his neck. He grabbed me and hugged me so tightly I could feel each of his finely chiseled muscles kneading into my body, reminding me of so many sweaty nights in his arms.

He was a handsome man, six feet three and strong, with ebony skin as smooth as milk and beautiful almond-shaped eyes the color of mahogany. Yet he was rough as sandpaper. He lacked sophistication, something anyone could tell as soon as he began to speak.

"Did you miss me, gurl?" he said in his deep baritone voice, kneading his thick hands in circles on my back.

I paused to gather my thoughts when I noticed Herman was now standing up, his arms folded across his chest. He was frowning so deeply, indented lines rippled across his forehead.

"Of course I did," I said, resting my head on his shoulder. Herman was shaking his head, as if to warn me. Some of the regular women had their heads together, whispering.

"Well, Daddy's home now. Gonna take care of his baby tonight," Willie said.

He pulled my face into his and kissed me hard. When he tried to force his tongue into my mouth, I resisted, keeping my lips tight.

He raised his voice. "What's wrong with you? You got yo'self somebody else?" His fingers clenched my chin as he gazed deep in my eyes.

A chill came over me, but I hastily fought it away.

"No, Willie," I said softly, and draped my long arms around his shoulders. "I'm so glad you're home."

CHAPTER 3
CARRIE

The summer heat would not let up. Even in the evenings, everyone complained as they sat on the porch fanning, wiping beads of sweat from their brows and sipping ice water. "It is too hot. We need rain. Even the devil wants a sip of water today." If you had to get something done, you needed to start early. I tried to stay inside, especially on Saturday mornings, but Momma wouldn't hear of it.

I ignored the faint call for as long as I could. Then it started closing in on me, getting stronger and louder, rippling in my ears.

"Carrie! Carrie Parker!" I turned over to snuggle deep in the bedcovers, placing my pillow over my ears to filter out Momma's voice.

"Chile, you better get up. You oughta go to bed at night, you night-oil-burning rambler! You heard me calling you!"

As was the case every Saturday morning, I was being forced to get up way too early. I removed the pillow, eased open one eyelid, and Momma was standing directly over my head with her hands on her tiny hips, her face stiff with authority.

"All right. I'm getting up," I muttered, trying to keep my tired eyes open long enough for her to turn and walk away.

When she did, I closed my eyes again.

"What did you say, girl?" she inquired from across the room.

"I mean, yes, ma'am," I mumbled, holding my breath until she left, and then pulling the covers over my eyes and snuggling tight in them one last time.

"It's time you got up. We got things to do this mawnin'." I could hear Momma's fading voice as she walked down the hallway toward the kitchen.

In the country, there was always something to do, even if it was sweeping dirt in the yard.

I could barely raise my head off the pillow. Every night I stayed up practicing my school work as my teacher said I should over the summer break. Making up sentences was more difficult than it sounded, and I still did not feel as though the work enhanced my knowledge of nouns, verbs, and capitalizations. So instead, I wrote about myself, filled my notepad up with my cares, fears, and desires.

Our teacher, Mrs. Miller, was obsessed with learning. Repeating something over and over until it became second nature. At moments when the repetitions got out of hand, I'd lean over and whisper to my friend, Hester, "She's doing this because she had a bad weekend and is taking it out on us." Mrs. Miller was tall and statuesque, with bronze-colored skin. She wore her long, black hair pulled back into a flawless bun. She had everything in place, and whenever we forgot why we were in school, she'd point to the whipping strap she hung on the nail beside her desk. And she would not hesitate to use it.

I stretched my arms and let out a long, groaning yawn, trying to wake myself up. Rising with the chickens was not for me. Already I could feel the sun beaming through my bedroom window, burning my face. I could see Carl way out between the tall leaves of tobacco with beads of sweat trickling down his face, his collar moist with sweat, his back bent. Deep inside the overgrown leaves, my youngest brother, John, was coaxing mules down the rows. *Don't they ever quit?* I thought.

Before Momma called again, I sat up and swung my legs over the side of the bed. I stumbled over the books and papers that I had left on the floor the night before. I walked over to the wash basin, poured it full of water, and then splashed enough on my face to remove the night's sleep. My eyes were puffy, sleep creeping out of the corners.

Finally, I washed my face with lye soap and combed my hair back, parting it down the middle and making two large braids. I wet my finger with a little spit to slick down the untamed hairs sticking out at my temples. The smell of Momma's buttermilk biscuits and sausage crept into the bedroom and lured me into the kitchen.

I had barely started my breakfast when Momma announced that I was going to go with her to Mrs. Ferguson's house, the white lady she worked for. Twice a week for as long as I could remember, Momma washed and ironed for a couple who lived two miles down the road. The Fergusons were not rich when measured against some of the other white folks, but they were modestly wealthy compared to the colored folk I knew. Mrs. Ferguson always needed help.

"Mae Lou," she'd say, "I don't know how you can work like that. I can't do it. I've got just enough time to stay beautiful for Mr. Ferguson." And then she'd grin. I'd turn and roll my eyes so no one could see me. Until she'd married Mr. Ferguson, she had been used to the service of maids and butlers; her parents were wealthy slave owners and had once housed over one hundred slaves on their land, spread out over two hundred acres.

Momma rushed me to finish the breakfast dishes before we left. I had gathered water from the well twice, and still it was not enough. Rush, rush, rush. That's how Momma did everything. Rushing was all the women in her family had ever done. I was determined that was not the way I was going to do things. Momma preached too much about education for me to work so hard all the time. Slavery was abolished years ago, yet it still seemed to exist in some form or another, even in our own house.

"Gurl, you'd betta act like you want to work today. We got too much to do for you to be playin'. The devil loves an idle mind."

Momma pulled out one of her starched white aprons and cinched it around her petite waist. She pinned an old straw hat on top of the red bandanna she already had on her head. She had beautiful long black hair with a hint of gray, but she only wore it down on Sundays. "The Lord is the only one I need to dress up for," she would always say.

As we walked down the road to the Ferguson house, Momma hummed her spirituals, like she did in church. Sometimes she'd hit a note so high and out of tune, the birds would fly away from the trees and I had to keep from covering my ears. I knew it was her way of preparing herself mentally to do a job that she really didn't enjoy doing, though she would never admit it. Sometimes after everyone had left the kitchen, she'd read her Bible by the kerosene lamp. Sometimes she would read a novel scavenged out of the trash bin that Mrs. Ferguson had thrown away

When we came to a place where Momma noticed blackberries in a patch, she stopped humming and stepped into the brush.

"Let me pick us a few berries while they still in season."

She handed me a few. I loved the sweetness of blackberries, and thought of the many times Momma had baked a blackberry roll for me only to have Papa help me eat it.

"They are so sweet," I said, eating them right down.

As always, she said, "Just like you."

"Sweet, just like you," I repeated to myself and smiled. On that hot day, as summer was turning to autumn, I didn't know how few blackberry days of summer were left.

Momma started off again with her short, quick steps. I found myself breaking into a trot to keep up. After awhile my legs burned from my muscles struggling to keep pace. It was too nice of a day to be washing and ironing for some lazy white lady.

When we finally made it to Mrs. Ferguson's house, our shoes were filthy from the red dirt on the road. "Make sho' you dust that dirt off your shoes. We don't want to dirty da floors."

We went to the back door and Momma knocked several times. "Just a minute," Mrs. Ferguson responded from inside the house.

Her house was a big white antebellum one with a wide wooden wraparound front porch. The large, oversized windows opened the view from inside to the huge oaks and pines that shaded one side of her yard. On the back side of the property, apple and September pear trees hung full. Her home was secluded among the tobacco and cornfields. Alongside the rolling hills was a pond that reflected the well-kept landscape.

Inside, it was immaculately clean and spacious. The oversized mahogany fireplace in the sitting room gleamed from furniture polish, and right above it was a family portrait painted by a local artist. The hardwood floors were slick from a fresh coat of wax. The furniture was old with a traditional English paisley sofa and a high-back velvet cream chair in the sitting room. Her dining area had a typical drop-leaf table with eight chairs, and a china cabinet with the fine china her mother had given her on the day she married. A painting of a mountain set behind a mansion on a plantation hung on her dining room wall. Yet the shades were pulled down and the house had a cold, unused air to it. I hated being there.

As soon as we stepped onto the porch, Momma took the balled-up handkerchief out of her pocket and dusted off her shoes. Then she handed it to me so that I could do the same.

"Good morning, Mae Lou," Mrs. Ferguson greeted in her professional, boss-lady voice.

"Morning, ma'am," Momma answered.

"Glad to see you this morning. I put the clothes on the back porch for you, Mae Lou."

In her late forties, Mrs. Ferguson was a short, robust, well-dressed woman. Her red hair was always pinned up off her shoulders, and her fine lips painted with a coat of ruby red lipstick that was so thick it could be shared with four other women. From a distance, her lips were the first thing anyone noticed on her.

Momma fabricated a grin and I smiled sourly. I followed her outside to the back porch. We filled up the two big wooden wash-tubs with boiling water. One of the tubs was for the washing, and the other was for the rinsing. I didn't understand why the Fergusons did not have a washing machine. Most people who could afford one did.

Momma washed the clothes on a washboard and I dipped them in warm water to rinse the suds away. Then I shook them out and hung them on the clothesline. When they dried, we would fold them and Momma would take them upstairs to put away.

After we were finished, Mrs. Ferguson handed Momma some change. Momma wrapped it in a handkerchief and stuck it in her bra for safekeeping.

When we made it back to our house, I was wet from sweat and my dress clung to my skin. I knew Momma needed a rest, too; her eyes had started to droop.

All the next week, Momma worked tirelessly. To her, rest meant wasting time. So, on Sunday, Aunt Bessie convinced her to come along for a train trip to Washington, D.C. Papa was still living then. So I was shocked when she agreed to go.

The next weekend, instead of going to the Fergusons, Momma

took the trip. She caught the noon train with Aunt Bessie to Washington, D.C. When she returned home, her face appeared softer and her eyes danced when she spoke. And less than a month after Papa was buried, she took another trip. She returned glowing again and seemingly even more relaxed than after the first trip. This one must have been extra special. I found her on Monday morning smiling in the kitchen as she took sips from her coffee cup. There was something about the two trips that had made her different.

CHAPTER 4
PEARL

I woke up the next morning before the rooster crowed. My eyes fixated on the ceiling, following the cracks in the camel-colored plaster. The sun was breaking, and Willie was lying naked beside me with one leg hanging over the side of the bed, hissing loud snores with each breath. All week our love-making had been aggressive and rough. Inside, my heart was unwelcoming and estranged, searching for the passion that could unite us. Last night was like every night since he'd returned.

By the time we made it back to the apartment, Willie was riled up, breathing hard, twitching, his eyes asking questions and making accusations.

"Willie, this is your first week back. I swear to you I wasn't singing to that man. I was singing to the crowd." I poured a glass of water from the icebox and fanned a fly buzzing around my face. I had opened the window because the air was steamy and sweat was dripping down my bosom.

I walked into the bedroom where Willie was sitting on the bed fully dressed, and wagging his head from side to side in anger.

"It damn sho' didn't look like it."

"Come on, Willie; get that out of your head."

"Pearl, you better not be seeing no other man."

I stopped in front of the mirror, and saw his eyes blazing with anger. Another tower of rage was building, so I quickly unbuttoned my dress and let it fall off my shoulders onto the floor.

"Can you help me with this, Willie?" I asked.

Eagerly he sprang off the bed to assist me. His thick black fingers struggled to unlace my tight corset, which had kept the roundness of my stomach from protruding.

Willie was helpless when I was naked, and I knew it. I removed everything including my silk panties, and tossed them on the back of the chair. I stood directly in front of him as if I was posing for a photograph. His dark mahogany eyes roved up and down my frame, and I casually twirled around like a ballerina so he could take it all in. I guess I was an exhibitionist by nature, and it left Willie speechless, making him forget about Herman and the nightclub. I unbuttoned the top button of his shirt, and he helped me with the rest before unfastening his pants. I sat on the floor in front of him with my thighs parted so he could see what he'd missed in the last two years. As I helped him pull off the long army boots that went up to his knees, I couldn't help but notice the rising bulge directly in my face. After he slid his pants to the floor, I stood between his legs.

I kissed him lightly on the lips.

"Come to Momma," I whispered cunningly in his ear, and straddled my legs around his muscular thighs. Willie didn't know how to hold back, so I coaxed him along the way. He took my heavy breasts, first one and then another, into his mouth and suckled my nipples until they were sore. I ran my fingertips up and down his sweaty back, and he moaned, "Pearl, oh please, Pearl."

He kneaded my curvy hips, and lifted me onto his long, thick shaft.

"Slow down, Willie."

He was breathless with want. "I missed you, gurl. I can't stand the thought of you with nobody else," he murmured. Beads of sweat slid down his temples, and my breath grew shallow. With each thrust, I lost control. I rode him rough like he wanted me to.

When we were done, I snuggled into his thick, black arms. Still I couldn't help remembering his anger. I inhaled deeply from the thought of how easily he got pissed off. I thought the service would change him, maybe give him the patience he lacked when it came to a confrontation. When the United States' colored soldiers entered World War I in 1917, I pleaded with him to join. We had been married for only six months, but that was long enough.

In the beginning, I wanted to love him. The first night I met him, a cold thunderous downpour of rain with driving winds at the core swept leaves across the street. The walk downtown had ruffled my hair and blown it out of place. It was a dreary night, one I did not want to spend alone. I reapplied my lipstick, brushed my hair back in place, and found a seat at the bar. The crowd was thin, more couples than singles. All night men bought me glasses of gin and tonic, but none had the courage to join me at the bar. Willie was the only one. By the time I'd finished my third drink, the bartender was pouring me another.

"Who's paying for this one?" I asked the bartender.

"Not me, the man over there."

He pointed at a big black man, whose dark skin was buffed and shiny, standing on the other side of the bar. When I glanced in that direction, I noticed the man staring back at me. The haunted look in his eyes made me a little uneasy. As he strolled toward me, each chiseled muscle appeared to move with the rhythm of his stride.

He introduced himself. "I've been watching you all night long."

"Oh yeah?" I said, missing the warm comfort of a man. I had split with my ole man two months prior, and with the help of gin, even with my apprehension, this new man sounded like a good replacement.

"Can I visit you sometime?" he asked.

He was gorgeously distinctive, and his robust baritone voice vibrated in my ears.

I stayed in an apartment house on the north side of D.C., and even with my singing gigs, could barely pay the rent. The apartment was located in an upper-class neighborhood of colored professionals. It had taken me nearly twelve years to save enough money to move into that neighborhood.

I don't know why, but I answered, "Yes, why not." The entire night after that, he admired my beauty.

Willie started visiting me once a week. We would walk around the corner hand in hand, and sometimes he'd take me to a picture show. I liked him. He was a hardworking country boy who held down two jobs. All the other knucklehead Negroes I'd known had been bullshitters. They'd be infatuated in the nightclub, sending me drinks of gin and tonic and telling the waiter to get me whatever I desired, and soon after I agreed to go out with them, the irresponsibility would surface. I'd end up at cheap restaurants snacking on saltine crackers, wishing I had never met them. Even so, I couldn't fall in love with Willie. He was too uncivilized for me.

"Will you marry me?" he asked one night after I had given my best performance. I'd sung my heart out until beads of sweat dripped down my temples, and the waves in my hair had started to fall. The local colored newspaper, which was published by Howard University Press, said I'd brought the house down and I quote, "Bessie Smith, move over. Pearl has arrived."

I was in a good mood the next day after hearing about the review, and that night Willie came by. He was wearing a country flannel shirt, trousers and brogan boots.

"Come in," I said, still overcome with joy after reading the review.

Willie came with two boxes. "Pearl, ain't no reason for you to keep singing from place to place without some support."

"What are you saying?" I asked, pouring him a cup of coffee and calculating in my head the odds of finding someone who would take care of me. I'd had many men, and settling down couldn't have been further from my mind. I didn't want to be tied down. So far, Willie had been very accepting of my profession. I was thirty-one years old. Most women my age were married and had children. I was still pursuing my dream.

"Willie, I'm not the marrying type. I sing in nightclubs and my best tippers are men."

He studied my face with his penetrating eyes. "I don't care how you make a living, gurl. I want you to be mine."

Genuine love is all I had been searching for my entire life, so I broke down and said yes, without asking questions or thinking things through. The next day, I put on a cream-colored chemise dress, my Mary Jane shoes, and a cream pill hat, and Willie and I marched down to the courthouse and were married.

I never expected him to become so possessive. On the nights he didn't work, he'd come to the club, sit at a front table and threaten any man who made a pass at me. One night, he left a patron screaming, "You no-good son of a bitch," as he headed for the door with blood dripping from his lip and an ugly lump on his head.

"Keep yo' damn hands off my wife," Willie threatened another man who'd whispered in my ear one night when I had bowed to the crowd and started back to my table.

"Man, I don't want to hear none of that," the man said in response.

Before the music started to play, Willie grabbed the guy by the shirt collar and threw him against the wall. Then Willie threw a punch in the fellow's face, and without blinking, he pulled a switch-blade on the guy. Once the owner saw that, he threatened to call the police. I begged the owner not to call, since cops didn't like coloreds. "Come back and sing once ya get rid of yo' crazy husband," the owner told me.

So when the Colored National Guard started recruiting soldiers, I convinced Willie to join. Willie wasn't too accepting at first. He had reservations about a colored man fighting for a country that basically treated coloreds like shit. But he loved the idea of being a soldier and traveling to some foreign country, even if he never got to fight. Most colored soldiers who enlisted were supply men, clean-up crews and cooks. Willie said that some would be able to fight. Besides, his cousin in Harlem, New York, was joining the 15th New York Voluntary Infantry Regiment. So Willie decided to ride the train to New York and join with his cousin, who had once lived in Washington. I promised to be faithful while he was away. Volunteers were joining from all over. It was the perfect outlet for someone like Willie. Now after two years, I wondered if he had changed at all.

That first night, Willie and I had a drink before leaving the club. The ice never melted in his Scotch on the rocks and I gulped down half of my third gin and tonic.

"It's time for us to go home, gurl. Been two years since I done did the do," he said, grinning from ear to ear. Then he rubbed my thigh. I cringed inside. It felt different than it did with Herman, who had sent a warm wave over my flesh earlier in the evening before I performed. He was gentle and smooth.

"How about a dance before we leave?" I said, since Willie didn't understand anything about getting a girl ready. He lacked the "in betweens."

"Don't you want to be with yo' man? I've been gone a long time, gurl." He squeezed my leg so tightly I almost slapped his hand.

"Of course I do."

"Why you gots to be so proper? Talk dirty to me. Let me know how you feel."

"Willie, after we get home, I promise." I watched Herman dancing slow, cheek to cheek, with the petite country girl.

"Do you know that nigger?

"Who are you talking about, Willie?"

He nudged his head toward Herman. "The one over there who's been staring at you all night."

"No, I don't know anybody, Willie."

"Why the hell is he lookin' over here then?"

I tried to laugh it off. "Come on, baby, I've been getting a lot of attention all my life."

"You's my wife."

That threatening note in his voice awoke bad old memories. "Calm down; our night is just beginning," I whispered in his ear.

Willie and I danced cheek to cheek one more time before we decided to leave.

Roy saw us and ran to open the door.

"Good night, Miz Pearl," Roy said, holding the door.

"Look like I got back just in time," Willie mumbled in my ear.

We lived only blocks from the club, so we walked hand in hand down the street. We walked right past Herman and the lady he'd been dancing with all night, as they stood outside talking.

When we retuned to the apartment, Willie went inside first. Like he'd never left, he went through all of the four rooms, including the bathroom, and examined them for signs of deception.

"What's wrong, Willie?"

"Nothing; I want to know what's been going on 'round here."

"What do you mean, Willie?"

A frown rippled across his stiff face and his mahogany eyes bore into mine. “I don’t like the way that man looked at you. And I don’t like the way you sang for him. Seem like somebody’s been messing up ’round here.”

His vigilance hadn’t let up all week. While Willie slept, I put on a plain plaid straight skirt and white blouse and went to the corner store to purchase food for breakfast. Willie loved country cooking, hot grits with butter, fried ham and eggs. Yet my mind wasn’t on cooking. I was thinking about how much I missed Herman’s touch.

CHAPTER 5
CARRIE

After Papa's death, everything started to go wrong. Momma stopped acting like herself. My brothers started arguing because Papa wasn't there to settle them down. And then I learned I wasn't even related to any of them.

I found out the first day of school. Students gathered under the old pine tree outside the schoolhouse to tell stories about their summer vacations. One girl had gone to see her grandma. A boy bragged about riding in his uncle's Studebaker. Another had gone to Washington, D.C., which was every child's wish. For my brothers and me, school was actually our vacation. We could escape working all day in the tobacco field, summer garden and the winter garden of turnips, cabbage, and collards.

School had its ups and its downs, but for me, it was mostly ups. It was where all the children of Jefferson received their first experience with independence, enough freedom to dream.

Everything we wore on the first day of school was brand-spanking new. All summer Momma had sewn burlap and cotton dresses for me, and trousers and shirts for my brothers. To top it off, she'd ordered us new shoes right out of the Sears mail-order catalog.

When we arrived at school, the first person I noticed was Anna Smith. She stood out as bright as a big yellow crayon. As always, she was surrounded by several girls who were listening intently to what she was talking about as if she was the mayor or someone important. When she glanced my way, all of a sudden the joy of my first day drained from my face.

"There she goes again," I said, and sighed. When she pointed her chubby finger at me, I wanted to run. But instead, I threw my head back, squared my shoulders and strolled right past her. I heard her whisper to her friends, "That's her." Snickers broke out from the group, and I quickened my stride.

Ringing her cowbell, Mrs. Miller yelled, "Children, come into the schoolhouse now. It's time to begin!" I was a bit relieved.

My brother, John, spoke up. "Now, don't pay Anna Smith no mind this year, Sis. She got to have a problem, staring at people the way she do." Then he turned back toward her and gazed at her so deeply that she was forced to look away.

"You're right," I agreed, and privately smirked as I strolled inside the run-down schoolhouse with both of my brothers by my side.

Hester saw me when I came through the door, waved her hand and patted the empty seat beside her. "I saved a seat for you," she said as I eased into it. Hester was like a big sister, even though we were the same age. She wasn't a big talker, more an observer who knew what was going on. She spent a good deal of time looking out for me and giving advice. Hester's skin was a beautiful mocha chocolate, and her hair reached almost down to her waist. She was what folks called a Black Indian. She simply said she was mixed up. We didn't live too far apart, but we only saw each other during the school term. She was the first to get a boyfriend and the first to become a woman. I usually followed Hester in about everything, except learning. I loved to read, and Mrs. Miller had grabbed Momma's hand one Sunday after church. "If Carrie keeps on studying the way she has been, she could teach school one day."

Since we had become teenagers, Hester and I had spent our

recess combing our hair or whispering about boys, especially talking about the crush Hester had on my brother John.

When Anna walked through the door, I cringed. I wanted space between us. But all sixteen of us students were in close quarters. The younger children sat in the front of the classroom at an old scuffed-up oak table that had been around as long as the school, and the rest of us sat at desks behind them. Mrs. Miller's desk faced the class and the wood-burning stove was in the back.

Mrs. Miller had been away from Jefferson County only once. The two years she'd spent at Howard to obtain a teacher's diploma was long enough to her. According to Mr. Miller, who was as happy being a farmer as she was teaching school, he'd laid claim to her long before she left for college. He was uneducated himself, but for his wife's sake, he'd listen to her read all day long. She adored him. Their two children sat in the front desk in class, close to Mrs. Miller, so she could give them an evil eye if they ever decided to get out of place. I admired her, and each day that I sat there and practiced, and read, I was that much closer to vacating Jefferson for a teaching diploma of my own. She was my role model.

Traditions of education had been passed down to Mrs. Miller from the women in her family. Her great-grandmother learned to read from her slave master's wife, so the story went. Mrs. Johnson, behind her husband's back, taught a few of her house slaves basic words, and gave them books to hide under the floorboards in the slaves' quarters. This started an educational revolution that was passed down to Mrs. Miller, and she continued to enlighten us any way she could.

Mrs. Miller took roll, as we did each morning, and started a review of the alphabet. She divided the class into different groups, mixing those who could read with those having problems. My stomach turned a somersault when Mrs. Miller said, “Carrie, join the group in the left corner of the room.”

As I dragged my chair in the direction of the group, I tried to hide my feelings. Anna began to snicker at me, along with two other girls. Ignoring them, I opened a book and began reading. I glanced out of the corner of my eye and saw Anna nudge a thinner, dark-skinned girl beside her. I became tense and defensive, balling up my fist as I held the book. I even stumbled over a few of the words. Finally I asked, “What are y’all laughing at? Is there something funny around here?” I rolled my eyes to let them know how I was feeling.

“Nawl, only you,” Anna said, and then she glanced at her buddies for approval.

I sat straight up. “I don’t understand. What am I doing that is so darn funny?”

At first no one said anything. And when I thought I’d taken control of the situation, Anna said, “Well, you think you’s better’n me, but you ain’t. You’s just like the rest of us.” She slapped the arm of the girl sitting next to her. “You don’t know e’rythang. Bet nobody told ya that you’s be my sista.” In reply, I snapped my eyes shut, and when I opened them again, I rolled them way back in my head. It was the silliest thing I’d ever heard.

“Gurl, you heard me. Now what ya say? You can‘t talk? Cat got yo’ tongue?” Her voice was raspy and bitter.

I leaned over and locked eyes with her. “Don’t you have anything else to do but dream? You wish I was your darn sister.”

By then, everyone nearby was listening in, including the little children.

My first reaction was to give her a further piece of my mind, but I kept my cool. I didn’t need the attention of the entire class. What kind of sick person would make up something so stupid?

"Listen, girl," I said softly, once the other group had turned back to reading, "There is no way we can be kin. I don't even know you. All I know is that you don't like me, and I don't know why."

Anna raised her voice. "You's right 'bout that. I don't like ya like my ma don't like you. That's why she gave you up. She ain't want you; you her bastard." An outburst of laughter broke out amongst the other girls.

My mouth flew open, and I started to tremble. I raised my hand to slap her but caught myself. Instead, I held my hand extended and then forced myself to withdraw.

"Gurl, I know you ain't crazy," Anna said, and held her hand up to ward off the slap.

"No, I'm not, but you are," I said.

I struggled to get through the group reading session, biting my lip to keep from going off. The girls stopped laughing and playing long enough to read aloud in the group after Mrs. Miller calmed them down.

The rest of the day was almost unbearable. Anna's words kept dancing inside my head. I didn't feel any different from the rest of my family, and all of us were treated the same. But for some reason, I knew Anna hadn't made it up. Once, Hester had asked me if I was Anna's cousin. She thought we favored. The more I thought about it, my brothers and I did not favor at all. They were lean, tall, chocolate, and very handsome. I was short, stubby, and peach-colored, with sharp, keen features, like those of Mrs. Ferguson.

On the way home, I wondered how much my brothers had overheard. John never missed anything.

"What that girl say to you?" he asked, on cue.

"Nothing," I quickly said.

"She said something," he said, shaking his head. "I don't want to have to shut her up."

"Did you hear anything?" I asked both of my brothers.

"Naw, I don't pay her no attention," Carl answered.

"Why were you so quiet in there?" John asked.

"I'm tired."

"Too tired enough to get Anna off you? 'Cause that can be handled."

I resisted allowing my protective brother to get involved. I was afraid he might forget the oath he'd promised to Papa that he would never ever hit a woman. Besides, as quiet as I kept it, I wanted to whip her butt myself.

Momma was cooking when we got home and the aroma of chicken frying and black-eyed peas stewing greeted us at the door. The aroma normally would make me salivate, but I couldn't think about food. All I wanted was to rest and protect my bruised ego.

"Chile, you'd better eat. We don't waste food 'round here," Momma warned me at the table.

"Yes, ma'am," I said.

I tried to shake the thoughts Anna had stirred around in my head, but was still thinking about family after we finished eating. My brothers went outside for their chores and Momma ordered me to get a pail of water from the well.

I smacked my lips. The only time she talked to me was when she needed something done.

"Did you hear me?" she asked.

"Yeah, I heard you," I mumbled.

She turned around sharply. "What did you say?"

"I said, yes, ma'am." Under my breath, I mumbled, "Why don't you do it yourself?"

Times like these, I wished our well had a pump like the Fergusons had. Also I wished we weren't so *dad-blamed* country, living out in the wilderness away from people and activity.

I didn't know how to tell my momma that I really needed to talk to her, and that I had about all I could take from Anna Smith.

"Chile, why are you moving so slow 'round here this evening?"

"It's 'cause I want to," I said audaciously, doing something I knew was disrespectful. Before I could move, she slapped the living hell out of me. The sound echoed throughout the house, at least in my ears. She left her handprint on my cheek, left my skin stinging like it was on fire. I grabbed my cheek, felt ashamed, but couldn't keep my mouth shut.

I blurted out, "You're not my real momma anyways." My stomach dropped. I knew what I'd said was out of line. I was too distraught to run for my life, so I stood there. My knees locked together.

A frown spread across her face. Her eyebrows arched and her beautiful round eyes transformed into slits. "Where on earth did you get such a notion? Chile, you and I are 'bout to come unbenefited!" Those were Momma's famous words when she was mad. She stood beside the sink with her arms folded across her chest and waited for me to say something back to her. I was silent. I knew her next move would be a lick across my behind.

At last, Momma put down the dish towel in her hand. "Sit down. It's time we talked." She pulled out a chair at the kitchen table. I sat down, too, and waited for Momma to start.

She pointed her finger at me. "You've got something stewing around in your mind. And whatever it is, it is making you do things that are out of the ordinary. I want to know what is going on."

I sniffed and snorted back tears. "There's this girl at school and she said that I'm her sister. She makes fun of me and some of the other girls laugh at me, too."

"Now, I done told you children about people. You know everybody don't mean you no good. And you should not listen to that type of person."

"But, Momma, she won't leave me alone."

"She'll leave you alone."

"Momma, are the things she says true?" Teardrops dripped from the corners of my eyes. I wiped them with the back of my hand, but I couldn't stop them from flowing.

Momma got up and hugged me. Though I was surprised, I emptied myself in her bosom.

She gazed at me with tears in her eyes, too.

"You know, Chile, the Lord is still in control."

I slid closer to her and listened.

"I was twenty-one when I got you. And I didn't think 'bout all of this happening. Didn't know you'd go to school with any of Minnie's children; didn't know they'd know, and I didn't think they'd tease you 'bout something you didn't know 'bout."

As she told the story, I started to well up again, since I could feel the pain Momma had as she talked.

"You were just under two years old when I got you," she said, and tears welled up in her eyes.

"I had two young boys of my own and Minnie, your real momma, had one younger than you and another on the way. I got you 'cause one day at church I heard 'bout a chile that was burnt. They said it was an accident; said the man had knocked a pan of boiling water on the chile. But Mrs. Jackson, another member at the church, said it was really that he didn't want no illegitimate chile in his house." She gestured to no one in particular. "I don't know. I wanted to help. So I went to see your momma. And when I seen you, I asked if I could have you."

As Momma told the story, I began to realize how special I was.

"Minnie told me her husband didn't like you too much. He

didn't like feeding nobody else's chile. Lord, you were puny. You were burnt all over your body, especially on your hands and face, like you were asking to be picked up. I left with you that day. I carried you home and you became my little girl. I went down to the courthouse and filed the papers. Folks used to tell me the ugly slick scabs covering your face and hands made them sick at the stomach. But it didn't bother me one bit. My people were from Africa, knew how to heal wounds. I used shea butter, aloe vera, bitter leaf and even tobacco from the earth to heal you. You see now they don't need to run."

So this began a new era in my life. I had other kinfolk, and I was determined to find out what they were like. It was all fortunate, because while I was visiting my new relatives, I was able to avoid our new guest at home.

CHAPTER 6
CARRIE

"Good evening, young lady, your momma in?" He talked fast and his smooth voice unsettled me. I felt a cold chill travel through my limbs, and a tingling in my fingers. The feeling was always a warning to me that something strange was about to happen. I'd last experienced it the day Papa died.

"Yes, she's in," I said through the crack in the door.

Momma quickly appeared at the door, too, and stood behind me as I greeted her guest. He wasn't a bad-looking man, but he lacked substance, absent of any distinctive features. He didn't have nice thick hair, white teeth, or skin smooth as milk. He was short compared to Papa, who was nearly six feet five inches tall. The only distinctive thing about him was his clothes. He had on cuffed plaid trousers and laced shoes. Most of the men we knew wore boots, except to church. His fingers were long and thin and edged with clean fingernails that made them too delicate for work.

"Come in," I said, and turned toward Momma. "He wants to see you."

"I can see, Chile," Momma said. She threw open the door, and he followed close behind her into the front room. He took a seat on the Davenport sofa and crossed his thin legs. Momma sat down beside him. I stood at the door, grateful that he hadn't sat in my papa's seat. Momma glanced over at me and gave me her infamous stern face. I received her signal and went into the kitchen.

In less than ten minutes, he was walking into our kitchen behind Momma with a smile spread from ear to ear. Momma invited him to sit while she attended to the food already cooking on the stove.

He quickly found a seat at the table, and this time it *was* Papa's chair. Momma pulled out a chair and sat down beside him. He subtly touched Momma on the hand, and she let him. Feeling a need to guard her, I took a seat, too, and cut my eyes toward them. With her eyes fixated on him, she ignored me. After another few moments, she got up, reached on the shelf and grabbed two cups.

"Want some coffee, Herman?" she asked.

"I don't mind if I do," he said, adjusting himself in Papa's chair.

She filled both of their cups to the top and offered him cream and sugar.

It was wet outside, and the wind whirled through the trees. Sadly, my papa wasn't around to liven up the house, fill up the stove and bring warmth to the room. Instead, Momma chunked two logs into the stove and opened up the flue, and our home, to a stranger.

"We're going to be eating dinner soon. I hope you stay."

"Mae Lou, thank you for inviting me to eat. It's been a month of Sundays since I had a woman cook a meal for me." He removed his jacket and placed it on the back of the chair.

"It's been a while since a man has eaten with me, too."

I struggled to keep from screaming. She shouldn't let that man eat here, in Papa's chair. I got up from the table, poured a glass of water, took a deep breath and sat back down.

"Don't you have something you needs to do?" Momma said, noticing my distraught face.

I got up and checked on the chicken she was frying in lard.

Not enough time had passed. Papa had only been dead three months, and like some teenager, she was already having company. My eyes became slits and I bit my tongue, knowing I would have to eat with them.

My intuition told me there was something sinister about this man. The way he'd gazed at me the moment I opened the door made me want to slam it in his face. But how could I have done that? Papa always said if we'd listen, God would warn us about things.

When John and Carl joined us in the kitchen, both of them stopped short. They peered down at Momma and her new beau without speaking.

"Why are y'all staring? You act like we never have visitors."

John came closer to the table. "We wanted to make an acquaintance," he said. Carl shrugged his shoulders as if he didn't care, and I assumed he wanted to ignore it.

Herman, as Momma had called him, hastily stood up, reached out his hand and introduced himself. "Herman Camm."

The smiles on my brothers' faces instantly dwindled and disappointment set in.

Momma stunned me that Sunday. She had moved on and was no longer grieving over Papa. All this time she had been thinking about courting another man. And it was only the first of many visits from Mr. Camm.

If that wasn't enough, Anna Smith approached me the next morning at school.

"You've been walking 'round here for a month acting like I still ain't kin to you. I done told you we sisters."

I had always relished the old pine tree in front of the schoolyard. Sometimes I'd prop up against it and gaze through its leaves at the gray sky and let all my thoughts drift with the clouds. I had propped up against the tree when she walked up. Now she wouldn't let me think.

"Anna, you have teased me for so long, it is hard for me to believe anything you say. And if I am your sister, why do you treat me so bad?"

"You's walking 'round here like you's better'n me. I wanted to make you suffer."

Once again, I saw that she shared the same keen features as I did. We did favor, and yet she had on the dingiest clothes of anybody in class. Her braided hair was wiry and unattractive. I had on nice clothes that had been ironed, and my hair was braided neatly into two cornrows. I could sense her jealousy and the insecurity of being dirt poor.

"Ma told me 'bout you a long time 'go. I had to think on it before I said anythang. I wanted to make sho' you's as nice as she think. She been asking 'bout you. She wants to see you, Carrie."

I was outraged. "Why do she want to see me after all these years? I'm fifteen years old. Where has she been all my life? I'm practically grown." I tried to be sarcastic, but my voice trembled. I didn't realize that it would be so hard for me to deal with. Deep inside, I wanted Anna to say it was all a misunderstanding, a foul joke.

"She can't 'ford you. You came just like my baby, un'spect'ly. She say she want to know her firstborn, that's all." As the sound of her raspy voice penetrated my ears, all I could think about was the secrets they'd held all these years.

"Anna, I don't want to be bothered with your momma. She has not been there for me, so why should I go see some woman that I don't even know? She gave me away. I didn't leave her!"

Anna bristled with anger. The vein in her neck trembled beneath her skin. She put her hand on her hips and moved closer to me.

Her breath blasted my face. "You don't talk 'bout my ma like that. She wants to see you. She good peoples."

Before I could respond, Mrs. Miller called everybody inside. As Anna walked away, she turned around and rolled her eyes at me.

I still didn't want Anna to be my sister, but as her words sank in, I realized I did want to meet my real mother. If nothing else, I wanted to see what we shared.

So after school, I went home with Anna. Her house wasn't very far, a mile north of the schoolhouse. As we turned onto this little dirt trail, my breathing sped up. The path was crowded with overgrown weeds, shrubbery, and vines that blocked our view of anything even a few feet in front of us. Set back amongst the trees was a small house with gray paint puckering off its sides. Chickens were scattered around in the yard, along with a lot of small children with snotty noses and unattended hair. At first glimpse of Anna, they all came running, including some of the chickens. One of the children grabbed Anna's leg and studied me from top to bottom with tiny, round, concerned eyes.

As we entered, I found the house crowded with chairs of no consistent type, a Davenport, tables, and clothes scattered throughout. Sitting at the kitchen table was a lady who was my mirror image. Despite myself, my heart swelled at the sight of her. She was swollen with child. She gazed at me and a smile illuminated her face.

"That's Ma, right there," Anna said, pointing.

"Come here," she said, welcoming me.

I moved closer and held out my hand for her to shake. But instead, she pulled me in close and hugged me so hard her hands seemed to knead into my spine. Then she kissed my cheek and bit it.

"Ouch," I said and Anna and her ma giggled like silly children.

"Nice to meet you," I managed, stunned by both the resemblance and the greeting I had not expected from a stranger.

"Thank the Lord you's here," she sang out. Anna pulled a chair out from the kitchen table for me to sit in. The aroma of beans cooking filled the air. She shooed a fly from around her food. Several of the children had come inside and were sitting on the floor staring at me. The robust stink of the dirty children and their musty clothes overpowered the aroma of food cooking.

"I didn't think you's gonna come."

"Yes, ma'am," was all I could say.

"I'm so glad Anna Mae brung you here. I'd always wanted my chirren to know their oldest sista."

I frowned, not feeling any kinship to these ragged children.

"What's wrong?" she asked.

"Nothing," I lied. Aside from the scent, I was having a hard time being there. It made me sad to think that for fifteen years she had never once come to visit me, and she'd lived right in the same town the entire time.

"Are you hungry?" she asked.

"No, ma'am, I'm gonna eat when I get home."

Still smiling, she wobbled to her feet and stirred the cooking beans. We looked so much alike, it scared me. She was even slightly bowlegged. The only difference: she was much lighter than me. She could probably have passed for white if she dared. Anna and I both shared her keen features.

"You can call me Minnie, though I wouldn't mind if you called me Ma. I'm sure Mrs. Mae Lou wouldn't care." Momma would, I was sure of that. Anyhow, there was no way I was going to call her Ma. The only momma I knew was Mrs. Mae Lou, as she called her.

"I heard you's a good student. You like school, huh?"

"Yes, ma'am."

"Wish you could git Anna Mae to like it. That darn chile be hating to do her work." Anna looked at me and snickered.

As the ice began to melt in the room, Anna's daddy walked through the door.

"Whose child is this, Minnie? I ain't never seen her around here."

Minnie's smile slowly diminished. She barely got out the words. "She's Mrs. Mae Lou's girl."

"Hmmph." He cut a cold eye my way, and immediately I felt his hostility.

"Anna, it's time for me to go." I stood up and walked toward the door. Mr. Smith swished past me, opened the door and walked out. The door slammed in my face. Before I left, Minnie said, "If you's git a chance, come again, okay?" Now I could see pain in her eyes, even fear.

Minnie stood in the front door and watched Anna and I leave the yard. We hadn't gone ten feet before an older lady with a cane hobbled down the path into the yard. She smiled when she saw me.

"Lordy, Mae Lou done raised a fine-looking young lady," she said, resting on the cane for support.

"What you doing up here, Ginny?"

"Yo' mammy tole me that you's gonna bring Carrie here the last day of yo' lesson. I want to make my acquaintance, too."

I recognized her. She was the lady that had hugged me many Sundays at church. She'd always be standing at the door with the ushers. I'd noticed her laughing and talking to Momma on the church grounds.

"You know me, don't you?"

"Yes, ma'am. You go to church with us."

"I's yo' auntie, and I'm so glad to see you." Then she hugged me, like she'd done every Sunday she was in attendance.

Then Minnie yelled from the doorway, "Ginny, that there chile gots to be home. She ain't got time to be gossiping with you."

"Now, why I's got to be gossiping?" she mumbled, turning to me. "Ev'rytime I sees you, yo' skin done got prettier and prettier. Can't see a burn nowhere. Mae Lou is a miracle worker."

Anna didn't say a word. Minnie was still in the door, now with frown folds across her forehead. Mr. Smith, short and the color of red dirt, propped himself up on the shed wall beside an old wheelbarrow in the yard and gazed intently at us. A cigarette dangled from his lips, smoke billowing in the air.

"I better make it home," I said.

"Y'all chirren go on for it get late. Ev'rybody needs to be home 'fore dark." Ginny paused, then added, "Annie, now show Carrie where's I live, in case she want to stop by and visit me, too."

The next day, on my way to Hester's, I took an abrupt turn over to Ginny's place. I remembered what Anna had said the day before.

"Now remember she ain't got all her screws. She has a touch of ole-timer's disease, so don't believe ev'rythang she says."

"Why don't you come with me when I visit?"

"I's don't really like Ginny. She gives my daddy a hard time."

"Why?"

"'Cause she lonely."

When I approached Ginny's house, she was rocking on the porch, like she knew I was coming. The sun was casting a shadow through the big oak in her front yard. The house was in need of repair, a fresh whitewash of paint. Yet her yard was neat—no grass growing to my kneecaps as it did at Minnie's, and everything appeared to be organized and in place.

"Chile, I didn't 'spect to see you so soon. I figured church would be the onliest time." She had a few front teeth missing, and her cane was hooked over her rocker for quick access. She was certainly Minnie's sister. They shared the same nose and thin lips and hazel eyes. She was a lot darker, though.

"Ginny, I want to talk to you."

"I s'posed you would." She picked up a Mason jar of ice water and took a drink. She tilted back in the chair and studied me as if she could see right through me. I swallowed hard because she made me nervous.

"Want som'thin' to drank?" she said.

"No, ma'am, I want to find out something about me."

"Chile, take a seat up here. No sense in gett'n yo clothes all dirty." Then she spat a wad of chewing tobacco in a cup and wiped her mouth with a handkerchief she had in her dress pocket.

"Ginny, tell me about how I was burnt?" I got straight to the point, even if it sounded rude.

"Chile, I didn't mean to stir up no trouble, now. I thought you knew. Mae Lou ain't tell ya?"

"Momma explained it to me, but I still don't understand everything. Why she didn't want me?" I waited on edge for her to chew the nasty snuff she kept under her tongue, and then spit into a jar.

She cleared her throat, "Did Mae Lou tell you 'bout us?" Ginny asked.

"Yes, sort of. She told me I was adopted."

"Well, now I's know where to start. When Mae Lou took ya, you's been burnt by somebody up at Minnie's. No one knows who did the stuff, but chances are, it was her ole man. That man ain't doing not'in' but holding Minnie down. She'd just met 'im and was 'specting another baby when she done married 'im. He's a rough boy, thanks he's bad and all, got some Indian in 'im. Well, we got some, too. I ain't scared of the boy, but Minnie is."

"And you think he burnt me?"

"Nawl, I's don't really know for sure, but he's no-good like that. He cut a boy down yonder 'while ago. Sheriff didn't do not'in'," she said, frowning. "But he gonna mess with the right one and they's gonna send his ass to kingdom come." Then she got up, went in the house to check on her cooking: chicken and turnip greens.

When she came back, she handed me a chicken wing and a biscuit and bit into one herself.

"Now listen here. Mae Lou is one decent lady. She and Robert, Lord bless his soul, they good peoples. Minnie couldn't find nicer peoples to have you." She was right about that. When I had left Minnie's, I thanked the Lord for my parents. Minnie didn't have anything. Her house was too small for all the children she had.

"Is Minnie's husband my father?"

"Nawl, Chile, that's why you's ain't there. He ain't want no chirren that won't his own 'round. He told Minnie to get rid of you. She ain't listen, though. Then all of sudden, you burnt. Chile, you's almost dead when Mae Lou came. Somebody at the chu'ch told her 'bout that mean son of a bitch, 'scuse my English. Mae Lou nursed you back."

She devoured the chicken and biscuit down quick, even with missing teeth, and sipped the ice water.

"Yo' papa left 'round here while Minnie's carrying you. He came back for you and Minnie, but she wouldn't go. She done got tangled up with that nigga."

I listened intently, though my stomach turned somersaults from all the spitting and chewing of tobacco. Even still, Ginny had something special about her. Her eyes poured out the wisdom of someone who'd been around, seen a few things, and danced in a few holes.

"Why do you think people keep so many secrets?" I asked her.

"Ev'rybody trying to look good, even if they's lived a helluva life themselves. I learned a long time ago to please myself. And one day you will, too."

I was enjoying my time with my new aunt, but even so, I could see she was getting tired. I got up to leave. She nodded, understanding, and said, "Now don't be no stranger."

CHAPTER 7
PEARL

Willie was a different man after his ship landed on American shores. The proud heroism that had inspired him to hold his head up high disappeared once he found out that no jobs existed for colored soldiers. World War I had left a bitter taste on many of the colored soldiers' tongues, Willie included. After searching for work for a month, his bitterness only intensified. Often, after a day of walking the streets and hearing the same words, "Come back next week," he would have an uncontrollable outburst.

"Why did I fight in a damn war for a year and a half?" Willie asked, slamming his fist down hard on the bed.

"Willie, you got to go to places you wouldn't have been able to see otherwise," I said, standing in front of the beveled mirror on the armoire, brushing the waves in my hair and pinning it up into a chignon.

He sat on the side of the bed, wearing only a T-shirt and long underpants, his head hung low. "To hell with that! Seems like I's in better shape 'fore leaving for the service. I had two jobs and they didn't pay too bad, either."

I didn't respond.

He looked up at me. "I fought just like them white boys. I was in those awful trenches, too, Pearl."

Willie was no stranger to hardship. Had been on his own ever since he'd left Fredericksburg at fourteen and headed to the city. Other coloreds were doing the same, leaving their farms for better jobs.

"I know it was rough, but at least you were able to save some money from the service," I said.

He looked at me with despair in his mahogany brown eyes. "The factory jobs are taken, and the people over at the government office keep telling me to check back. The money I have won't last long if I can't find work."

I walked over to him. "I can pay the rent, Willie," I said, rubbing his shoulder.

Frowns rippled across his sweaty forehead. "I ain't gonna let no woman take care of me. I'm the man. I wear the pants 'round here."

I sat down beside him, and put my hand on his knee. "I sing at the club three times a week. I get my regular pay plus tips. I don't do too badly. Besides, I paid the bills when you were away."

"Didn't you hear me? I ain't letting no woman run me. I am a man," he said, raising his voice.

Many times his stubbornness got in his way. Often he was too rowdy for me, and getting him to listen was a task of its own. "Calm down," I said in a soothing tone. "Something is going to happen. A job will come through. Now come on; it's almost time for us to leave."

I opened the armoire and pulled out the royal blue dress Willie had brought me from New York. It was made out of chiffon and the waist was low, emphasizing my heavy chest and round hips. "It's what the women in the city wear to a party," Willie had said the night he returned. I knew he was depressed, so I wanted to do anything I could to cheer him up and make my life easier.

"You know something, Pearl, they called us Doughboys. Can

you believe a grown man being called a boy? I didn't like that, either."

I gave him a hug and a kiss. "Forget about all that tonight, Willie. Come on to the joint and let me sing to you."

At last he smiled. "All right." He went to the small armoire we shared. As he searched for something to wear, I pulled out a white, button-down shirt and I held it up to his chest. "Put this on."

He put on the shirt with gray pants and gave his boots a spit shine.

"You look good, baby," I told him and his broad chest started to rise again. I spun around so he could admire the dress he'd bought for me.

"Gurl, you are so beautiful."

We arrived at the joint around eight o'clock, and it was filling up fast. Ever since the soldiers had come back home, the place had been jam-packed. Some nights patrons stood around for the entire night, simply to be in the company of the soldiers. They were perceived as worldly, and many of them were single. The ladies always outnumbered the men here, and on occasion a scrap would break out between the women over the attention of one of the soldiers. As usual, I ordered a gin and tonic and strolled back to the table I'd taken as my own a while ago. Willie remained at the bar.

He had come to all of my performances for over a month. He seemed to relish the time at the joint, where he fraternized with the men with whom he had spent the last two years. Although he didn't let me out of his sight, he had managed to contain his jealous rages because he knew one of us had to have a job. He'd even controlled himself around Herman.

Roy came over as usual.

"Miz Pearl, you want something else 'fore the set?"

"No, baby, I think this will do for now."

"You don't seem like yo'self tonight."

"Oh, I'm all right."

"Well, if you want something tell me, Miz Pearl."

Roy had been the only man Willie felt comfortable with talking to me. I couldn't tell if it was Roy's mannerisms or the fact that he was so naïve and young, too tender for me to touch, that set Willie at ease. Maybe it was because Roy stuck to the same routine, bringing me drinks and asking me how I felt.

"Now, that boy has a crush on you," Willie had commented one night after Roy walked away from our table.

My nerves were rattled by his mood, and I was afraid to speak. I was certain anything I said would set him off.

"I ain't got to worry 'bout him, though. It's the ones I don't see that I need to know," he mumbled, "like the men you saw while I was gone."

I bit my bottom lip, and then eased the words out, "Willie, please. These people know I'm married. They remember you."

He looked around with a scowl. "Ain't nobody up in here but hound dogs. All of 'em searching for a coattail to get under. I'm a man, Pearl. I know these things."

I ignored him and kept smiling as some of the patrons noticed me and waved. Willie was so nosy and distrusting of me, I wished I had never married him.

I did see why the attention bothered him, though. Willie was easy on the eyes, too. All of the women smiled at him and I knew they wanted him. Even with his country shirts and boots, his tall stature and good looks forced the ladies to stare. Still, I had my eyes on someone else.

That night Herman sat at the center table in the front row. When I saw him, all of the feelings I had for him intensified. He stared right into my eyes. When I began his favorite song, I closed my eyes to keep from gaping at him from the stage, all the while wondering if Willie noticed the connection Herman and I shared.

Willie had been standing at the bar, occasionally glancing at me. I would acknowledge him and wave every so often. But when Herman strolled through the door with cuffed trousers, a white shirt and hat, I inhaled. The sight of him had thrown me off balance. I had missed the way Herman made me feel before a set, how he rubbed my thigh and kissed me on the forehead and said I was the prettiest woman in the place. I couldn't take my eyes off him.

Willie strutted toward the stage. Two women whispered as he walked past them. Yet he only had eyes for me. He smiled with his thick, weathered hands wrapped around a glass of scotch and water. He stared hard at Herman; but the smooth lover man never acknowledged him.

Willie was a good man, maybe too good for me, but I craved Herman like an alcoholic craves whiskey. The time I'd spent with him had been too fast and edgy.

The next morning, as always, Willie got up early. He put on a white shirt, trousers, and boots. From the window I watched him cross the street and head toward downtown, past the three men standing on the corner. I watched him until he was out of my sight and then I got dressed. I walked three long blocks south behind the school yard, through the alley, and past the corner store. With each step I prayed that Willie didn't turn around, that he didn't forget something and have to return home. Most days he'd go to several places before coming back, and I wanted him to take his time today. When I reached Herman's brick tenement house, a regular from the club came to the door as I was entering. He spoke and winked his eye at me.

I walked quickly down the hallway. Herman lived in the last room on the left. I tapped lightly on his door, trying to avoid waking up any of the other renters. Herman opened the door, still in his underpants. "Come on in, baby." I slid in like any sinner, and was relieved when he shut the door behind me. Even though it was mid-morning, it didn't bother me at all that he was home while other men were out making a legitimate living; that was how hustlers lived.

Many of our nights together had been spent at my place, when most of the town slept and only howling dogs roamed. So morning visits made me feel uncomfortable and frantic.

"Good morning," I said and started to undress.

Herman helped me remove my bloomers and corset.

Once I crawled into his bed, it felt so natural. He started stroking my back as soon as I was in his arms.

"Pearl, you know that woman from the country you seen me with?"

I turned slightly to see his face. "Yes."

He stumbled over the words. "I like her. I like her a lot."

I moved from his arms. "What do you mean, Herman?"

He sat up in the bed. "You're with Willie now," he said, as if that explained everything.

I started to become alarmed. "I thought you cared for me."

"I do, but I need somebody, too." He held out his hands. "I'm going to marry her."

CHAPTER 8
CARRIE

One night Momma called us in for a meeting. John had just come in the door, grinning after spending the evening with Hester, even though their date had been supervised by her parents. Carl had finished his chores. I was in my room writing in my diary. Mr. Camm had dropped in for one of his visits, and had stayed for dinner and rested his full stomach while reclining in Papa's chair.

Carl, John, and I joined Momma and Mr. Camm at the kitchen table. He was as comfortable as any man could be in somebody else's house. He was smiling, leaning back in the chair, the toes of his shoes elevated as if he lived here. He looked at me, winked and cut a sly grin. I turned my head away.

Momma quickly got to the point. "Me and Mr. Camm are gonna get married," she said and smiled at him. No sound came from anywhere. Not even the chickens cackled under the window sill. My brother Carl turned three shades darker, shifted in his seat and cleared his throat.

"When did all this come about?" he asked.

"Well, Herman's been coming around for some time now. He's already like one of the family." She glanced across the table at Mr. Camm, who immediately offered his take on the news.

"Yes indeedy, I thought it was 'bout time me and Mae Lou tied the knot, came together as a family."

"How can you be thinking 'bout marriage? Papa ain't even turned cold in his grave," John blurted out. That was expected, since he was never one to hold his tongue.

"You hush yo' mouth, boy! Mr. Camm is good to me and he wants us to be his fam'ly," Momma snapped. John flared his nostrils and shook his head. He'd said what I had been thinking, but didn't have the courage to say.

"Well, congratulations," Carl said and banged his fist on the kitchen table so hard that the table shook.

Momma didn't say anything, but she cut her eyes in his direction. I couldn't help gazing at Mr. Camm. He'd slithered his way into Momma's life and now our home. He was slick, like the fox Papa shot that was sneaking around our hen house. He seemed to enjoy the feuding, his beady eyes moving from Momma's face to Carl's.

"I'm sorry, Momma, I want you to be happy," Carl said.

John mumbled something under his breath and I smacked my lips.

"Now, we done talked to the reverend, so we gonna do it real soon," Momma said. With that announcement, not even a gust of fresh air could clean the foulness in the room.

"Carrie, you mighty quiet," Mr. Camm said, peering at me from across the table.

"Congratulations, Momma," I forced from my lips.

"I know that ev'rybody going to git along," Momma assured us. To add insult to our feelings, Mr. Camm put his arm around her shoulder.

He was smiling from ear to ear, like any vagrant would who had finally found a stable home in which to lay his head.

Where on earth had this man come from? Now he was going to stay?

On that Sunday, they got married. It was freezing cold. The wind whistled through the bare trees and that morning I'd hoped it would snow. If it had, church would not convene and the wedding would not take place. So when the reverend finished his sermon, and opened up his prayer book, and announced he was about to perform a wedding ceremony, a chill went through my entire body. Some of the skeptical church members frowned and whispered, "A wedding? Who's getting married?"

When the reverend asked who would give Momma away, Carl took his time as he walked to the altar. The reverend said, "Son, come on now, we got a wedding to do."

The congregation cheered at the sight of Momma. She was beautiful. Her hair was hanging down to her shoulders in curls. She was dressed in off-white from top to bottom. Her lips were rose and her face dusted with nutmeg face powder. Mr. Camm was wearing the same spiffy suit he'd worn the first Sunday he'd come to pay Momma a visit.

When they began to say their vows, tears slid down my face, because I'd never seen Momma look so beautiful.

"I now pronounce you man and wife," the reverend said and most of the church cheered. But close to me sat two church members who mumbled loud enough for me and anyone else nearby to hear.

"That man ain't right for Mae Lou."

"He done been around town. Been spending his nights somewhere else, if you know what I mean."

"I hope he don't hurt her, 'cause he's a ladies' man."

"Ain't that the truth."

Afterward, Aunt Bessie and Ms. Ruth served fried chicken, potato salad, ham biscuits, peach punch, and the wedding cake.

Mr. Camm shook hands, grinning as usual. After grabbing Carl's and John's hands and literally forcing them to shake with him, he walked over to me.

"Little lady, ain't you gonna give yo new pappy a hug?" Before I could respond, he'd grabbed me and pulled me close to him. He was scrawny but strong. I nearly choked before I pulled away, managing to smile.

On the way home from the church, John said to me, "Papa has only been gone a few months." Momma turned around and gave him a stern look. I kept my eyes fixed straight ahead. Inside, I wished I had been bold enough to say the same thing.

Momma had made the biggest mistake of her life.

CHAPTER 9
CARRIE

Carl was young and on the verge of manhood when he fell in love. He strutted around like a peacock. Although all the girls in school had eyes for him, Mary was his choice. She was a short, peach-colored girl like me with short, curly hair. She was quiet and timid. At church, Carl sat with Mary and her family. It used to be hard to get him up on the fourth Sunday morning for church, but soon he was waking up the rest of the house.

Every other Sunday evening, he would put on his church clothes and ask to drive the family buggy to Mary's. And if Momma didn't allow him to use it, he'd walk all the way. He took special care of his appearance, something he had never cared about before. He would bathe and shave, doing all he could to look presentable, shedding his regular overalls and T-shirts for his Sunday trousers and a white dress shirt.

When Carl finally told us he had proposed to Mary, none of us were surprised. The wide smile on his face told us what her answer was, too. Carl had been saving the extra money he made working for the Fergusons in a ceramic blue cookie jar, kept stashed under his bed.

"I'm going to buy a couple of cows and a pig with the money," he told me.

"Why don't you use it to leave from around here?"

He was puzzled by that suggestion. "I like it here, been here all my life. I'm used to this."

"Young people don't have anything to do in the country."

A smile lit his face. "Oh, there are plenty of things to keep you occupied."

"What, may I ask?"

"For one thing, you could spend more time reading and working. You know what Momma always says about an idle mind."

Mentioning Momma wasn't the right thing to say to me. Right now I was barely speaking to her.

Carl didn't notice. "Pretty soon you and everybody else are going to be plenty busy helping me clear the land near the creek."

"How's that fun?"

"At least you'll be helping your brother. The faster we build a place for Mary and me to live, the faster we can get married."

"I can't wait," I said sarcastically.

"At least you will have me close by."

That was a comfort, but I said, "I don't want you to leave at all."

"I'll be right across the yard."

"Why can't y'all move in with us?"

He glanced toward the kitchen, where Mr. Camm was sitting. "Now you know that wouldn't be right."

"For me it would."

"Like I said, we'll be across the yard, and you're welcome at any time."

At the same time, John was counting down the weeks until he could get out of the county. And as quiet as I kept it, so was I. One night he went to Momma and asked for her support.

Momma was sitting on the porch rocking in the chair Papa had built for her. She often sat out there and admired the changing of the season.

When John came and sat down in the chair beside her, she smiled.

"Momma, I want to quit school and go up to Washington with Uncle Joe." Being blunt was his middle name.

"Oh yeah, and what else do you want?" she said with a growl.

"You know how bad coloreds get treated around here. We can't get jobs doing nothing but farming or handyman work."

"And what's wrong with that? People take good care of their families with handyman work, as you've named it."

John wasn't going to back down, though.

"Momma, I want to leave."

"I hope you thought this thing out 'fore coming to me," she said.

"I need to grow. I can't grow around here. People are in the same condition they were in before slavery was abolished."

"And how would you know that, son? Most of the peoples you are talking about made it possible for us to farm and do handiwork. We've come a long way."

That wasn't good enough for him. "But I need to go."

She gritted her teeth. "Boy, I thought you had some sense in your head. Now you go to talking like a fool. I let Carl quit school to help 'round here. Now you want to quit. You gonna finish school and get your paper, and then we can talk." Then she leaned back in the rocking chair and started to rock.

"I need a break, Momma. I'm tired," he said humbly.

Momma began to hum in reply.

She often hummed or sang when she had nothing to say, or when she was frustrated and annoyed.

John disliked humdrum country life more than I did. He never understood why colored folks still felt as if they needed to serve whites. Many times Momma had to stop him from letting his tongue run wild and causing the family embarrassment.

One Sunday morning in church school, Miss Ruth, our teacher, slapped John right smack dab on the lips. Miss Ruth had been talking about how much God loved us and John questioned her.

"Well, Miss Ruth, if He loves us so much, then why is it that coloreds have less than the whites?" Carl nudged him in the side, tried his best to get him to be quiet, but John was so riled up, he didn't seem to notice.

"Now, the Bible say wez all God chirren and He loves us one and all," Miss Ruth said. She was a robust woman, and she squinted when she spoke. She couldn't read and John knew that. She always wanted to teach, but the only place that it was okay to teach without being able to read was church.

"Now, Miss Ruth, can you show me that in this here Bible?" John held the Bible up toward her and smirked at the rest of us.

She grabbed the Bible, opened it to the fourteenth chapter of Proverbs and pointed her finger at the text. Despite her illiteracy, she knew that the fourteenth chapter was about foolishness and the use of the tongue. She'd learned about the Bible by listening to others recite the words.

John stopped talking long enough to read the scripture. When he finished reading, he understood what she had been trying to teach us, but it was too late. Miss Ruth reached over the pew and backhanded him right in the mouth. His head hit the back of the pew with a thump. I had to catch myself to keep from laughing out loud at him.

He apologized, but it was too late for that as well. Momma and Papa had also been listening to his foolishness. Papa was jacking him up by the collar so hard Momma had to grab Papa's arm and pull him back. Sighing loudly, Papa took out his handkerchief and wiped his brow.

Momma wasn't defending John now, though. Setting her feet

on the porch floor, she said, "John, I thought I'd taught you right. Now you know ain't no colored man gonna find a decent job without an education, and I expect you to finish your schooling." Then she stood and walked back into the house. The screen door slammed behind her. John was left speechless and frozen in place. Eventually, he threw his hands up in the air and turned away, mumbling something to himself.

I was the only one who had no chance to escape. And I needed out more than my brothers. Though Mr. Camm had just married Momma, that didn't stop him from turning his lustful eyes on me.

Momma walked around blissfully through the house. It made me uneasy when I thought about how she'd never done that when Papa was alive. When I came in a room where she was, I would catch her smiling like a schoolgirl in love and immediately, she'd wipe the smile off her face and a frown would replace it. I'd shake my head.

Nothing seemed to move Mr. Camm. He was laid-back, even lazy. He watched Carl work tirelessly and never bothered to help. Because Carl had taken on Papa's chores, he had to drop out of school. Mr. Camm would plop down in a chair under a tree and watch Carl do all the things that fell under the responsibilities of a man of the house. He'd light a cigarette and blow smoke rings until they dissipated in the wind. Most of the time, he was in the way. Papa had been so different. Even before we were dressed in the morning, he had already eaten breakfast and found something to do.

Mr. Camm's laziness wasn't what disturbed me the most, though. One Saturday morning when Momma had gone to Mrs. Fergusons' and left me home, Mr. Camm strolled into the kitchen. While I put food away, he kept staring and grinning at me. He rubbed his head and grinned.

"What are you doing in here?" he asked.

Fear always came over me whenever he entered a room, and I said quietly, "I'm doing the things Momma told me to do."

"You're just trying to get my attention."

I ignored him and continued to stack Mason jars under the kitchen cabinet.

"Why are you ignoring me?"

"I'm trying to get this done before Momma gets back."

When I stood up straight from stacking the jars, he came up right in front of me and blocked my path.

"Excuse me," I said, shivering but trying to slide past.

"You don't need to go around me."

I stood there and waited for him to get out of my way.

He remained where he was, as if he wanted me to do something else. Eventually he did move.

"You scared of me," he said, laughing as I passed him.

I went straight to my room, locked the door and waited for him to leave the house before I came back out. My hands trembled as I sat on my bed. I pulled out my diary and wrote about what he'd done. After several long minutes, my heartbeat finally returned to normal.

When I heard the squeaky kitchen door slam shut, I knew Mr. Camm had gone outside. I finished writing in my diary and returned to the kitchen to complete the list of chores Momma expected to be done. The sooner I finished, the sooner I could get to washing and pin-curling my hair for church.

I had been in the kitchen only ten minutes when Mr. Camm snuck back in the house. My brothers were outside working with their backs bent, pulling weeds, continuing the difficult work that had stolen Papa from his family.

"You're still in here?" Mr. Camm asked as if he and I had a casual relationship.

"I told you. I've got to finish up before Momma comes back. She should be coming soon," I said, by way of warning him.

He gazed at me with his dark, beady eyes and then opened the pantry. He grabbed the hammer which hung on the nail inside, but he didn't leave. He leaned back against the wall and gawked at me from across the room.

I grabbed the broom and vigorously swept the floor, hoping that he'd leave.

Tears welled up in my eyes, but I didn't release them. I was annoyed at the way he watched me. His eyes traveled from my emerging chest down to my feet. The close attention made me nervous. I'd been nervous about him watching me ever since he moved in.

At last I couldn't take the staring, so I propped the broom up in the corner of the room and started walking out the kitchen. Like a cat, he pushed up against me and I almost lost my balance. I broke my fall against the wall.

"Leave me alone," I said.

"You fell against me," he responded, still piercing me with his eyes.

"No, sir, I didn't," I said as I hurried down the hall.

He stood in the door and called after me, "It's a matter of opinion." Then he let out an uproar of laughter.

I was left shaking after the encounter, and gave up on finishing the chores. I'd take the punishment if Momma delivered it.

His actions made me want to get a knife. When he stood against the wall eyeing me most evenings after dinner, all yearning and lustful, I wanted to kill him.

The thought of my brothers leaving home troubled me, and sometimes, late at night, I'd cry. I didn't ever want to be alone with Mr. Camm in the house. Carl was in love with Mary, and John was thinking about moving away and getting a government job. Carl had already started working with Mr. Ferguson some days, spending more and more time away from home. And it was obvious that Mr. Camm wouldn't leave me alone.

CHAPTER 10
PEARL

"I'm ready to go," Willie said as soon as I sat down. I had belted my heart out and the crowd had cheered and begged me to sing an encore.

"Can I finish my drink? I just finished my set, Willie." I took a sip of my gin and tonic, watching the men swing wild women around and do the loose legs jiggle. I loved to dance and so did Herman. We'd dance the entire night away. We had actually closed the joint once or twice. I didn't want to go home tonight. Herman was on the floor dancing with one of the ladies who came in regularly, and if Willie had not been there, it would have been me on the floor with him.

"Come on," I said, "let's stay a little longer."

"No, I'm ready now," he said, and stood up. He had fire in his eyes.

I reluctantly stood up as well, and left my gin and tonic half-full on the table as Roy walked over to check on me.

"You're leaving early tonight," he said. "You all right, Miz Pearl?"

"I'm all right, Roy. Good night."

He nodded at me and mumbled, "Good night, Willie," through a frown of confusion.

Willie threw up a hand, even though the vein in his neck pulsated visibly and his nostrils were flared. He was mad.

On the walk home, he didn't say but a few words, even when I tried to convince him to talk.

"What's wrong, Willie?" I asked.

"Ain't nothing wrong," he said, and grunted.

"I thought you wanted to hang out with your buddies tonight."

He pulled me by the hand and propelled me faster down the street. His nostrils were wide and his face swollen from a frustration he could not control. I hoped the cold night breeze would settle him down before we made it home.

Washington, D. C. was lively for a Wednesday night, and as we swiftly walked down the cobblestone street, we could hear the chatter and laughter of people passing by. It was a colorful and diverse neighborhood adorned with lovely shrubbery and trees. Decent people of all professions lived here. It was like a big family. Sometimes, late at night, I could hear the echoes of fun and laughter through my bedroom window.

Our pace slowed before we made it to the apartment, and Willie's heavy breathing ceased. My heart started to race when he put the key in the lock.

I walked inside, got undressed, took a sink bath and put on my nightgown. Willie went into the kitchen and poured himself a glass of water from the icebox. He sipped it and plopped down in a chair and sat there as if he was in a trance.

Thirty minutes passed before he finally came into the bedroom. He stood in the frame of the door and stared at me.

"Aren't you coming to bed, Willie?"

He paused, and then said, "Do you want me in there?"

I was getting tired of begging him to tell me what was on his mind. His sudden eruptions had my nerves rattled. I was tired of walking around on egg shells, scared to even talk to the men at the club who had supplemented my income with good tips while Willie had been away.

"Willie, come to bed if you want to. I'm going to sleep," I said grumpily and slid deep under the covers. When I reached over to cut out the lights, he scared me, yelling, "You'd better leave them lights on!" in his stern, baritone voice.

All of a sudden, I felt a chill pass through my body. The tension was so thick I would need a knife to slice through it. I didn't like the feeling, and reminded myself that Willie had never raised a hand to me.

I sat straight up in the bed. "What is wrong with you, Willie? Something is going on with you."

"You don't know, Pearl?" he asked, and moved toward the bed.

"No, damm it, I don't."

"Let me start," he said ominously, and sat down at the foot of the bed.

I was silent, scared to move, waiting for him to continue.

"That nigger, the one you been singing to at the club."

"Come on, Willie, we've been down this road before."

"Gurl, don't make me mad. You know him and I know you been seeing him. Do I look like a damn fool to you?"

Fire was in his eyes, and he was moving erratically and pointing like a madman. I didn't know what to do. I wondered if one of my patrons had said something. Or was Willie speculating as always, trying to get me to confess?

"I haven't been seeing anybody but you."

He gave me a hard stare. "Gurl, when I married you, I knew you's the kind a woman a man need to keep an eye on. You's pretty and you know it. And you get off on the attention of other men."

"Willie, all women are like that," I said, confused.

"But not for every damn man." He raised his voice even louder. "The night I came home, you were singing for him. And you've sang to the son of a bitch every night he's come in. What the hell you want me to think?"

I pretended to be weary. "I don't know what you are talking about."

"Pearl, you's a goddamn liar!" he yelled.

The neighbor knocked on the wall. "Keep it down over there."

The walls were not thin, yet Willie's thick, baritone voice could wake up the dead when it was loud.

"Calm down," I said to him.

"There you go again. 'Calm down.' You's my damm wife. You ain't got no business smiling in other men's faces. You should have mo' respect for yo'self."

"I work."

"Gurl, let me finish. I used to get mad when we first met, with men watching you and lusting over you. Now, I know it is yo' business. But, Pearl, I am a country boy. I believe in old-fashioned thangs, and I don't want my wife acting like a damn whore. You are my wife. And the way that dude look at you, you know him more than you letting on."

"I don't know nothing."

"I tell you what," he said. "You can keep lying if you want to, but I'm going to kill his black ass."

I stiffened with alarm. "Willie, you are crazy. That man hasn't done anything to you."

"He's seeing my wife."

"I told you, I don't know him."

"Okay then," he said, and he stood up. "I hear he lives around here, and I'm going to find him." He stormed out of the bedroom.

I jumped out of the bed and followed him into the living room. His eyes were troubled and beads of sweat were sliding down the sides of his face. He patted his pocket searching, I knew, for his switchblade.

"Where are you going?" I asked.

"Back down to the club. Tonight was the last time you going to see that son of a bitch."

Willie always carried a knife on him, and even though I didn't know of a time he had used it, I always feared he might. I dashed in front of the door and blocked him from leaving.

"Willie, stay here. Don't go down there getting in trouble."

"Why are you worried about him? What the hell he mean to you?"

He tried to push me away from the door, but I wouldn't budge.

"Move, Pearl, 'fore I hurt you."

I yelled, "Leave that man alone, Willie! Stay away from him."

Without warning, he slapped me so hard I tumbled to the floor. I hit my head on the knob on the way down. My head stung from the fall, and blood started dripping down my cheek. "I told you not to mess around on me, Pearl. I told you, gurl."

He was so enraged, he hit the wall with his bare fist and put a dent in the plaster.

I got up, blood dripping from the cut above my eye. I ran into the bathroom and pressed a wet cloth against my head to stop the bleeding and hopefully prevent swelling.

Willie sat down on the bed, shaking his head. "I'm sorry, Pearl. I didn't mean to hurt you."

All I could think about was my safety. "I'm leaving here tonight."

I pulled out my suitcase and started throwing clothes out of my drawer into it.

Enraged again, Willie lifted it up off the bed and heaved the suitcase across the room. It fell to the floor with a bang and my clothes tumbled onto the floor.

"You ain't going nowhere. You're my wife. You don't leave me!" he yelled.

Tears welled up in my eyes. I had never felt so trapped in my life. Without speaking, I bent down and started picking up my clothes and unwillingly shoved them back in the armoire drawer.

Willie coldly watched me pick up clothes with one hand, holding the wet towel on my face with the other.

When I had conjured up enough courage, I told him, "You need to leave, Willie. Get out of my house."

He said firmly, "I ain't going no damn where and neither is you. So get used to it. Why don't you think about a way to satisfy yo' man, and keep yo' mind off that nigger at the club?"

My face and my voice had been my money-makers. My looks had gotten me jobs and my talent had kept me working. Now it all had been compromised. The left side of my face was deep red and swollen. I had a small cut above my eye. And the more I thought about what Willie had done, the more upset I became.

I put the suitcase back under the bed.

Willie finally took off his clothes and crawled in the bed. He patted the space beside him. "Get in."

Both fear and rage swept over my body like a howling wind.

Willie had become a bitter man, and I was dazed by my craving for Herman. I was no longer thinking like a sane woman. The sight of Willie naked made me angrier than I had been when he slapped me. I didn't know how I could sleep with him.

I went into the washroom and put some petroleum jelly on my face. The swelling was subsiding, but a small bruise was forming over my eye.

I crawled into bed and snuggled as close to my edge as possible without falling over it.

Willie put his hand on my back. Tears welled up in my eyes and dropped onto the pillowcase. I had always been slow to cry, but I could not imagine spending the rest of my life with him. He was a detriment to my career and my chance at real love.

I flinched as he started rubbing my back.

"You are my wife, gurl."

I pleaded, "Willie, please go to sleep."

My words fell on deaf ears. He rubbed my legs and tugged at me until I stopped resisting. I gave in out of fear. If he hit me once, he might try again.

He got on top of me, licked my neck and then my breasts, and rubbed his hands against my vagina. My nipples reacted and so did my clitoris.

"You know I love you, gurl," he whispered deeply in my ear.

At least he was quick. Inside of me, I couldn't let myself go.

I lay there like a stiff and let him gyrate up and down on me for the last time.

I fell off to sleep after a while, and so did Willie.

The next day was Thursday. Willie got up early. He put on the same striped shirt, black pants, and brogans. "Pearl, you be here when I come back."

I turned my back toward him. "Where am I going? I don't sing tonight and besides, you've messed my face up."

"I'm going to find work so you can quit that job. I want my woman home and with children."

The idea left me numb. I was thirty-three years old. I never desired to be domesticated. That was precisely the reason why I had worked so hard on my singing career. And Willie was not going to change me.

Out the window, I watched him turn the corner. I put my clothes on, threw what I could fit in my suitcase, gathered money from the jar I had hidden under the bed, and took off down the street to the club.

Roy was there cleaning up from the night before, washing down the tables. He noticed my bruise. "What happened to you, Miz Pearl?"

"I need to get to the train station," I told him.

He poured a drink. “Calm down. Drink this,” he said.

I drank the entire glass in one gulp.

“Please, you got to get me to the train station,” I said. “I can’t be here when Willie comes back.”

Roy quickly became protective. “Stay here, Miz Pearl. You’ll be safe here.”

He locked me in the club. While he was gone, I poured myself another shot of gin and sipped on it until I was lightheaded.

In less than twenty minutes, Roy returned. “I got my uncle’s car.”

Roy drove me to the train station, and as a generous gesture, he paid for my ticket to Jefferson.

I was going to pay a visit to the country.

CHAPTER 11
CARRIE

The piece of land Carl chose to build on was in the perfect place. Shadowed between tall Virginia pine trees and surrounded by beautiful willows and oaks, it lay less than a tenth of a mile away from Momma, and after all the trees were cut down, only fifty feet from the road. Behind it was a creek that reflected the sun, moon, and even the stars on clear nights.

Every Saturday and Sunday afternoon, after everything was in order, all of us went over to Carl's property and helped him remove the unwanted shrubbery and trees. Momma always said that if one of us had a task, we all lended a hand. I admired that about our family.

One of those afternoons, I walked up to Carl. "Why are you working so hard? Mary's not going anywhere," I teased.

"I'm doing what any decent man would do. Besides, I'm ready to be with Mary," he said. Carl had never spoken with so much emotion about anyone. Until he met Mary, I'd never even seen him look at a girl, even the ones that pursued him, with such love and affection.

"What do you mean you're 'ready'?"

"Forget it. You'll figure it out one day," he replied, smiling. "So stop asking questions." He started again slinging the gigantic sickle across the leaves and brush.

"But why—"

"Carrie, can't we get it done? Why don't you stop asking so many dern questions?"

"Fine."

It was a big job, clearing land. I pulled up roots and weeds until my back ached. Sticker briars stuck to my dress and stockings. John steered the mules to turn over the largest weeds and bushes. At times, Mary's father would also help.

Right after we finished on that particular day, Carl said, "I need everybody's help. We've got to move all of the green stuff lying around into one big pile to be burned."

Mr. Camm stood up, adjusted his hat and put his hand on his hips. "Mae Lou, I'm gonna ride over to town for a minute. Be back in a little while." Everyone knew that he was going over to the Watering Hole, a juke joint three miles south of us. Momma did not say a word; she kept on throwing weeds in the big pile.

We didn't see him again until he staggered in the door around four o'clock in the morning. He was so drunk his scent preceded him into the house, the stink of whiskey and nasty women. His shirt was hanging over his pants, part inside and part out. He didn't even shut the door behind him. Momma put the latch back on the door, and he staggered in the direction of their bedroom.

"Herman, you are not going to keep coming in my house all times of night," she told him.

"Oh, come on, baby," he slurred, bracing the wall for support as he struggled toward their room. When she caught up, he leaned over and kissed her on the neck.

She pushed him away and he slipped, almost falling to the floor.

After their bedroom door closed, I could still hear the rumble of voices battling inside.

"Let me tell you. Ain't gonna be no staying out all night and then coming home to me."

"What you talking about, Mae Lou? I love you."

"Herman, sit down. Take yo' clothes off and get in the bed. It is almost daybreak."

"Come on, Mae Lou, you know I love you."

"Get yo' hands off me. I can't tell you what to do. You's a grown man, but I can't have you coming in here all times of the night. And if you don't like it, you gonna have to get out."

"Mae Lou, let me get some rest. I don't want to hear this tonight."

"Listen, Herman, this is my house and I ain't gonna let you or nobody else bring me down. You gonna have to come home at a decent hour or else."

"I hear you, Mae Lou, get under the covers."

"I done told you to get yo' hands off me. You drunk and you smell."

The sounds diminished. *That scoundrel*, I thought, and climbed back in the bed. Every weekend he had some place to go. When the sun went down, that's when he came alive, hitching the horses up for their twilight stroll to his favorite spot to get drunk. The Watering Hole was noted for loose women and a good time. Momma used to say that only floozies hung out in places like that. I supposed Mr. Camm was one.

The next morning, as Mr. Camm sat down for breakfast, the stench of whiskey braced me like a stiff wind from across the table. I covered my nose and mouth with a napkin to prevent the smell from interfering with the taste of my food.

"I put some water in the bedroom this mo'ning, so you can wash up," Momma said, her nose turned up. "Whys don't you go back and wash a little 'til breakfast is ready."

Mr. Camm smacked his lips and tottered right up from the table, almost knocking the chair to the ground. He mumbled, "I can't believe this shit," and walked back to the bedroom.

Five minutes later, he reentered the kitchen. The stench was now subdued and we could eat our food without choking. I wondered to myself about it all. How could Momma put up with such a drunk? I'd known from the start that he would disappoint Momma. I knew it, and those thoughts made my blood warm.

After breakfast, we all headed back to Carl's land and started clearing the brush. Mr. Camm spent the whole day working with us. I'd always heard that sometimes it's best to work off a good drunk.

My mind didn't stay on Mr. Camm for long. A far more handsome helper came along. As soon as I saw him, I murmured, "That man got it all."

Every time Simon visited Carl, my heart trembled. When our eyes met for the first time, embers of heat kindled throughout my body. His almond eyes were deep-set and magnetic. He was handsome, at least six feet tall, with broad shoulders and built like an athlete. He had perfect teeth that sparkled when the sun hit them, and smooth skin like a cup of coffee blended perfectly with a hint of cream. He and Carl had become the best of friends, and the new house had become their hang-out. For that reason alone, I was elated.

Where had this man been all my life?

This is how it all started. At first he didn't say much, simply watched me from a distance. I went out of my way to be seen, sashaying in front of him as he helped my brother clear land. At times I stopped to pick up a twig only a few feet away from where he stood, hoping he liked what he saw.

Simon was Mary's brother, but I'd never seen him in church. He stayed over in a neighboring town taking care of his sick grandma. As much as I hated being in the sun, its rays didn't seem to burn as hot whenever Simon was around. I made myself extra useful. On the days when Carl worked during the week, I would finish my homework and politely offer my help wherever I could.

"Why are you hanging around here doing extra work every day? You normally try to hide from anything to do with working outside." Carl smiled when he pulled a handkerchief out of his back pocket and wiped the pearls of sweat dripping down his face. His collar was covered in a ring of wetness.

"Don't you need help?" I asked.

"I think you're hanging around here trying to get some attention. Look like you got your eye on Simon."

"Well, since you mentioned him, does he have a girlfriend?"

"What? Why do you need to know that?"

"Just asking," I said, acting as if it didn't matter.

"You better watch yourself," Carl warned me as if he had taken Papa's place and I needed his approval to date.

One hot summer day, after working hard, I sat down on a tree trunk to rest. When I lifted my head, I caught a glimpse of Simon staring at me from behind a stack of weeds and twigs. My cheeks flushed and my heart fluttered. When our eyes met, he smiled. I lowered my head, pretending I didn't notice him. I wasn't sure if it was his mesmerizing stare or his even white teeth that attracted me. Or was it his chiseled body? It was anything my mind imagined it could be. And I did imagine.

He strolled over to me, his shoulders squared, and my heart started to race.

"I see you here every evening with your brother. You don't seem like the kind of girl who should be working out in the woods."

I was so shocked when he finally said something to me, I started to stutter.

Because I wasn't prepared to respond, the silliest things flowed from my lips. I didn't have any experience with boys.

Whenever the boys at the schoolhouse talked to me, I was always too shy to respond. In my opinion, none of the boys in my class were mature enough to be with me anyway. I liked playing with them, but not when they'd show they liked me by teasing and calling me names, then sneaking around and hitting me on the arm to get my attention. When I got my period, Momma had given me the big sermon about boys. For an hour, she lectured and pointed her finger at me before she was confident I'd finally gotten the message. "Boys can be bad for you," she said, and her words still lingered in my head. "Don't let 'em ruin your life. Your focus should be on staying in school and learning all you can. The rest will come in due time."

"I finished school two years ago," Simon told me. "Been away for a while. I was in Lynchburg taking care of my sick grandma. Now I'm back down here."

"Are you glad to be back?"

Carl stopped what he was doing and stood there intently listening to every word that came out of my mouth. I didn't care, so I turned my head and continued. I wanted to know Simon better.

"Somewhat, but I don't plan on staying here. I got plans of my own now," he said. He moved closer and gazed directly in my eyes. And the closer he came, the more I became flustered.

"Me, too," I managed. "I'm going to leave once I finish school and go away to college. I think I want to settle in a big city, maybe teach school."

"I hope it's not too far. I can't get to know you from too far away," he said, grinning, and I nearly fainted right there. But I took a deep breath and remained composed.

"Hey, there's too much work to be playing," Carl called out.

I picked up a handful of twigs and tossed them into the burning bonfire. Then I walked back over to where Simon was working and continued my conversation. "So what are your plans?"

"I'm trying to get a job with the Negro Leagues. I don't care if it's with the Richmond Black Sluggers or that new team, the Birmingham Black Barons. Anybody that will take me, I'm gone." Then he picked up the sickle, and as he started swinging it like a baseball bat, every chiseled muscle seemed to burst out of his shirt. I caught myself staring.

Momma loved baseball and so did I. Whenever traveling teams came to town, it was a big event. Folks gathered at the empty field for the big game. Families laid out food on the grass. Others dug holes and fired up a barbecue pit, roasting pork and steaming fresh butterfish and trout. Many times we had to vacate our own beds to give the players a place to rest. Momma always welcomed them, since the closest town wouldn't allow coloreds in their boarding houses. Now a baseball player wanted to talk to me.

I couldn't wait to go to school the next morning. I had to let Hester and Anna know that I had my eyes on someone. Many times I'd felt left out when we discussed boys. First, it was Hester's John. Then it was Anna's James. The one boy who had taken a liking to me was not my type. My brothers teased me because Junior had the biggest front teeth anybody had ever seen. After two years, he finally stopped sending me love notes and tagging me, and started writing another girl. Now, I had Simon to talk about.

He was smooth, too. Sitting in the kitchen with my brothers, I overheard him talking to Carl. Though I was supposed to be in my room, I listened in the hallway.

"What's with Carrie, man?" Carl asked.

"I like her. She seems to be all right. I've been checking her out."

"Yeah, I've noticed. Don't mess up now," he warned. "She is my sister."

"Oh, I won't. Just want to get to know her and be her friend."

"Come on now, just friends."

Simon let out a chuckle. "Man, I've only had one conversation with your sister so far. I promise I'll be respectful."

"You better be."

Simon laughed again. "Was I hard on you when you came to the house to see Mary?"

"That was different."

"Okay, if you say so. I do want to know her better, though."

Our friendship started growing, and the only person who couldn't tell was Momma.

In class I begged, "Hester, you've got to meet this guy."

"Okay, but I can't come this evening. It's a school night, and my parents would have a fit if I went to your house after school. I'm already in trouble with them for coming in after the sun went down."

"What happened?"

"John and I took a walk and it took a little too long. My parents chewed me out. Momma even swore, told me she was going to kick my ass."

"I hope they're not still mad."

"No, they're okay now, but I don't want do that again on a weekday."

"How about you come after church on Sunday?"

A smile appeared on her lips. "I'll have to because you won't shut up until I do. This guy has done something to you. You didn't act like this when Junior was after you," she said, giggling.

"This guy is different. He's mature and handsome. You've got to tell me what you think."

"If I told you I didn't like him, would you stop seeing him?"

I knew that wasn't possible. "I wouldn't say that."

"I know you wouldn't, so trust your own gut when it comes to your feelings."

"I will, but you're my best friend."

Hester's shoes were covered with dust when she made it to our house that Sunday; in lieu of going home, she'd walked the two miles to our house alone, because I asked. I gave her one of my plain dresses to put on since she'd messed up her church clothes.

"Where is he?"

"He's not here," I said, hoping he'd show up.

Carl didn't wait on anybody; he'd already started laying the foundation for his house when John joined him. Hester, Momma, and me joined them and started adding more weeds and shrubbery to the pile already stacked over two feet high.

We had been hard at work for over an hour before Simon came. I was so anxious to see him, I blurted out, "You finally made it," as if he owed me an explanation. He was ready to work, dressed in overalls, a straw hat and all. My pulse jumped even seeing him in common clothes.

"Yeah, I couldn't let my future brother-in-law down. He's got too much to do. Besides, my sister needs a nice place to live," he answered, smiling at Carl.

"That's right, get to work. You're late," Carl teased. Then he placed his hands on his back, took a deep breath and went right back laying stones for the foundation.

Hester touched me on the shoulder and whispered in my ear, "Yes, he is gorgeous, but not as handsome as John." We both giggled like we did every day in the schoolyard.

Momma was amazingly strong. And even though she only weighed a good one hundred ten pounds soaking wet, she had the strength of a bull. She was right beside us working as hard as any of the men—so hard she didn't even notice Hester and me giggling like a couple of laughing hyenas. If she had, she would have given us her infamous stern and cold look, which meant disapproval.

Mr. Camm found a shaded tree and propped himself up against its trunk. From behind the swaying tree limb and leaves, he intensely eyed Hester from across the yard. Everywhere she moved, his eyes would follow, as a hungry dog does its prey. He panned her frame, as he'd done me, from head to toe. And he didn't stop when he saw Momma looking. I felt sorry for her, because she had been exposed to something that embarrassed me and I wanted this to remain a family secret.

Hester turned toward me. "Your stepfather is staring at me. What is wrong with him?"

"Ignore him," I said.

"I would, but he is making me nervous. I sure hope he don't stare at every young girl he comes in contact with," she said, and rolled her eyes his way.

"He does. So don't pay him any attention; he does that to everybody. It's creepy, though."

"I hope he know it is impolite to stare at someone so hard."

"Oh, forget about him."

He was the last person I wanted to talk about. When I turned, he was still staring. He was a low-down skunk who couldn't be embarrassed.

Soon the sun began to slide beneath the clouds and paint the sky ginger. John made sure that Hester got home before dark. He took her home in our buggy and returned as the sky turned gray and the crickets started singing.

Still, we kept working. When everyone was hot, I volunteered to go for water. Simon said he'd help, too. Clearing land was a laborious job, and everyone was thirsty. When we made it to the house, we rested on the Davenport in the front room. Without any warning, Simon grabbed my fingers and clenched them. Then he reached over and kissed me on the lips.

It was my first kiss. So romantic and pure.

I was the only passenger to disembark. Most of the passengers were headed to Richmond or even farther south to places like Charlotte, North Carolina, and Atlanta, Georgia. As I placed my foot on the red clay, old memories resurfaced in a rush. When I caught a glimpse of a cardinal flying through the trees, I smiled because I always felt as though red birds brought good luck. The greenery was thick, rows and rows of pines. Everything looked the same as it had when I'd left.

"You gonna be all right?" the colored porter asked when I stepped down from the train.

"Yeah, I'll be okay," I said, admiring his weathered, deep chocolate skin with folds of wrinkles layered around his eyes. I couldn't help wondering what kind of blues they told.

"Ain't nothing 'round here but road. Now you be careful, ma'am," he said, and stepped back up in the train car.

"I know," I mumbled, and waved.

I picked up my suitcase and started down a path I'd trod many times as a child.

The noon sun was high, and the grass was withered from the cold. The air was fresh and filled with scents of earth. When I passed pastures with grazing animals, their musty odors floated through the air like wind. The walk was eerie, and by the time I arrived at my parents' small farm a mile down the road, I was slightly spooked.

I took a deep breath and headed up to the front door. On the front porch were two weathered, ash-colored rocking chairs.

I knocked and the door opened. "Lord have mercy, look who's here."

My mother was a dark-skinned, thick woman with tiny feet and fingers. She had a round face with deep dimples and black hair mixed with gray. I favored my momma a great deal, folks used to say, but had taken my complexion and height from my daddy.

CHAPTER 12
PEARL

My home had been the nightclubs of Washington, D.C., filled with stories told through the rhythm of the blues. And now the blues were real. It had been years since I had crossed my mother's doorstep. When I first left, I missed my family and their support, but after a while I became used to the independence. Now I was headed back to a place I had despised since I saw the first street pole with a lantern in Washington, at sixteen years of age. As I traveled south into Virginia, I thought about the career I had left behind and the men who I allowed to have such a great influence in my life.

I knew little about Herman, only that we were born in the same hometown. I couldn't even remember his family, had hear the last name Camm mentioned only once. Like most peopl who lived out in the country, we were isolated. My best frien was my older sister, and my only male contact back then was n brother, who ignored us girls and treated us pretty bad.

Willie, on the other hand, had a sister who was five years ol and lived in Washington. Before Willie left for the service, would often visit her, but since his return, we had not seen he all. In only a month, my routine had been completely mud up and now I was headed back to a place I no longer knew.

When the conductor yelled, "Jefferson County," I retr my suitcase from under the seat.

"Don't just stand there. Come in, child."

We held each other for at least a minute.

Then she waited until I had sat down. "Why do you have that bruise over your eye?"

She was never one to waste time. When she had something to say, it was quickly on her lips.

"It's a long story, Momma."

She looked at me as if I was still a child. "Now take yo' time. Think long and hard and then tell me the damn truth."

I shook my head.

The house hadn't changed in years. Pale gray paint and white curtains still were the core of her decorating scheme. On the Davenport was a throw cover she'd made out of scraps of material. Around her fireplace was an assortment of white plates with a blue paisley design. An old photograph on the mantel showed me and my siblings one Sunday after church when I was twelve years old. I remembered her begging the white photographer to let her pay for the portrait in installments. I was reminded that nothing had changed. She sat with her chubby arms crossed over her chest, anticipating my answer. Next, she would grind me for the truth.

"Momma, Willie and I had a fight, words and shit."

She was surprised. "The last time you wrote me, Willie was still in the service. When did he get home?" And she peered at me like she always did, thinking I made up stories simply for the sake of lying. She was wrong. They were only for survival.

I took off my shoes, wincing at my sore feet. "He's been home for over a month now."

"So why in the hell did he hit ya? What lie did you tell this time, girl?"

"Why do you always have to believe the worst about me?"

"I know my child. You are always hiding some sort of shit."

When she spoke, it was as if I was still her little girl. Most time getting whippings for telling "stories," as she called them. However, from my point of view, my stories were exaggerated truths, although I realized that excuse had never gotten me anywhere with her.

"Willie put his hands on me for the first and last time."

"Tell me what happened. Did he find out you been seeing Herman?"

"We are just friends," I protested.

Her lips tightened grimly. "Child, you are way too old for this. Telling lies like you did when you were a little girl. I thought I'd whipped you enough for that. Now you gonna go and get yo'self in trouble. Willie is a good man. He would do anything for you. I can't see that boy lifting a hand to you."

"Well, he did," I said with attitude.

She assessed the truth of what I was saying, then relented. "Willie better not come down here with no shit like that. I know you did something, though, 'cause he never hit ya before."

"We were only married six months before he went into the service."

She allowed that was true. "You really never know a person till ya live with 'em."

"He's good, but he's got a temper."

"Now, I told you not to take no wooden nickels from nobody. If he ever raises a hand to you again, you got to leave him where he's standing. But then again, don't go 'round 'voking him, either. I know ya, child, and there's mo' to this story."

"Momma, can I just feel safe at home?"

She nodded, but followed that with a warning. "This is the country, child. We treat each other right 'round here. Ain't nobody better than nobody else. Now I know you got some uppity ways, and if you gonna stay here, forget that you been in the city most of yo' life. We move a little slow."

"Why are you saying this nonsense to me, Momma?"

"I told you to think big. And I'm glad you do, but don't put the people down around ya."

"I don't do that."

"I want you to know."

I shook my head.

"Put yo' things in the bedroom, and come get yo'self some of Momma's home cooking," she said.

Annie May Moore, my mother, always demanded attention, and she got it. She worked in the church and stood contently beside my father on the farm. She knew her children, paid attention to everything they did, analyzing us and insisting on the truth. Lying to her was worthless. Since I had been her youngest, my siblings felt she always gave me more breaks. Whenever I talked back to her, instead of slapping me as she did to them, she would simply listen. My aunt said it was because Momma used to be like me.

We spent the evening talking about Washington, D.C., the lights of the city, the nightclubs I sang in. After a while, my father turned his nose up. "That ain't no life for a married woman."

We snickered because my mother had gotten as much joy from listening to the stories as I did from telling them. She had wanted to know every detail.

The next day, a Sunday, we got dressed for church. Like old times, I convinced Momma to put on some lipstick and nutmeg powder. She did and admired her beauty in the mirror. Daddy hitched the horse to the buggy. I waited and prepared to step back in time. Most people here couldn't afford cars. The church was a good two miles down the road, as I recalled walking there many times as a child.

"Whoa," Daddy said when we arrived, and the wagon came to a stop.

After Momma and I got out, Daddy coaxed the horse over beside the graveyard, where two other buggies were hitched. It was the fourth Sunday and everyone, including my siblings, attended church. Most of the community had helped build it. My grandparents had helped lay the foundation for the building. Even the land had been donated by a family in the church. The pews and floors had been built with lumber from the trees off the sharecroppers' lands. The pulpit was in front of the church, with a podium. A potbelly stove off to the left kept it warm in the winter, and opening the window sashes cooled it off in the summer. The outhouse was in the back of the building. In the summer months, the yellow jackets buzzed around, and often people were stung while eliminating. Even snakes had been known to find shelter in the outhouse. The deacons always took responsibility for keeping the church in shape, including the outhouse.

"That's her," a lady said, pointing her crooked finger at me.

She and several other church members came over to us. "Annie May, yo' daughter is home. You come to sing for us?"

"No, ma'am. I'm here visiting Momma for a while."

"You used to have a beautiful voice when you were a little girl," one of the ladies said, "and you used to love to sing verses. We'd love to hear you do a tune for us this mo'ning."

I glanced at Momma, who had moved on and was standing with Daddy, talking to a man on the church steps. She saw me and winked.

"You remember 'Marching to Zion,' don't you?"

"Yes, ma'am."

"Good. You walk in the church with the choir."

Before I could further protest, the other woman laid a hand on my forearm. "You're such a pretty girl. We so glad you want to sing for the Lord."

My muscles tightened, and I bit my lip, actually wanting to sing out, "I'm a sinner." My momma had deliberately left me to fend for myself. There was no denying a herd of desperate and demanding old ladies with hats cocked to the side on their heads. So I followed them up the steps and down the church aisle to the choir stand, singing, "We're marching to Zion, beautiful, beautiful Zion..."

I kept in step with the ladies, rocking from side to side with them as we came down the aisle.

My father, mother, and siblings sat on the second pew of the small wooden church. The community gathering place, I called it. Everybody came, including the babies. The deacons sat on the right, facing the preacher who had been there ever since I was a child.

I was starting to feel comfortable when Herman strolled to the front of the church and waited while the country woman from the nightclub walked down the aisle. What was he doing here? I started to hyperventilate.

I took a deep breath and rolled back on the pew close to Momma.

She put her arm around me. "You all right?" She was the only person that knew about him.

"I guess so," I answered, my lips quivering as I tried to keep from crying.

After the service, Momma took my hand, and we walked over to Herman.

"I knew you weren't no good," she said to him.

"Ms. Annie, I do care," he said to her, and then, turning to face me, added, "Sorry." At that point his new wife intruded in our circle, glowering at me. She knew who I was.

CHAPTER 13
CARRIE

I never liked a liar. Momma had always said, "A liar is worse than a thief." Yet, I was sneaking behind her back, not once or twice, but sometimes as much as three times a week. I'd meet Simon in the evening under the tree in the schoolyard, and then I'd tell Momma I'd been studying with Hester. In truth, the only lessons I'd learned were about Simon.

The old pine tree became our spot. Even in the fall, when its cones and needles blanketed the ground, we met there and let the wind blow through our hair. Our whispers were safe under the tree.

Simon told me, "I'm getting tired of us acting the way we do. I come to your house and we pretend we're casual friends. We are more than that, and I don't like sneaking around, especially behind your momma's back. We're starting out the wrong way and I care too much about you to keep this nonsense up. Besides, you are a grown woman."

"I don't like lying, either. I'm not a liar by nature. But Momma won't understand; she never does. I thought it would be easier on everyone if we waited a while before letting her know."

He disagreed. "All we're doing is making our lives hard. Besides, you will be sixteen soon and she should understand."

"I'm going to tell her. I really am."

I wanted to keep it our secret, though. *It would break my heart if Momma made me stop seeing him,* I thought. She had warned me many times about girls sneaking around with boys and then coming up with a baby. "If any child comes in this house with a baby, they're going to have to get out of here," she'd said to me one day, right after John had teased me about Junior in school. "You gonna get your education first." Yet, every time that I saw Simon, I'd get a tingling feeling inside. My girlish crush had turned into the womanly arousal that Momma had warned me about. No more sly grins, but sultry hints of passion instead. Warmth stirred through my loins. When he pulled me close, the thumping of his chest against mine sent me to another height of ecstasy.

Simon never pressured me for more, even when we found it hard to stop. He never put his hands on my thighs and in my bloomers like Hester said John did. He was more respectful than that. But sometimes I had that feeling. And when I did, my cheeks would turn pink, and I'd have to force myself to think about something else.

Simon respected me. Knowing it made me feel special because he was not a lay-down-in-the-woods, shame-your-name type of fellow.

"I want something to look forward to on my wedding night," he said. I gazed into his almond-shaped eyes and was mesmerized. Had he pursued it further, I surely would have given in, and later regretted it, as Momma had predicted.

"You are special to me, Carrie, and I want our lives to start out in the right way. I believe marriage should come first. That's why this fooling around ain't going to work."

"I know, but I can't help it."

In two months, I would be sixteen. Most girls were married by that age. Yet I settled for a date with Simon to church or an occasional picture show in town. Every time I got home after spending time at the schoolyard with him, my eyes dropped with shame. The minute I'd see Momma, the guilt would clog up in my throat. But it was never enough to make me tell her how I'd been sneaking around with Simon.

On another note, she did come closer to finding out how much I was dodging Mr. Camm. Sometimes he'd block my path and other times he would stare at me. It always happened when Momma was away at the Fergusons' or outside hanging clothes or lying down. Soon as she'd come into the room, he would change his demeanor as the wind did on an unpredictable March day. He was always around and taking up space that should have never been his to enjoy. He turned my stomach.

Momma almost caught him one Tuesday evening after she'd gone into her bedroom and left me in the kitchen washing the dishes. Instead of joining her, he sat in the high-back chair in the front room. After a minute, he walked into the kitchen.

"Please move," I said when he stopped directly in front of me.

"Why don't you stop whining?"

He thought I'd give in to his sleazy attentions. "I need you to move so I can get by."

"I ain't going nowhere," he said, his beady eyes shifting around the room, in case Momma came out of the bedroom.

"Can I go around you now?" I insisted.

"You know you like it." I saw him fondling the crotch of his pants.

I pushed him, and he still didn't budge.

"Please, leave me alone," I whispered. I didn't want Momma to know how much of a pervert she'd married.

"Just shut up." With one firm stride, he pinned me against the kitchen sink. Alcohol wafted into my nostrils.

I lifted my leg up as high as I could and came down on his foot hard.

"Ouch! You little..." He stopped, instantly retreating when Momma entered the room.

"What is going on in here?" Momma asked.

"Nothing," he responded quickly before I could speak.

I wanted to scream. I was so upset, all I could do was walk out of the room. My breathing was hard, and even after I settled down in my room and pulled my diary out to write, I still wanted to knock him out cold. Momma had kept me from killing him. He had wanted to do something so despicable. And the closer he came to crossing that line, the angrier he made me.

The last thing I wanted was to be accused of making things up. Ida, who was around thirteen or so, lived a few miles up the road, not far from the church. She had accused her uncle of trying to come on to her. After the news got out—and rumors travel fast in the country—I overheard Momma telling Papa at church, "Ida made the whole thing up, Robert. She's a little liar."

And when Miss Topsie accused Mr. Tom of taking liberties with her, Momma and Papa had both laughed and said she'd made it up. She kept her wavy black hair shorn close, and slicked down with a bang. She was beautiful. Her flawless, caramel-colored skin, thin waist, wide hips, and big toned legs made all the men stop and stare. When she'd come to church, the reverend would clear his throat because of her mesmerizing beauty. A time or two, Papa even gawked and Momma had tapped him on the shoulder. "Pay attention to the reverend."

All the ladies whispered when she walked through the church door. Some even sighed, and others uttered, "Look who done walked in the church." The church women knew that she was the kind who could take a man on a sultry trip away from his family. Men begged for her attention, but none like Mr. Tom.

One of the deacons in the church, Mr. Tom, simply yearned for her. Every time he saw her, his imagination would take him to heights he was ashamed to mention. The thought of her made his nature rise. He'd catch himself and look the other way. The entire congregation noticed, myself included.

Now, Miss Topsie wasn't real easy. She wanted a man who could do something for her like pay her rent, take care of her farm, and buy her clothes. She lived in a nice house and had a farm that was well kept by the men she hired. But Miss Topsie liked her meat a little rare. She liked being a mistress to white men with overloaded pockets and a craving for dark honey. Mr. Tom always felt that he could be the one to change her ways. He even bragged to one of the other men, "Once women get with me, it is hard as hell to walk away."

He'd told another deacon, "Ain't no white man can do her like I can."

The deacon replied, "You ain't got no money, Tom."

"What the hell does that have to do with anything? I can have any of these women on the church grounds."

"Man, that woman doesn't want you."

One day, Mr. Tom blocked Miss Topsie's stride when she stepped foot on church grounds. When he approached her and made his advances, she'd put her hands on her wide hips and softly but decisively said, "Tom, you ain't my type."

"What you mean, I ain't?" Mr. Tom said, nasty enough to make her angry.

"You ain't for me. Now go on and leave me alone." Then she dismissed him like he was a child.

"Tom is a damn fool. That woman ain't thinking about him," Ms. Ruth said, in earshot so that Mr. Tom could overhear her.

Mr. Tom detested being turned down, since most of the single, churchgoing women always advanced on him. He was a fine man, the color of the bitter chocolate my momma used in cakes and from what the women said, twice as sweet. He was 6 feet three inches and towered over nearly all of the men, except for Papa. Women cooked for him and sewed and did whatever he needed, but none could excite his nature as much as Miss Topsie.

When Miss Topsie left him standing on the church grounds, begging in front of some of the other lustful women, he vowed to make her pay. He mumbled, "I bet you's gonna find out 'bout me." She lifted her head and sashayed over to the reverend.

That same evening, Mr. Tom beat her home. He eased himself in through the cracked bedroom window and slid behind her front door, counting on the shadow from the closed curtains to disguise his face. He had his way with Miss Topsie, or so she alleged, right in her parlor. Her guest area, she called it. "He held me down and mounted me like you would a horse and let out all his frustrations on me," she told the reverend.

Miss Topsie called on her white men acquaintances, but none of them wanted the stale taste of nigger on their breath. They simply refused to help. They didn't need their wives thinking that they were defending no nigger woman. Then Miss Topsie turned to the church. Not one of the members supported her. Mr. Tom denied ever being with her. Like always, a deacon was perceived as a saint. But I suspected she was telling the truth, and so did the other parishioners, despite their unwillingness to support her publicly. After that, she left town.

I knew that Momma would say the same thing about me. So far, Mr. Camm had kept his hands to himself. I would hate to think that he'd do more than what he was doing now. Whenever he winked at me, I turned my head. He was dirty. The same with the time he pinned me against the sink. I waited patiently for him to move his smelly carcass out of my way.

As I wrote in my diary, he stuck his head in the door. I jumped to my feet. "I know you want me," he said quietly.

"No, sir, I was trying to get by."

"I know y'all women. I know y'all." He stood there, grinning.

"Momma wouldn't like the way you act," I threatened him.

"You's better keep your mouth closed," he hissed, pointing at me with veins popping out of his neck and a frown so evil even the devil himself might be afraid.

"Leave me alone," I pleaded.

"I ain't did nothing to you *yet*. You keep on and you gonna see," he warned me.

As he left I ran to the door, slammed it and threw the latch on. I sat on my bed thinking about how my family had changed. My most confusing thoughts were of my momma, who hadn't seen the things everyone else had been whispering about.

The very next day Mr. Camm was in the backyard sitting beside the wood pile when I came home from school. He stopped me moments before I could step in the house.

"Put your books down and get me the wheelbarrow."

Reluctantly, I set my books on the porch beside the back door. I rushed into the barn as swiftly as possible to get the wheelbarrow. Just as I came out, he was on his way inside the barn. I was relieved I'd made it out before he came in.

"You think you fast, don't ya?"

Out of breath, I answered him, "No, sir. I was doing what you asked me."

I pushed the wheelbarrow out into the yard. I glanced over my shoulder and saw him staring at me with eyes turned to slits of disgust. I rushed inside the house, my chest heaving. I found Momma cooking in the kitchen. I started to relax when I saw her standing there. She had been gazing at us from the window.

"Why are you out of breath?" she asked.

"I was getting the wheelbarrow out of the barn for Mr. Camm."

"What on earth is he doing with that?"

"I don't know."

She pulled back the curtain and peered out at him. Mr. Camm was outside fumbling with the wheel on it. He appeared to be busy, but I knew nothing was wrong with it.

"Look like he's fixing it. You's look like you seen a ghost, chile; sit down."

I sat down at the table. "He startled me when I saw him in the door of the barn."

"He caught you off guard," she said, shrugging.

I had to tell her. I couldn't run no more. I inhaled a big breath to gain enough nerve to tell on him.

"Momma…"

As I was about to say more, he walked into the kitchen.

I flinched.

"Lord, you scared her," Momma said to him.

"Oh yeah?" he said, gazing intently at me and silently daring me to open my mouth.

I got up and went to my room. I shut the door firmly, took out my diary and started writing.

Simon was waiting for me under the tree later that afternoon. My face lit up when I saw him. But it was getting too cold for us to be sitting under a tree. It was frosty cold, and the clouds hung low, full of moisture. The wind was whipping through the naked trees, and the branches were swaying. Simon had in his arms an old quilt we could use to stay warm. I smiled in relief. As soon as we sat down and wrapped ourselves up in the quilt, he whispered in my ear, "Carrie, let's do it. Let's get married."

"Marriage, to me?" I nervously echoed his sentiment.

"I want you to leave with me. You always talk about getting away from around here. Now is the time. We can go and build a life together. I got accepted by the Richmond Black Sluggers. I'm going to be a professional baseball player."

How could he be leaving? I sniffed back tears as long as I could and then I cupped my hands over my face and released them. "You can't leave me."

"We can go together," he said gently.

"I hope so."

I knew in my heart that Momma was not going to let me go, but I held on to the hope.

Momma wanted me to go to college and return to Jefferson, maybe become a teacher. I didn't want that. I wanted Simon and a chance to see the world. I would never be happy in rural Virginia. I wondered how I could convince her otherwise.

When Simon pulled me close, my heart began to race. And when he put his tongue inside my mouth, I almost forgot about waiting. I wanted to submit to him that very instant. I had to get Momma's approval, or I would go crazy.

CHAPTER 14
CARRIE

I never liked cold weather. Winter lingered for far too long. We had to huddle around the cast-iron stoves for warmth. On the ground was at least a foot of snow, and the farm animals were all confined to the barn. The wind whistled through the trees, as I stepped outside to gather the eggs from the hens. I was wrapped up, yet the wind swirled around me. The rubber galoshes I wore on my feet kept out the wetness, but they did nothing for the stinging cold.

I hadn't seen Simon in two weeks, and I missed him. The weather had been too bad for anyone to travel. The only footsteps slowly disappearing in the snow were mine. We had even missed church. I hoped that the cold spell would let up. I could see drops of water falling from the crooked icicles on the roof.

Everyone was sitting at the kitchen table when I returned with the eggs. Momma had boiled water for coffee, and the aroma of biscuits baking in the oven could be wafted throughout the house. She cracked six eggs and beat them together and poured them into the hot cast-iron frying pan with a little bacon grease.

Mr. Camm blessed the table and we all began to sop our biscuits in the scrambled eggs and sip on the hot coffee. Everyone was trying to keep warm, and no one in the house was traveling farther than the fireplace in the front room or the wood stove in the kitchen.

It didn't take long for the house to get warm. Momma went around picking up things and dusting, placing each what-not in its proper place. She had a lot of nervous energy. She rarely found the time to sit and rest, which was probably why she remained so petite.

For once I was happy to pitch in. When she asked me to hang the clothes she was washing by hand in the kitchen sink, I saw it as an opportunity to talk to her about my plans.

I had hung a clothesline in my room so I could dry my personal things. It also came in handy when the bad weather came and we needed to dry other items in the house.

As soon as Momma pulled out the first garment to hang, I started to talk.

"Momma, you know I have been working hard in school." She didn't respond. "I am hoping to go to college in Richmond next year."

"Good," she mumbled, and continued putting items on the clothesline, shaking them with vigor so that the wrinkles fell out.

John had already gotten accepted into Howard University, in Washington, D.C., and the entire house celebrated, Momma the proudest of all of us. I hoped she would have the same excitement over my feelings for Simon.

"Momma, you know Simon and I are good friends."

"Yes, I can see that," she replied.

"He is a real nice guy, decent like Papa."

She paused, a wet shirt suspended in her hands. "Where are you going with this, chile?"

"I like him a whole lot."

"I see." She cleared her throat and waited.

"I will be sixteen next month, and I was wondering if he could come see me," I blurted out.

"I've noticed him helping Carl. He seems to be a decent fellow and he is Mary's brother."

"Momma, he is real nice."

"You's don't need to convince me. It's what you think that matters. I suppose that you're close enough to sixteen to have a suitor."

"Yes, ma'am," I said happily.

"Tell yo' brother to let him know it's all right to come co'ting you."

I wanted to hug her but I knew she didn't like emotional displays. I was glad that I'd told her that much. I handed her an apron to hang on the line.

"Simon is leaving to go play baseball with the Richmond Black Sluggers," I said, carefully choosing the right words. Words I felt wouldn't change her mood. So far I was winning.

"Well, what will you do then?" she inquired.

I dropped my head. "I want to go with him," I uttered, knowing that I'd strike a nerve and might even get slapped.

Sure enough her mood changed. Her eyes became slits as she stared at me. "You ain't gonna be going nowhere with no man."

"Momma, please," I cried. "We are going to get married."

That news made her angrier. "I s'pose you've been seeing him behind my back. Been doing things grown-ups do." Her voice was louder and more intense.

"Oh no, ma'am." I paused, trying to think of a reason. "He told me that day we went to get water. He said that if he left to play with the team, he was going to ask you to let me marry him." I felt so stupid. I was lying to her again.

"That boy didn't even know you that day," she replied disbelievingly. "I want to talk to that boy. Why hasn't he asked me? You went to get water, not to get married. I's been around this here earth a long time, long enough to know when I'm being lied to. And don't you forget it."

Her comment stung; the truth always hurt. "Momma, I told him that he should talk to you first."

She was furious with me. She swung a shirt so hard on the line, splatters of water struck my face. She was not going to tolerate any sneaking behind her back.

Momma picked up the wash pan and turned around. For a moment, I thought she was going to go upside my head.

"Chile, I thought you wanted more than this. I thought you wanted to be somebody. I didn't think you wanted to live in a man's shadow. Why can't y'all chirren see?"

I didn't say anything. I didn't know what to say.

The last time Mr. Camm pinned me between the kitchen table and the stove was the last day I came straight home from school. After being threatened in my own home, I tried to stay away. John insisted on escorting Hester home each evening after school. They always walked home, snuggling up together, sometimes stopping and kissing along the way. He begged me to wait for him on the schoolyard until he came back. Sometimes I followed behind them and smacked my lips every time he moved closer to kiss her. Anyhow, Momma would whip both of us if I came home without him.

Other times when he'd leave with Hester, I would walk home with Anna. I didn't like hanging around the schoolyard and getting cold. John didn't like me leaving without him, though. He wanted me to be sitting in the same spot waiting when he returned from Hester's.

"Why are you going home with her?" John said, gazing at

Anna like she was still our enemy. Anna stood with her hands on her hips, ignoring him.

"It's too cold," I replied. I wondered when I would get up the courage to tell him who she was. I secretly wondered if he knew.

Minnie had enough children for two people. She had a total of twelve and number thirteen was still attached to her breast. Between caring for her own children and Anna's, she had her hands full.

I put my worries aside the day Anna told me about her baby.

"Carrie, I had her when I was thirteen years old. Ma told me it's all right to be 'specting at my age. She was young when you's came. But now's it's bad. I'm tired all the time. I'm too tired for learning."

"But Anna, you need an education. You are not going to be able to do nothing for your child if you can't get a job. One day you might want to get away from here. You can't do much out in the world if you can't read."

"I know," she said, kicking up snow dust on the path. "I can't take care of no baby and schooling, too. Ma said she'll help me, but I be tired. A baby is a lot of work."

"Listen, if I can help you, I will. I'll do all I can to help you read. But I ain't too good with babies. Where's her daddy?"

Anna dropped her head. "He ain't want no baby. He just used me. He left to go to the service. He said he'd be comin' back, but he hasn't; ain't even sent her a doll-baby."

When Anna first met James, he was a young man, no more than seventeen himself. He started coming around to Anna's house with a cousin. Anna, only twelve at the time, started thinking about him too much. He was different than any of the teenage boys she'd come to know.

"James was a fine man. He could speak better than Mrs. Miller.

He be dressed in nice clothes and most times he didn't have on bib overalls."

"He was smooth, huh, Anna?"

"Yep."

Anna said the first day he called out to her, he was standing in her yard, propped up on the picket fence that was halfway torn down.

"Girl, do you live here?"

"I was shy. But when he called out to me, I felt good."

"Was he handsome?"

"He had all of his teeth and he dressed real good. When I looked at 'im, my heart sped up."

She told me he wasn't real handsome, but he had something sparkly about him, and the sight of him sent warmth through her limbs.

So when he approached her, she responded, "Yep, I live here."

"Hey, come over here. I want to talk to you," he said so smoothly.

She moved to him. "What's your name?" he asked her as soon as she stopped.

"Anna."

"You got yourself a boyfriend, Anna?"

"Nawl."

"Well, I don't have a girlfriend, either."

"So what you wants with me?"

Anna said he grabbed her hand and pulled her close to him. He had said he didn't like wasting time. After two, maybe three visits, he had her heart. He started whispering deep promises in her ear. He said things like, "I need you" and "I want you."

"He held my hand and whispered sweet stuff in my ear. I liked him."

"Sounds like a good guy."

"Well, at first. He come two times a week. We'd talk and he'd listen to me better than any of my sistas and brothas. Then the day came when I laid over behind the shed and felt the aches and trembles of him pushing against my womanhood. Felt the thrill of a grown woman, and it be like honey," Anna said with a fervent smile on her face.

As time passed, he came less often. He came once a month, then once every two months until he left for the service in World War I. He didn't even stay long enough to experience the joys of bringing a newborn into the world.

"Anna, she's still a baby. He might fool you and come back."

"I don't think so. He doesn't care 'bout us," she said, discouraged. "Now it be me, Ma, and the baby."

"What about your daddy?"

"I can't count on him."

I reached over and rubbed her shoulder. She looked at me with a faint smile. I enjoyed talking to Anna. She was a lot easier to talk to than Minnie, who had yet to tell me she was sorry or tell me how it all happened. Every time I was there, she'd be quizzing me about my life, but didn't share too much about herself. Whenever I came close to finding out more about Minnie, Mr. Smith would interrupt her. One day I tried to talk to him. "How are you doing, Mr. Smith?"

"You talkin' to me?" He turned around to look at me.

"Yes, sir."

"I's fine. I got myself too much work to do; ain't got no conversation for you."

I decided that day that he could rot for all I cared. Besides, Ginny already told me about his no-good butt.

Two weeks later, the snow had melted and the ground was still wet when Simon came by. At the sight of him from the kitchen window, a warm surge traveled through my body. When he came inside the house and asked for Carl, Momma spoke to him and kept on cooking. I expected her to at least give him some sort of threatening look, but she didn't.

I whispered, "Hi," like an innocent child. Momma turned around and cut her eyes my way, and then she clucked her tongue. I knew what she meant. But in my heart, I wanted to hug him the way we did under the tree in the schoolyard. He gave me one of the biggest smiles and touched me on the shoulder as he went by me. I didn't move, scared Momma would chastise me in front of him.

Simon followed Carl out the door. I peeked out the window at them huddled around the woodpile, Carl using his hands as usual to make his point as they talked, Simon calm and poised. Simon and I had made an agreement to never spend time in the same room together, not until we told Momma about us. He had felt if she caught on to us before we told her, she'd lose respect for the both of us.

"Why didn't you say something to him? Seems like anybody you want to marry, you should be able to talk to," Momma commented.

"I don't know."

"It's okay to talk to Simon 'round me," she said dryly. "I don't like you sneaking behind my back. It's not ladylike."

I started putting on my coat and scarf. Everything she said was right.

"Ask him to come in. It is too cold for you to stand outside."

I smiled. "Yes, ma'am."

I couldn't believe how nervous I was. I looked up and saw Mr. Camm standing by the kitchen door with a menacing frown on his face. He made me more tense.

When I opened the door, I poked my head outside and motioned for Simon to come inside. Carl and Simon walked back inside, rubbing their hands from the cold. As Simon came near, I whispered to him, "Momma said we can talk, spend a little time together."

He saw Momma was watching my every move and said, "Thank you for allowing me to visit with Carrie." Momma nodded in his direction, but she didn't smile. Mr. Camm's eyes were dark, mean and evil. The way he watched us made my skin crawl.

"Y'all go on in the front room and talk."

As I was walking toward the front room, I heard her direct Carl, "You need to go in there, too, and sit for a spell."

Carl came in and sat in the chair across from us. At first he gazed at us from across the room and smiled. Then he said, "Man, can you believe that at eighteen, we still get treated like little boys."

"Hey, it's the same way my pops do to you."

"It is crazy."

"I know."

Both of them grinned.

Simon sat beside me on the Davenport, and we slid apart to make sure at least a foot was between us.

"That's good," Carl said, chuckling.

Minutes later, though, Carl's eyes were drooping. He began adjusting himself in the chair, trying to keep his eyes open. The fireplace was popping and sizzling from the wet wood drying. I was glad to see him resting because all he'd been doing in the last year was working.

Seizing the opportunity, Simon reached over and grabbed my hand. "I missed you," he said.

"Me, too," I replied, scared to show too much emotion in front of my brother.

"I was so happy when the snow melted." He shifted his body toward mine, placing one leg on the Davenport.

"I talked to Momma about us," I whispered.

"I can tell. You surprised me when you asked me in. I bet it wasn't easy."

"I was afraid at first, thought she was going to kill me. But I was tired of the lying, too."

"Did you tell her that we wanted to get married?"

"Yes. But like I expected, she didn't give me her blessing to leave."

Carl had fallen asleep by now. He had leaned his head to the left and was snoring soundly.

"Do I need to talk to her?"

"I think so. But I really don't think it will help."

I moved closer and puckered up so that Simon could kiss me. He grabbed me hard and dotted kisses all over my face. When he kissed me on the neck, a shudder went through my entire body. I wanted to cuddle in his arms and lie down. We moved back into our places, though, still holding hands, fearful that Momma would walk in or Carl would wake up.

"I've got to talk to her," he said. "I love you. The two weeks apart was hard for me."

"Me, too… I kept hoping the snow would melt."

"My sister and I were miserable. She missed Carl as much as I missed you. So when the sun started melting the snow, neither one of us could wait to get out of the house."

His grip on my hand tightened. "You know I'll be leaving in three weeks, and I want to take you with me."

I felt a stab of pain in my heart. I knew how hard and stubborn Momma could be. My chance of going with Simon was as dim as the rest of my dreams of leaving Jefferson County.

Carl didn't sleep long, fifteen minutes at the most.

After he woke up, I went into my room and finished changing the sheets and sweeping the floor.

Simon waited until I'd finished my morning chores. "I need to talk to you," he said solemnly.

I looked at him and waited.

"Your momma said no."

"Momma doesn't want me to be happy. She never understands anything." Tears welled in my eyes, but didn't fall. I already knew what her answer would be.

He pulled me close to him. "No, she wants you to have an education. But I'm gonna come back for you as soon as you finish school." He paused before adding, "If you still want to be with me, that is."

"I want to be with you, but what if you find someone else?" I pleaded out of desperation.

He shook his head. "At night I lie awake thinking of how it would be if we were married. How I would take care of you and what kind of life we could make. So you see, you're the only person I care about."

He took me in his arms. "I can't tell you how hurt I am, but I have to respect your momma. She's looking out for your best interests."

"But I want to go."

Feeling someone watching us, I looked up. Mr. Camm was staring at us with a big smile on his face.

CHAPTER 15
PEARL

Momma begged me to go to church, sing with the choir, get involved. But instead, I went to the joint. Folks called it a "hole in the wall," a shack hidden deep behind the maples, tall oaks, and pines, and it had a scandalous reputation. It was a place to shed stress, or cry out and shout without judgment. And in the same spirit of fellowship, it was also a place to be entertained. Singing in clubs was where I naturally found contentment. Only there could I unravel and let loose.

"A decent woman ain't got no business in a place like that. It's a hellhole, I tell you," my daddy said as I painted bright red lipstick on my lips. He was a stickler for rules, though he narrowly followed them himself.

"Leave her alone. She needs to get out amongst people. She's been in the city all these years," Momma reasoned.

"What's wrong with church? There's plenty of decent women in the church, plenty of peoples to be around," he bellowed back at her.

"Daddy, I'm a grown woman now. I'm not your little girl anymore."

He couldn't understand, "Why can't you sing for the Lord? All my family sing for the Lord."

"I can sing anywhere, Daddy."

He hissed and walked out the room.

"Oh, he'll be all right," Momma said, shooing Daddy away with her hand. "He wants the best for you."

"I'm thirty years old plus. I'm not his young girl going off to the big city for the first time."

Momma giggled. "I remember that. He had a fit when you left for Washington. Didn't speak to me for over a month or so, accused me of persuading you to leave. When he gets something in his head, he never changes."

"Daddy is always worried about what people think. Momma, I am a nightclub singer. I've been doing it since I was sixteen years old. This is who I am."

"Hey, we will always be your parents, no matter how old you get," she said, then frowned. "But when it comes to men, you need help."

I never felt I needed their help. But this time Willie hadn't given me a choice.

"It is getting dark outside. No woman needs to be out there without light walking down the road. That's how peoples get taken and even lynched."

"The joint is closer than the church. I've been there before."

"Take the buggy; it'll be dark soon."

"You know how Daddy is about the horses at night."

He had two horses, and they served two purposes only. One was for traveling and the other was for tilling the land. Neither was in the best condition. Daddy had been given one of the horses and a buggy when the white family he worked for upgraded to a Model T Ford. It was greatly appreciated, since I could remember the days during the war when money was so scarce, he eventually had to sell the buggy he built with his own hands to a family down the road. His earnings had been just enough to purchase flour and sugar from the seed and feed store in town where he bought things on time.

"Do it, and take a torch with you so you can see," Momma said.

The joint was different from the nightclubs in Washington, D.C. Inside was an open space lit by kerosene lamps with rough wood tables and chairs. The walls were plain, no pictures or color added for personality. It was a place to congregate. The bartender sold jugs of homemade wine and corn liquor to its patrons. The food they sold was prepared by some of the women in the area. Nothing fancy was required for a place where sinners could associate with one another. And then on the fourth Sunday, everyone would go to church, and kneel down and ask God for forgiveness.

Smiles greeted me as I entered the place. Some of the faces were familiar, but most I no longer recognized. I sat down at an empty table. Even though I was a stranger to Jefferson now, I felt at home in the joint. The old crank record player was spinning. People danced cheek to cheek, and I started to unwind and feel a sense of lightness. I had only seen Herman twice since his wedding. His explanation for getting married, it never really made much sense.

He'd come calling at my momma's house the next Sunday after I returned home. He was still dressed in his Sunday suit and a wide-brimmed hat. He had said it was a friendly visit. After a few words of small talk with Momma, and tolerating my daddy's cold stare, we took a walk together down the road.

"I know a place we can go," he said and grabbed my hand.

I shrank away. "You are a married man now."

Squeezing my hand, he said, "You know I can't get you off my mind. Besides, you're married, too."

"I'm not going back to Willie."

"Oh, he's a good man. He can't please you like I can."

We went down the path toward the creek and found a place that had been cleared. Herman removed his suit jacket and spread it on the ground so I could sit.

He pulled me close to him. "We will always be together."

He leaned into me and the warmth from his breath sent waves of desire through my body. I inhaled. As my temperature started to rise, he slowly slipped my dress off my shoulders, exposing my large breasts to the sun. I waited as his full lips gently kissed my shoulder, neck, and cheeks. It was paradise. He moved over me and pushed his tongue deep inside my mouth. I was light-headed, high on passion. I was in touch with nature, felt purpose and fruitfulness. He massaged my naked body from top to bottom. He gently bent me over and I braced myself on a tree stump. He cupped a breast and rolled his tongue up and down my back. He gently pulled my bare behind into him and thrust his manhood into me. After a while he turned me around and guided me to the ground. The leaves swirled around my body as every muscle began to contract. With each movement I lost control. My body quivered as he exploded inside me. At that moment, I wanted to spend the night with him, stay with him always.

"You all right, baby?" Herman had said, casting a shadow over me.

I glanced around. Three couples were seated nearby, staring into each other's eyes. Two of the men I recognized, and knew were married to a woman different than the one they were with. One of the men smiled at me and winked. It was a makeshift rendezvous spot that served to bring illicit folks together.

Herman sat down, his eyes blood red. The stench of liquor was still on his breath. In his hand were the remnants of a pint of corn liquor. Nonetheless, I was elated to see him, spend time with him, even more now since Willie was not around.

"I told the dude that runs this place about you. I told him you might want to help him out."

"Help with what?"

"Singing. He needs somebody."

"I don't know if I'm going to stay around here," I told him. "Everything's so slow and living with my parents is not working."

"We can always be together here. If you go back up the road, that nigger is going to cause us some problems."

I wasn't as worried about that now. "Who knows if we will ever be together again? I've been here for almost a month, and he hasn't shown up yet."

"He ain't going to give you up. He love you, girl, like I do," he said, and kissed me on the forehead.

"I don't want to talk about him. I want to have a good time." I poured myself a drink of corn liquor and diluted it with water. It was a different taste from the smooth taste of the gin I loved to drink. I had seen Bessie Smith drink one and from that point on I did, too.

That was the beginning of my singing at the juke joint. Every time the blues started to play, Herman and I went to the dance floor. We swayed to the music. The men and women stared. I was accustomed to the attention, yet occasionally throughout the evening, I would catch Herman eyeing other women, most of them young and innocent. It had bothered me. In Washington, he had done the same thing, and one night a woman said to him, "She's not even old enough to be your damn daughter." He pushed her off.

"Your wife is going to catch on to us one day."

"She is a church-going woman. She wouldn't step foot in a place like this."

"Do you think she's better than me?"

"No, she's the kind of woman that will take care of a man, feed you and all that."

I batted my eyes. "So what am I?"

"You take care of a man in the most important way." I could tell the liquor was talking. "You make a man holler for more." He reached down and squeezed my thigh.

I moved my leg.

"What's wrong with you, girl?"

"Not a thing."

His rattling on was making me uneasy. Liquor had that effect on Herman. There was no way a plain country girl could please him the way I had. Cooking and cleaning were for a domestic. I was a city girl, glamorous and gifted.

Folks danced everywhere in the joint. Some stayed near their tables and others provocatively in the back. I put my head on Herman's shoulder, closed my eyes and swayed with the rhythm of the music. I could feel the beat vibrating through the hardwood floor. I was in my groove. When I opened my eyes, I twitched. My heart started racing.

"What's wrong, Pearl?" Herman slurred, still holding me.

"I think I just saw Willie."

The man disappeared in the crowd. I kept staring, waiting to catch sight of him again.

"He ain't up in here. That nigger knows his limitations."

I had a strange feeling that somebody was watching me. But I didn't see Willie or anybody else I really knew. After a few minutes, my anxiety dissolved and I laid my cheek back on Herman's shoulder and closed my eyes.

CHAPTER 16
CARRIE

Simon pushed me up against the tree and wrapped his entire body around me. My breaths shortened. My heart raced, and my whole body steamed with the fire he ignited in me. I gripped his back with both arms, and held him tight. It was two days before my sixteenth birthday.

"Things are happening faster than I thought they would," he said. "I have to go to Richmond. I've got to find a place to live."

It was the first time Simon had ever come close to touching my private parts. He rubbed my thighs through my stockings and dress. He ran his tongue over my lips and down my neck, and my knees buckled.

"I don't want you to let anyone touch you while I'm gone. No fooling around behind my back." He kneaded my buttocks and pulled me closer.

"I want you," I said as my body melted inch by inch with his touch. Even though I was nervous, I was willing.

He lowered his head and started to put his lips on my breast. Then he stopped.

"I can't do this," he said. "I want our wedding night to be special."

My cheeks flushed pink as Simon awakened feelings in me I'd never experienced. I smiled and knew that everything was worth waiting for.

"Don't forget me, Carrie."

"I can't," I said. "I'll look for a school in Richmond."

We took our time walking home, stopping every so often to embrace and kiss. More than once I considered giving up my virginity right where we were standing.

I knew that it would be a while before I would see Simon again. The realization saddened me. After promising we would keep in touch through letters, he walked me all the way home so he could say good-bye to Carl and the family.

When he threw me a kiss from beyond the fence, I hugged the porch rail tightly. Teardrops gushed out of my eyes like a spring rain. He turned and I could see a lonely teardrop sliding down his cheek. I threw him a kiss and went into my room and cried myself to sleep.

After a month, I received my first letter. It was short, not much more than a paragraph.

I'm almost settled in now. I miss you. I love you and I hope that you will be here with me next year. Love, Simon

I pulled out my pen and paper and immediately wrote back to him, letting him know that I wanted to know the details of life in Richmond. I wanted to know about the tall buildings, the street-cars, and the lights. I told him that I loved him, and that I hoped he could come home for Carl's wedding.

At dinner that night, Carl said, "As soon as the weather breaks, I'm going to go ahead and move in the house. I want to iron out all of the kinks before Mary comes."

A selfish part of me wanted to keep him home for my protection.

Carl and Mary set their wedding date for spring. Carl had spent most of the winter building a nice place for them.

By this time, Mr. Camm was spending most of his nights away from home. Often he'd come staggering home, smelling like women and smoke. He'd stumble through the house looking for his bed so he could sleep off the remnants of too much corn liquor. When he couldn't find it, the Davenport became his resting place.

One Saturday afternoon, Momma went to the Fergusons' to serve a party. I wanted to go with her, but she made me stay home. I begged, "Momma, I'm sure there is something I can do."

"There's plenty to do right here."

I didn't want to be alone with that man. Less than an hour after Momma left, Mr. Camm got up. Smelly remnants of the night were still on him. He came into the kitchen after sleeping most of the day away. He sat at the table and made himself a cup of the stale brewed coffee, left on the stove from breakfast. The smell from last night's corn liquor was an abrupt shock to my nostrils, and I had to cover my nose.

I continued to start the dinner like Momma had instructed. I was standing at the sink washing a few utensils when he walked past me, pushing up on me from behind. I stumbled forward and grabbed for the wall.

When I turned around, he said, "Sorry. I lost my balance for a minute." He grinned as he stumbled back to the table. I clucked my teeth, not believing his apology. He'd bumped into me intentionally as he'd done many times before.

I hated being in the house with him. He was always in my way.

"I bet them boys like you, don't they?" he remarked.

I kept on washing the dishes.

"Girl, do you hear me talking to you?" He raised his voice and banged on the table. The cup and saucer clattered.

"Yes, sir," I said, startled. "I don't have any boys liking me. I have one friend," I said politely, even though it was none of his business. I wasn't his child.

"I saw you and that boy Simon gazing at each other," he said.

"He is my friend."

"I bet you're more than friends."

"No, sir," I said, and bit my bottom lip.

"You can fool yo' momma, but you can't fool me. I know y'all doing things grown-ups do."

"No, sir, we're not."

He glanced at my stomach. "Time will tell."

I took the potatoes off the stove and set them to the side to cool. I finished washing the dishes.

"Where are you going?" he asked as I turned to leave.

"I'm going to my room," I mumbled, looking back. I went into my room and hooked the latch on the door. From down the hallway, he yelled, "I know you want me, girl."

He made me very uncomfortable. He gazed at me like I was a piece of meat. Instead of occasionally, he was doing it all the time when Momma was out of the house, even out of the room.

I was sick of it.

When I heard Momma come in the door, I unlocked the latch and came out of my bedroom. Mr. Camm was sitting in the front room pretending to read. I had never seen him read anything before. I wasn't even sure that he could read.

Plates rattled in the kitchen as Momma set the table. She didn't like to eat past five o'clock in the evening, since everyone went to bed early. I sat down at the table. As Mr. Camm blessed the table and called out the Lord's name, I thought he was the biggest hypocrite I knew.

CHAPTER 17
CARRIE

A knot formed in my stomach as Momma closed the squeaky front door behind her. Suddenly, I was overcome with an air of helplessness. Inching my body out of the bed, I felt nothing but stillness all around me. Another Saturday that Momma had to leave. I quickly made certain the old rocking chair was secure under my bedroom doorknob, careful not to make a sound as I checked it. I hurried and washed in the old tin washtub. As usual, I braided a cornrow on each side of my head. I put my journal under my pillow and made up the bed.

I removed the old rocking chair and looked down the hallway, making sure that I didn't see Mr. Camm. I opened the door real slow, hoping that it would not squeak and wake him. As I stepped out on the porch in the direction of the barn, I heard him call.

"Good mo'ning."

"Morning," I said sullenly.

I had a funny feeling about the day, like something awful would happen. I took off in a hurry toward the chicken coop to gather the eggs. Every few steps I glanced over my shoulder. I hoped that he was not watching me. I grabbed the eggs as fast as I could from the smelly hen's nest. I was determined to spend as little time as possible in the chicken coop, not wanting to be trapped. I slowed down when I crossed where Mr. Camm was standing, hoping not to draw attention to myself. Didn't want to let the son of a bitch know I was scared of him.

Once I was inside, I grabbed the broom and started sweeping the hallway and the kitchen, continuing to make sure I was alone. Just as I began to feel safe, I heard the kitchen door squeak as it slowly opened. I shivered as Mr. Camm came inside. My chest started to heave again, and my breaths came short and fast. I braced myself against the wall and inhaled deeply to calm down. My legs trembled like shivering leaves moved by a brisk wind.

"Ain't you gonna fix us something to eat?" He moved closer to me. He stank of corn liquor and sex.

"Momma left some fat meat and biscuits on the stove," I said.

"I want you to fix me some of them eggs you got there," he demanded.

I clenched my fist. "Yes, sir."

I prayed, *Father, please make this man leave me alone*. I swept up the dirt from the floor and washed my trembling hands at the sink. Mr. Camm pulled out a chair and sat down at the table. Leaning back, he gazed at me, sliding his tongue over his lips. His stench made me gag, but I forced the choking sensation back.

I grabbed the cast-iron frying pan hanging on the wall and poured bacon grease in it. I cracked two of the hen eggs that I had gathered that morning and beat them together. Mr. Camm's eyes were focused on me, panning my body from head to toe. It disgusted me, the way he leaned back in Papa's chair with an air of authority. Scrambling the eggs, I put them on a saucer with a dry biscuit. I handed the saucer to Mr. Camm and poured him a stiff cup of coffee, hoping that he would sober up.

"Sit down, girl, and talk to yo' pappy a spell," he said, between the loud sips of coffee.

"I'm not hungry," I said, trying to remain cool.

"Sit down anyway. I don't like to eat alone."

I closed my eyes and took a deep breath. I slowly dragged the chair, scraping it against the floor. The screeching sound made him cringe. I poured myself a cup of steaming hot coffee and set it beside me. As the steam vapor billowed in the air, I thought about how it could burn him. How it would become a weapon if I needed to defend myself. He remained still, his red eyes peering at me across the table.

"Momma should be back soon," I said, trying to deter his focus.

"Why you worried 'bout her? She ain't going to be back no time soon."

"Just—"

"You don't worry 'bout her," he said. "*I* need you now."

Every so often he would lick his lips and clear his throat. I avoided eye contact, afraid he'd see the fear and disgust that was written all over my face. I felt I was confined in Hell.

He gulped down his coffee and finished most of his eggs. As he was standing from the table, he commented, "You ought to learn how to talk to peoples." I didn't say a word. I kept gazing out the window, watching the trees' branches wave in the stiff breeze. He pushed his saucer toward me and I slid back from the table, and stood up.

I had trouble concentrating on my chores the rest of the day, trying to anticipate what Mr. Camm might do. Although my hands had finally stopped shaking, my stomach was still knotted up, pulling my muscles in and churning with every brush of the broom.

I swept the back porch first, checking for him. Then I went on the front porch and, thankfully, he was nowhere in the area. For the moment, I felt relief from the tension in my neck. He had wandered off. It was not unusual, since most Saturdays he'd wander off and come back at the pit of the night, or the next morning. I hoped he had done the same today.

I'd held my water all morning, waiting for an opportunity to use the outhouse without him seeing me. Momma didn't believe in using pots during the day. I ran out to the outhouse and pulled the door shut. I held the door with one hand and my dress with the other as I released a long stream of urine.

I was out of breath when I came back in the house. My stomach growled from hunger, but I was too nervous to eat. On the way back from the outhouse, I had picked up a stick a little larger than my arm for protection. A part of my mind told me to get the shotgun and keep it at my side, but I knew that Momma would whip me if she caught me with her rifle. Besides, I didn't want to kill him, only fight him off.

I wanted to leave and walk over to Mary and Carl's house, but I feared Mr. Camm would be hiding in the bushes waiting to ambush me. I was so frightened of the man, I had a hard time calming down. Morning was turning into noon, and I was getting tired of guarding the door like a Union soldier. I was scared that if I went into my bedroom, he'd somehow get in. The terror of having Mr. Camm around had totally exhausted me. Then I moved my chair behind the table so that I could lay my head down.

Before long he came back. He walked right in on me. Startled, my eyes flew open. I shifted my position at the table. He was stumbling and moving slow. The strength of his stink was heightened and it flowed with him into the kitchen. Hopefully, he wouldn't bother me because it was too late to pick up the piece of wood I'd brought back in the house.

"Was you sleeping, deary?" he slurred, his shirt hanging sloppily outside of his pants.

"No, sir." I got up from the table and gave him a hard stare. My instincts told me to pick up something to use as a weapon, but nothing was close enough to reach.

My escape route was blocked by his smelly body. He cocked his head to the side and waited for me to react. I was walking toward the door, hoping to escape, when he lunged toward me. My whole body shivered uncontrollably. I backed up into the table, almost tilting it over.

Plates rattled.

He reached to grab me but lost his balance and tumbled to the ground. He quickly got back up.

"Mr. Camm, Momma should be back soon," I warned.

"Shut up."

"But Momma."

"She ain't coming no damn time soon. It's me and you, so get used to it."

I balled up both of my fists and waited for him to approach me.

"Come here," he slurred, his arms open and waiting for me.

My adrenaline kicked in. "You better get out of my way."

He stood there and didn't budge.

"If you touch me, I will tell Momma!" I screamed, hoping to put a little fear in him.

"I don't care. She'll never believe you. She know that you's a little liar, sneaking behind her back with that boy, Simon. Do you think she'll believe a little liar like you?"

I tried again to get around him. He grabbed my arm and swung me close to him, pressing on my bottom. I pushed him back. With both hands, I hit him in the face and ran to my room. He came right behind me. As I pushed from inside the room to close the door, Mr. Camm pushed harder with his shoulder on the other side. I tried to scream but couldn't. I didn't think Carl and Mary would hear me anyway. Still, I screamed at the top of my lungs. Mr. Camm gathered strength and charged through my door. He grabbed my shoulders and swung me around onto my bed. My heart pumped so hard that I thought it was going to burst. I tried to kick but my legs met only thin air. I struggled with Mr. Camm for as long as I could. He wasn't as drunk as I'd thought. I kicked so hard that I fell on the wood floor. He jumped on me and held me down with one arm pinning my hands. Tears rolled down my cheeks. I knew that I was in deep trouble.

The smell of corn liquor and sex nauseated me. He forced himself between my legs. I squirmed mightily, trying to break his hold on me. He was too strong. He held me down and tore off my bloomers with one hand. I tried to bite his arm, but couldn't reach it. He took his other hand and grabbed my right breast like he was trying to pull it off.

"Help...please help me! Please, Mr. Camm, leave me be." No one was around to help me.

He pulled his pants down as I squirmed underneath him. He slammed me back down. I tore his shirt and almost got my hands around his neck. He maneuvered on top of me.

Pain shot up my legs into my stomach as he pounded himself inside me. I screamed, "Oh God, Oh God, Oh God, please help me!"

When he was finished, he got up and pushed me aside. "You better not mention this to anybody, you little slut." He pulled up his pants and grinned at me, lying there on the floor crying. Then he staggered out of the room.

Aching with intense pain, I inched up off the floor and closed my bedroom door. I pushed my bed against the door, scared that he might come back. I couldn't stop crying and shaking. I was panting and breathing like an animal. I couldn't calm down. I went to the washbowl and tried to wash the pain away. A stream of warm blood oozed down my legs. I washed all of my body over and over in the chilly water. I could still smell him on me. I sprayed the air with some of the perfume Mrs. Ferguson had given me. It made the terrible scent worse.

I crawled up in the corner of the room and held my head down, punishing myself with what-if thoughts. When he left, I should have left. Why didn't I get up and beg to go with Momma until she said yes? What decent man would humiliate and rape his stepdaughter? What kind of animal had Momma married? I wanted to leave and never come back, but I had no money and no place to go. I laid my head on the cool floor and finally passed out in exhaustion.

CHAPTER 18
PEARL

I could not get over the feeling of someone lurking around watching me from behind an oak tree or around the side of the barn. When my momma and I went to town to purchase fabric, and we stood waiting for the owner to meticulously cut the piece of fabric, I could still sense a presence. I found myself glancing over my shoulder, peering out the side of my eyes at nothing and nobody. When we put the items in the buggy, I still felt someone was looking at me. At first I thought it was paranoia because of my boredom. Even though I had agreed to sing at the joint, the crowd could not give me the same elation as the ever-changing crowd in Washington, D.C. Then I realized my feelings of being watched were real and who the voyeur was. As the blue sky started to darken and the clouds rose across the sky and set off a turbulent storm, Willie showed up at my parents' house with papers hanging out of his back pocket.

He stood tall, with his shoulders squared, petitioning to come in the house. Momma warned him before he took the first step, "Now, Willie, we ain't gonna have no shit 'round here. You came to see Pearl. Now understand here, she my child and you better not raise a hand to her. The only ones with that authority is me and her daddy."

"Mrs. Annie May," he pleaded, "it was an accident. I didn't mean to hurt her. I didn't."

She pointed her chubby finger at him. "You wait right here. Don't step foot in here. Let me see if she want to see ya."

Willie waited impatiently on the porch, pacing back and forth.

I had been listening the whole time. "It's all right, let him in," I said with reservation in my voice.

"You sure?" Momma asked, and paused before going back to the front door.

"It'll be all right."

She went back out there and allowed him in the house.

I was sitting in a chair, dressed in a housedress Momma had made for me. In my opinion it was a far too common design. She had said my clothes were too dressy for the work in the country. Willie had on a blue shirt, black pants, and brogan boots. He had shaved, and for the first time in a while, I could see his dark lips without the mustache. It had erased years off his face.

He reached to hug me, but caught himself and held back.

"You look good, Pearl," he said and sat down in the high-back chair facing me.

My momma stood with her arms crossed, monitoring our conversation, like she had when I was a teenager and boys had come to visit.

She'd sit in the chair across from us with a patch quilt across her lap and a needle and thread in her hand, sewing swatches of different colors of leftover fabric. Occasionally, she'd glance at us to make sure we kept a good distance between us.

My lips didn't move. I sat right across from Willie on the Davenport and waited for him to speak.

"I know you mad at me. I don't blame ya for coming down here," he said. "I done been thinking. You's got yo' own career singing and I don't want to hold you back, since I know you do it for the money, Pearl. I want my wife back."

"I sing because I like it. And Willie, you're too damn hotheaded. You get mad too quick for me. I can't tolerate that."

"I ain't never gonna like no man with my wife."

When he spoke, the fire still smoldered in his eyes.

I glanced at Momma, and she shrugged. She agreed with him.

"There is no man, Willie. You need to get over that."

He didn't comment, but the muscles in his jaw constricted, as if I'd hit a nerve.

My daddy had liked Willie from the beginning. "He a country boy. He takes care of his family. Look at his hands. That boy got strong hands and calluses, been wo'king most his life."

Daddy never liked it when Herman stopped by and we told him we were good friends. "No man that's just a friend look at a woman like he do you."

Willie pulled the papers out of his pocket.

"I done did something for us, Pearl."

I really didn't care, but I wanted to hear what he had done. "What, Willie?"

"I bought us a piece of land right beside here. It's enough to build a farm and you can be with yo' people."

My momma started grinning. A smile so big, it spread across her entire face. "I'm gonna go on in the kitchen now. You want something to eat, Willie?"

"I am hungry, Mrs. Annie May."

"Give me a few minutes."

After she walked out, I told him, "Willie, I hadn't planned on staying here."

"I want you to be happy. Seems like yo' momma enjoy you here, and she is getting up in age."

"Willie, I really don't know." I knew that owning a piece of land was a big deal for coloreds, who had not received anything in the land of plenty. But living in the country did nothing for me.

"We can open our own club, if you want," he commented. A memory from the night at the joint flashed in my mind. In a panic, I wondered how long had he been in town. "When did you get in town?"

He avoided answering me. "Ain't you surprised? I came, got the land, and came straight over here."

"I don't know."

"I want you to be happy. Bessie Smith done did the town. You sound like her, Pearl, and peoples want something different. Just sing round here, maybe travel to D.C. sometimes. You can have yo' own place right here with yo' family."

Everywhere I sang, people would often comment that I reminded them of Bessie Smith. No matter how much I tried to sing the blues my way, everyone said the same thing.

"Let me think about all this, Willie."

"Do you think Mrs. Annie May will let me stay here with you for a little while?"

I hesitated. "This is my parents' place, Willie, I don't know."

"You's my wife."

Moments later, Momma walked into the family room. "I guess you gonna stay with us tonight. Come on in the kitchen and get you something to eat."

A conniving look beamed across Willie's face.

That night we lay in the bed beside one another, barely touching. It was quiet and pitch black. The only light around came from the moon high among the stars, casting a shadow through the thin curtain hanging across the windowpane. Willie reached over to put his arms around my waist, and I scooted away.

He moved closer. "Come on, gurl, you my wife." He grabbed my breast and fondled my nipple, even though I elbowed him twice.

"I can't tonight, Willie."

He didn't let my breast go. "Please, Pearl," he begged.

"I can't right now," I said, and moved closer to the edge of the bed.

"Look what you do to me, gurl," he said, referring to his swollen manhood.

"Go to sleep," I told him.

"It's been so long."

"Willie, give it some time."

Groaning, he rolled aside at last and tossed and turned the entire night.

My daddy appreciated having Willie in Jefferson. Willie rose early every morning and helped around the house, tending to the garden and picking tobacco on a farm nearby, coming home at night with blisters and bloody fingers from pulling and twisting the tobacco. At other times he did odd jobs.

With Willie in Jefferson, I could not see Herman. So after a week of Willie getting up early in the mornings and dressing in country overalls to go with my daddy to work, I got dressed, too.

I took the path down the road behind the Watsons' property and through the trees to the joint.

Herman was sitting at the bar. He had a drink in his hand and a cigarette hanging out the side of his mouth. His eyes were red and he was shaking his legs as he did whenever he had something on his mind.

"What's wrong with you, Herman?"

He was startled by my voice. "Ain't nothing wrong with me. Why do something have to be wrong with me?"

He seemed spooked, like he'd seen a ghost. "Why are you being so short with me?"

"Woman, please…"

"Why are you shaking?"

"I got stuff on my mind, Pearl. I'm tired of the damn questions."

The fear hadn't left his face, so I coaxed him. "Something isn't right. You drinking early in the morning. Talk to me, Herman. We used to share everything."

He pushed my hand away. "Like I said, I don't wants to talk about it."

CHAPTER 19
CARRIE

For three days, I couldn't eat. Every time I thought of what had happened, I became nauseated. I found it hard to concentrate on anything, fearful of my own self. Scared that even my family would turn their backs and abandon me. I didn't know what to do or who to talk to. I had no place to hide. I walked around ashamed, my eyes lowered to the ground. I had managed to stay out of the way of Momma's husband, knowing the sight of him would only heighten my anxiety. I found it hard calling him mister. *Mister* was used to show respect to men. How could I say mister to him?

Momma knew something was wrong. Each night she would pound on my door until I answered her. "Come on and eat 'fore the food get cold."

"I'm not hungry."

"Well, don't let me catch you in the kitchen later on. We eat together."

I had not eaten with the two of them since Mr. Camm stole my precious virginity from me. It was something that I'd always felt good about. Most of the girls my age had slept with boys, and even had children. My first time was going to be with someone special. Simon. Many times when the heat traveled throughout my loins and Simon felt the bulge of his own cravings, we'd stop. Marriage would be our permission to continue and finish.

I wasn't sure if I could control the deep-felt resentment I had for my mother and stepfather. First, Momma for inviting him into our home, and then Mr. Camm for being the cold, thieving, lowlife he was. Why didn't she leave him? Why did she need to have a man around?

I managed to mask my rage by making myself scarce, spending most of my time in my room, either reading, or writing or even praying. When I heard their voices, I drowned them out with my own. I would read out loud in my room, hum, anything to filter out Mr. Camm's voice. I could not stand it. If I didn't resist it, I knew that my rage would soon take over. The evidence remained on my thighs and breasts, bruises that I hid well underneath my long dresses.

Making sure that no one else was around, I grabbed two dry biscuits on the stove and poured some syrup on them. I ate one of them as I walked up the path to school and saved the other one for lunch. Every time I thought about what happened to me, my eyes would fill with tears. The warm breeze dried the tears that slid down my face, but the emotional scars would remain forever. I concentrated on the birds and the trees and Mr. Penn's apple trees as I passed his house. I held my head up as high as my conscience would allow. I tried hard to not think of how much I despised Momma's husband.

All my life, I'd been recognized by the church folk and others for my smile. I never let too much get me down. I had learned to take one day at a time. Never force things to happen, let things take their natural course.

I tried to focus on Simon, but the thoughts brought more tears to my eyes. What had I done to him? I wished that I had been born in a different family. First, I'd found out that I was adopted. Now this. What more could I take? Simon would understand, I tried to tell myself. If I could get through the next school term, then I'd leave.

At school, I isolated myself from Hester and Anna long enough to clear my head and refocus. During the breaks, I sat under the pine tree and hoped that they didn't bother me. I needed their company, but I wasn't ready to open up to them.

"Tell me what's wrong with you," Hester insisted, tugging my arm for attention. I wanted to share everything with her, but what would she think of me? Hester and I had similar expectations. We wanted more.

"I'm okay," I lied.

"Well, you sure don't look like it. You look like you lost your best friend."

"I'll be all right," I said, and Hester shook her head in disagreement.

I didn't go to Anna's. Instead, I walked home with Hester. I couldn't go straight to my house. Mrs. Ferguson was demanding more and more of Momma's time. She was coming home late a few times a week. I only had one evening chore, and it was the dishes. Then Momma would be home to protect me.

"Did something happen between you and Simon? You've been awfully quiet lately," Hester asked once we were in her room. All the way home, she would glance at me, wanting me to talk. And I couldn't because I felt ashamed and overburdened.

"I don't have much to say."

"Carrie, I've never known you to be this quiet. How are things at home? Is that man still messing with you? Talk to me." My heart ached to release it all, but I couldn't find the words. I bit my lower lip and wiped the water creeping out the side of my eye.

"Have you started your homework?" I managed to say. "Mrs. Miller wants us to turn it in on Friday."

"Are you sure you're all right?"

"I'm okay."

Hester and I lay across her bed and did our homework. When I started home, I had just enough time to get there before the sun slid beneath the horizon.

Mr. Camm was standing in the kitchen when I arrived. He gazed at me as usual, but this time it was different. I stood and looked him square in the eyes. I dared him to cross the line.

With his chest deflated, he turned and walked away with a make-believe grin on his face.

Tears beat my pen to the paper when I tried to write Simon. I couldn't find the words to say much. I managed to do what he normally did when he wrote me. Be brief. I told him that I missed him; I was well and hoped to see him soon. Then I licked the envelope and put it with the rest of the mail Momma had Carl take to the post office. I couldn't bother Simon with my problems anyway. He needed to concentrate on his game.

Pretty soon school would be out and I longed for Simon to pay me a visit. I had to find something to do during the summer, because I refused to be left in the house alone again with Mr. Camm.

On the way home from school the next day, I paid a visit to Mrs. Ferguson. She was not only the white lady Momma worked for, but along with the reverend, Momma occasionally sought her advice on matters of business. Momma knew that Mrs. Ferguson had some snobbish Southern ways, but she'd gotten used to them over the years. Mrs. Ferguson had even sought her advice in turn a time or two. They had a degree of respect for each other that went beyond a boss lady and worker relationship. Momma admired people of stature; people she believed were doing positive things. She admired Hester's parents, the reverend, and the Fergusons, and she looked down her nose at those she felt were doing the opposite, like the owner of the juke joint, the bootleggers and whores. She especially admired Mr. Ferguson, who had been able to provide well for his wife, despite not having the money of his father-in-law.

"Come on in," Mrs. Ferguson said from her back door.

I stood in her kitchen.

"What's going on, Carrie?"

"Mrs. Ferguson, I'm ready to work. I was hoping you had something I could do in the evenings after school."

"Mae Lou has been doing it all for me. She really doesn't need any help, since she comes more than once a week."

I persisted. "I thought maybe you knew somebody."

"Well, I know Mrs. Gaines was looking for someone to help her. Now, I can't guarantee anything, but she was looking awhile ago." She nodded her head slowly. "You stop by there on your way from school tomorrow, and tell her I sent you. And make sure you go to the back door." *Always the back door*, I thought. Despite that, I was grateful for her recommendations but frustrated that I had to do something I never ever wanted to do—clean for a living.

Momma was sitting at the table when I got home, staring out the window. For once she wasn't busy. It had been a long time since I'd studied her face. Her eyes were sunk deep in her head and darkened by a sadness, similar to the time when Papa had been sick. I wasn't sure if it was loneliness or pain from living with such a cold son of a bitch.

Momma had never liked for her children to wander too far from home. Even when it came to working, she felt that there was more than enough to do around the farm to occupy time. Making money was always secondary to her. As long as we were fed and clothed, there wasn't a need for us to work. She had said, "There will be plenty time for working once you finish your schooling," so I knew that I had to convince her that I needed a job away from home.

I sat down at the table. "Momma, it's almost time for me to go away to college." I was feeling uneasy about talking to a woman who'd nurtured and raised me my entire life.

"Yes, I know."

"It's about time that I make my own wages. John told me how much everything costs and it's real expensive."

For the last year our crop had not been real good and Momma wasn't making much profit. She needed money, although she'd die before admitting it. Carl managed to make enough for us to survive during the winter months, but not much over that. Mr. Camm was no good to us.

"Chile, stop beating around the bush, and tell me what you wants," she said.

"I want to work this summer. I can help pay my own way to school."

"What about your chores around the house here? I still need your help. Money ain't er'rythang."

"Momma, I'll get up early, and feed the hens, and gather the eggs before I leave in the morning."

"Where is a teenager gonna get a job 'round here?"

"I stopped by Mrs. Ferguson's and she knows someone who needs some light housekeeping."

"Now's you know better'n go involving Mrs. Ferguson in our business."

"Yes, ma'am."

"But I've got to admit it, you're moving in the right direction."

I was too frightened anyway to go out to the henhouse when

she was gone. I had daydreamed about killing Mr. Camm. I hated him with a deep-felt passion I'd never experienced before and imagined if he ever attempted to attack me again, he wouldn't live to see the break of another day.

"I think you are old 'nough to make your own money. I started wo'kin when I was much younger than you. I's didn't even get paid. Lord, times have changed." She shook her head and grinned. "Now don't go letting folk down that help you. They won't ever help ya again."

I smiled at Momma for the first time since the rape and said, "Thank you."

Even though the air was crisp, delight was everywhere. Everyone crowded around John and Uncle Joe, Papa's brother, as if they were celebrities of some sort. Country people are like that. John looked like he owned the college. In less than a year, he'd managed to adapt the sophistication of a citified colored man. He sported a freshly starched white shirt and dress trousers with a thin cuff in the bottom. His mustache was shaped around his lips and his hair was neat. And when he spoke, the words seemed to flow from his lips like a stream of water.

College must be good for him, I thought.

A year or more had passed since we'd seen Uncle Joe. He was the spitting image of Papa. Uncle Joe, although he was close to forty, still looked like a ladies' man, dark and stately with an air of sophistication. His hair was slicked back and his shoes gleamed from a recent shoe shine. The government had been good to him. At first he worked as a porter, but he didn't like the road, and the way the train shook made him sick to the stomach. Then he started cleaning up in a government building near the Capitol.

He moved up to the head of the maintenance department. Papa always said that he was good with his hands.

"Lord, Joe, we are glad you came," Momma said, eyes wide at the sight of him.

"Mae Lou, I had to make it to my nephew's wedding. Besides, he needed someone to stand in for his daddy. I couldn't miss it." He bent over and kissed her on the cheek.

"Well, I am happy you made it," she said again, grinning.

"Mr. Camm sure can't fill Papa's shoes," I whispered to John. He nodded ruefully.

Mr. Camm stood close, soaking in everything he could. His eyes had become dark and sinister, which was inappropriate for such a happy occasion. I stayed well out of his reach.

Uncle Joe and John put their things in the boys' old room. As I was fixing to go and help Momma in the kitchen, John knocked on my bedroom door.

He dropped down on my bed like old times.

"Is Hester coming?"

"Maybe...Why do you need to know, anyways?"

"Well, we're friends," he said, shoving me playfully on the bed.

Teasing, I said, "Maybe she has someone else now."

"Come on now. We're still close. I know about that boy in your class. She sent me a letter or two."

"By the way, bro, does she know about that girl you wrote me about from New York?"

"Now, I told you that girl and I are just friends. There was no need to worry Hester with that. Besides, in college, everybody sticks close, because the work is so difficult." I shook my head in disbelief.

"I'm leaving you to wonder about Hester. I'm going in the kitchen with Momma," I said, and slapped him on the arm.

Momma was standing over the stove stirring a sauce when I entered the kitchen. The aroma of sweets and greens cooking excited my nostrils. She told me to continue stirring while she shoved the rice pudding in the oven. My mouth salivated with the thought of tasting everything she was preparing.

"I need you to mind the kitchen while I walk with your uncle and Mr. Camm over to Carl's," she said. While she was gone, I finished adding the eggs, cream, and flavorings to the cake mixture. I'd known how to cook since I was a little girl. Momma had insisted I pay attention, telling me, "Don't no man want to marry a woman who can't cook."

Mary knocked on the door. She was carrying a box with two butter pound cakes in it. As she stood there in the sunlight, her glow radiated throughout the room.

"Momma baked these this morning," she said, handing me the cakes. She sat down, still smiling.

"Would you like some coffee?" I offered.

"No, thank you, I didn't plan on staying long. I've got so much to do."

"Is Simon coming home for the wedding?" I asked.

Her face softened at my concern. "We don't know, can't never tell about him. He likes to surprise us, always keeps us on edge. He hasn't written in a while. But Momma wrote him and so did I," Mary answered.

"I haven't heard from him, either."

"Oh, you will," she answered with confidence.

I wasn't so sure, but I changed the subject. It was Mary's day, after all. "So are you nervous?"

"Not really."

"Are you wearing white?"

"I have this beautiful white dress that Momma made for me. It has lace around the top..." She blushed the whole time she was describing her dress. Although I was elated for her, inside I wished it was my wedding.

"Carl is the most amazing man I have ever met. Don't tell nobody, but he's an even better man than my papa." I grinned because I knew that my brother was a good man, like our papa.

"He's a pretty good guy, even if he is my brother," I said.

Mary didn't stay long after that. She was worried that Carl would come back and see her before the ceremony.

"Don't need any bad luck," she said, smiling.

Momma was not real happy about them deciding to have their wedding at their new house rather than the church. She was so traditional. She had decided God didn't smile too kindly on non-church weddings, even if they lasted.

"In the eyes of God, weddings are sealed," she said.

"Isn't He everywhere, Momma?"

She ignored that remark. "Carl, me and yo' papa was married in the church, and so was Mr. Camm and me." At Carl's shrug, she threw up her hands in disgust and walked out of the kitchen into the front room.

Following behind her, Carl said, "Momma, we have prayed about this union. It doesn't matter where the ceremony is. I want to be like my grandpa and jump the broom."

"We're not slaves no more. Back then, they didn't have a church to get married in. But it's your wedding. I'll be there no matter what."

I thought some more about Simon, and wished he could come. Playing ball in the Negro Leagues could take you anywhere. Everyone's home became yours. He could be in the state of Virginia or in Georgia. But I wanted him here, even though I was no longer a virgin. When I thought about what happened, tears welled up in my eyes, and I struggled to keep them from falling. I had to enjoy the moment for Carl.

Momma and Aunt Bessie fried chicken, and Momma took one of the good hams out of the smokehouse and cooked it. "I wish the boy understood tradition," she grumbled.

"Isn't jumping the broom a tradition? That's what our people used to do."

"That was then. We ain't been slaves in years. Bessie, I can't believe you are 'greeing with him."

"I want him to be happy. Does a church make you happy?"

Momma paused to mull that over. "I guess you got a point."

"Why can't church be anywhere?"

It didn't matter much because the entire congregation had been invited to the wedding. We didn't expect them all to show up, but the ones who didn't have far to travel would be there. Besides, a wedding was a big event in Jefferson County.

By noon I was tired. We took the majority of the food to Carl's house and draped every table in white cloths Momma had borrowed from fellow church members. She decorated his front room like it was a white person's elegant house. Momma took some of her hard-earned money that she had hidden somewhere in the house and bought white candles.

At 2:45, everyone gathered together. Carl's stomach was turning somersaults.

I fixed him a drink of vinegar, water, and baking soda. "Drink it all down. You don't have much longer before the wedding starts." Frowning, he drank the tonic. After he finished, I had a drink as well because my stomach was also uneasy.

The weather was perfect. The sun was bright and it was around sixty-five degrees, not too hot and not too cold. It was like the day was invented for Carl and Mary. Everybody in the gathering looked so nice. Hester's long black hair had been paper curled and it was swinging down her back. I pulled my hair back in a bun with a little bang on top. Hester let me put on a little of the pink lipstick her mother had given her. Momma had on a white church hat that John brought with him from Washington, D.C. Mr. Camm was sober and had on his Sunday best. Everyone was ready but the bride.

At the sight of Hester, I thought about Anna. I wished that she could have come, but I knew that Momma would not like it. She'd warned me about being around the Smiths.

The reverend shook everyone's hand as he came through the door carrying his black Bible. Slowly, he made it through the crowd, bending down to kiss children and acknowledging all of the people who gazed at him in the pulpit on Sunday mornings.

"Boy, you got yo'self a nice-looking crowd here," the reverend said.

"Yes, sir," Carl said, grinning and looking a lot calmer than he had twenty minutes before. The tonic was working. John was standing close to Carl but eyeballing Hester like she was a new girl in town.

"It's time," Aunt Bessie kept saying. Finally, in walked Mary. She was the prettiest bride I'd ever seen. She had on a long, white dress with lace at the top. Her hair was curled under, and she had on rouge and lipstick. She had a rose in her hair and she held a bouquet of wildflowers. Directly behind her were her momma and daddy, who walked to the front of the room and took their places before the preacher.

Hester and I stood together. The preacher had started the ceremony when Hester nudged me.

"What?" I whispered.

"Look! Look toward the doorway."

Simon's smile greeted me.

"Oh, my God," I said. And after that moment, I did not hear another word of the wedding ceremony. The only part that I really remember was the kiss, which was long and mushy.

Afterward, everyone went outside to watch Carl and Mary jump the broom. All types of people had shown up for the wedding, friends and gossipers alike. Two ladies with wide-brimmed Sunday hats stood away from the crowd talking.

"I don't know what's so extraordinary about this wedding."

"Me neither, everybody is always gloating over Mae Lou and her chirren."

"Chile, you are so right, I bet her son's wedding will last a lot longer than hers to Herman."

"He done been with everybody in town. I don't know why Mae Lou fell for him."

"Let's keep it straight, Bert. I ain't been with him."

"Me either." They both let out a giggle and covered their mouths.

"Didn't think I was going to make it, did you?" Simon said.

I whirled around. "Well, I haven't heard from you in a while," I said, trying not to appear too anxious, but grinning like a Cheshire cat.

"I know. Sorry for that. I've been too busy to write. We've been traveling a lot. We've been to Rustburg, Farmville, Fairfax, Appomattox, and Washington, D.C. And the season is just getting started. It's a busy job. I didn't think I'd make it here in time." He leaned in closer. "Though I wanted to see Mary get married, I wanted to see you more. And you look so nice."

"You, too," I said.

He bent down and whispered in my ear, "Give me a kiss?" and I almost melted, right there.

"No," I hissed back, "somebody might see us."

"Why are you still worried about these people? Your momma gave us permission to see each other."

"I know, but she didn't tell me to be disrespectful."

"You're right," he said, even though so much was going on at the house, no one was really paying attention.

John and Hester had moved off to one side, and John had his arm around her shoulder. Everyone else was crowded around Carl and Mary, including the two ladies with wide-brimmed hats. The church folk all whispered about Mary's dress or Mrs. Susie's new man. Momma stood proudly with Mr. Camm right by her side. When the opportunity came, Simon and I walked back to my house. When we made it there, we sat down in the front room and kissed and hugged like we were the ones married.

"I hate it when you're away. I want to go with you. I can't stand it 'round here."

"Next spring we will be doing what they just did," he said.

"I hope that our day will be as special as theirs."

"It will. It will be more special." He kissed me so deeply, I lost my breath. I'd found myself staring at his oversized arms and flat stomach like he was a fine piece of art.

Thirty minutes passed before we decided to go back and join the rest of the wedding party. As we walked hand in hand through the path to Carl's house, I anticipated my own wedding night.

After the crowd died down and Carl stood admiring Mary's beauty, those still socializing knew it was time to leave. So they took their hats and said goodbye. Like many times before, Aunt Bessie and her family spent the night. Uncle Bill and Bessie stayed in my room and the children and I shared the floor in the front room. After the children fell off to sleep, I took out my journal and wrote about the wedding and how Simon had surprised me with his visit. I fell asleep with a smile on my face.

The next morning, it looked as if nothing had happened the day before. John and Uncle Joe had risen at sunup, packed their clothes and started back to Washington, D.C. Bessie, Bill, and their greedy children were finishing breakfast.

"We're gonna skip church this Sunday. It's been an exciting weekend. It was a mighty fine wedding," Momma boasted.

The sound of a horn jolted all of us.

We jumped up to see who could be blowing a horn, and we all peered out the window. A black Model T Ford was parked in the yard, and Simon sat behind the wheel.

"Good morning," he said, getting out of the car.

Everyone gathered around the car as if it was a miracle. Very few colored folks had cars and none we knew in Jefferson.

"I came by to see Carrie before I left, Mrs. Mae Lou."

"Oh, you did?" Momma said, examining the car with as much detail as any man.

"I was wondering if I could take Carrie for a ride in my new car."

Pausing like she was in deep thought, Momma reluctantly said, "Yes, 'viding she come back the same way she left." Everyone knew what that meant.

"I will," I said, and hopped in the car before she could change her mind.

It was seventy-seven degrees outside and the sun was shining bright as ever. We let the windows down and allowed the March wind to travel through our hair. We drove down the road to the schoolhouse and got out and sat under our tree. We talked as we had the first time we'd met here. He told me all about the league and where they would be traveling. He even encouraged me to do my schoolwork so that I could go to Virginia Union College in Richmond.

"Why did we come here?" Before he could answer, I asked, "Is it because this is our tree? This is where we first started seeing each other." I looked to the heavens. "Thank God Momma never found out." And we both giggled.

"Ain't that the truth?" he said.

"Are you seeing anybody else in Richmond?"

Simon answered my question honestly. "No, but there are a lot of women in Richmond. They are all sizes and shapes and interesting to watch." My faced turned red and he pulled me close. "Oh, girl, stop worrying. You will always be my love."

"Promise me that you will write to me. I hate not hearing from you."

"I promise to write, but don't get mad if it's only a line or two. I hate writing."

For the next hour, we didn't say anything. At one point, I started to mention Mr. Camm and quickly put it out of my mind so that I could enjoy the moment. We leaned against the tree and kissed and brushed against places of a forbidden nature.

Before we went back home, I convinced Simon to stop at Hester's house to show off the car.

"We might end up being sisters-in-law, after all," Hester said. "John and I are back together."

Simon leaned against his car as Hester admired it.

"Girl, I can't wait for school tomorrow; we've got so much to talk about."

"I was thinking the same thing."

CHAPTER 20
PEARL

Willie quickly found himself at home in Jefferson, inhaling the fresh air on a daily basis. It was a lot like Fredericksburg in that most of the people were sharecroppers and farmers. My family embraced him as one of their own. My father enjoyed having a son-in-law, and the country living made Willie blissful. For me, life had grown so mundane that going to church was a pleasure. The women in the gospel choir counted on me to harmonize their unsynchronized notes. On most fourth Sundays, Herman attended with Mae Lou, his wife. Despite that, he would discreetly wink or smile at me and I would do the same. Afterward, whenever I could, I would slip away from the house and meet him at the joint.

Willie had never been to my church, so he grinned when we all piled into the buggy to head there. He was dressed in his soldier's uniform, my father in his Sunday suit, and Momma and me in dresses and hats.

"Mrs. Annie May, I ain't been to church in years," he told Momma. "I prayed while I was gone, though. Prayed that God would bring me back safe, and he did. I didn't get a scratch."

"It is a month of Sundays between church meetings. Once a month is good enough for us all—and a little praying is good for everybody," Momma said, and then added, "Now, let me warn ya. Peoples going to want to know about the service. Just be patient with 'em."

Willie grinned from ear to ear.

"You a hero, son. It takes a man with guts to do what you did," my daddy commented.

Willie pulled his shoulders back and stuck his chest out. I only smacked my lips. I'd gotten tired of them treating Willie with so much love and respect.

Dinner was going to be served on the grounds. Everyone brought a dish of either fried chicken, peas, macaroni and cheese, turnips, collards, cornbread, or an assortment of pound cakes. The aromas drifted across the grounds and tantalized the taste buds of the hungry church members. Everyone was in good spirits, sharing their food, family, and conversations. The church yard was full of people. The little children ran after one another, and the rest of the people were either spread out on blankets under a tree or sitting at the picnic tables on the lawn. There were baskets full of food, and all of us waiting for the preacher to bless the meal.

When Willie got out of the buggy, people gawked at the sight of him. The Hell Fighter's uniform fit every curve on his body. He stood out amongst the crowd—six feet three inches tall and a sculpted body like a finely chiseled piece of artwork.

"Look like we got a man of service with us this mo'ning," the preacher said after blessing the food. "Welcome, son."

"Mo'ning," Willie answered.

"Sho' glad you could make it," the preacher said, shaking his hand.

For the first time since I'd returned, I was sharing the spotlight with Willie. He relished every moment, standing straight as an arrow.

"Anything we can do to help you, let us know. We take care of our own," the preacher said with pride, now patting Willie on his thick back. "God bless America." And sounds of approval echoed across the church yard. "God bless ya, boy," and "Glad you made it home."

Fitting in with the community was easy for Willie. When we lived in D.C., he'd raised chickens in the back of our apartment and, until he joined the Colored National Guard, had cultivated a small vegetable garden with beans, onions, and tomatoes, all of which he graciously shared with the other tenants. When he left, I let it all go, and proudly shopped at the market for my vegetables. I was a city girl.

Immediately after the choir sang a song, people started to move around. Some unpacked food and placed it on the tablecloths, and others laid it out on blankets in picnic form.

Willie was the center of attention, and a crowd of people, mostly men, stood around him as if he was a statue. He loosened the top button of his uniform, and wiped away the beads of sweat trickling down his ebony cheeks. Then the questions started coming.

"Let me ask ya, son," a man twice Willie's age said. "How was it fo' the colored boys in a foreign country?"

"My troop was in Germany and France. We fought right beside them white boys."

"I didn't know the coloreds did any of the actual fighting," Mr. Watson said.

"Some didn't. But I was in the trenches."

Then the old man interrupted. "No one knows what us colored boys done sacrificed for this country. This is our country, too." His voice cracked with emotion.

"I couldn't wait to get home, though."

"Me either, son, ain't no place like home." And the old fellow patted him on the shoulder and walked away.

Across the yard, Herman hovered over Mae Lou. Wherever

she went, he followed. She eventually walked right up to me. "Pearl, you need to leave other folks' husbands alone," she said, gazing hard in my eyes.

Caught by surprise, I glanced around at Willie. "I don't know what you're talking about."

Herman didn't say a word. He didn't even blink, only stood there like a coward, listening to her accuse me.

"Come on, Mae Lou," he said, and they walked off arm in arm.

Willie had seen us, but he was wrapped up with folks and hadn't heard a word Mae Lou said.

Mae Lou was one bold woman. She had been coming to Washington to visit Herman even before, when she was married to someone else. How in the hell did she have the audacity to confront me?

From across the church yard, Mae Lou and Herman appeared to be in a heated discussion. She would pull away and he would wrestle her back in his arms. Suddenly, she was quiet and back to her perfect self. I wondered if he'd told her I didn't mean anything to him.

Willie wasn't beaming with pride anymore. The sight of Herman had set him off. His smile was gone, replaced with a frown that came and went depending on who he was speaking with. We spent the entire day on the church yard, and I did everything I could to avoid Mae Lou the rest of the time.

Twice I saw Herman speaking to Mae Lou's daughter. And each time, the short, stocky girl with light hazel eyes moved away when he came near. As had been the case with me, his eyes followed her around wherever she went. All day she avoided him—turned up her nose and looked away.

I shook my head and turned away, found my family again.

Momma was glowing. She loved the company of a lot of people.

She was, like me, a city girl inside. Meanwhile, Daddy caught up on all the latest farm news from the men in the church.

On the way home, Willie was silent. He kept gazing out at the rolling hills and rows of chopped corn stalks as if they were calling his name. But Momma and Daddy couldn't keep their mouths closed. Dinner on the yard was the biggest event of the season, and some had traveled as far away as New York to worship with their families.

Willie went straight to our bedroom when we got home. So did my parents.

For three weeks, I hadn't let Willie touch me intimately, and his patience had started to fade. He removed his clothes. He hung his uniform behind the bedroom door on the hanging nail, and threw his underwear and socks on the floor.

It was still light outside, and the sun was still high. For some, it was early to bed and early to rise.

"Get in," Willie said.

"I'm so tired I can't keep my eyes open."

"I need to talk to you," he said, waiting for me to crawl in beside him.

Everything flashed before my eyes: Willie, Herman, and Mae Lou.

"You my wife, right?"

"Yes," I answered, puzzled by the question.

"Well, then show me," he said.

The way he demanded it made me worry. *What is really on your mind tonight, Willie?* I thought. I succumbed to him to keep the peace, but all the while I cringed at what lay ahead. If he saw Herman too many more times, we were all in trouble.

CHAPTER 21
CARRIE

The glare from the full moon lit up the inside of the house. From a distance a coyote howled. The sky was clear, yet the mood was solemn. Mr. Camm had left hours ago. Momma had been in the front room all evening listening to the wet wood sizzle as it dried out, and watching the sparks pop as the heat cut into the chill in the house. I sat in the front room with her, silent but enjoying her company. The last time we all had sat in the family room together had been before Papa died.

She looked at the clock above the fireplace and it said 11:30. She got up and went into her room. She came back with her coat on and a shawl around her shoulders.

"Momma, where are you going? It's late."

"Can't sleep. Going out for a spell."

"But you never go out at night."

"I know, chile."

"It's cold outside and pitch black."

She got her rifle and headed for the door. No one traveled without a weapon at night, and most women weren't seen out alone after sundown.

I made a quick decision. "I'm going with you."

"No, you need to stay here."

"I can't let you go out alone."

I put on my thick sweater and grabbed a quilt from my bed to throw across our legs. We got into the buggy and headed in the direction of the joint. The moon was bright and I looked to the sky and mumbled a prayer for our safety. I had never been to the joint before, and the closer we got to it, the more curious I became.

"Why are we going down here, Momma?"

"I want to check on Herman."

"He's all right. He drinks too much."

"I want to see for myself," she said stubbornly.

When we pulled in the yard, we could hear the piano playing from within, along with roars of laughter. Several buggies and horses were lined up on the side of the shack, plus the old car Mr. Camm had gotten a few weeks earlier. When Momma got out, she told me to stay in the buggy and wait for her. She left the rifle in the buggy with me and went inside the joint.

After a few minutes, I got out and followed her in. Women and men were huddled together in the corners or seated at the tables. The lights were dim and only shadows of heads were on the walls. It was hard to recognize the people in here. Momma went to the bar first and panned the patrons sitting around drinking liquor, looking for her husband. He wasn't sitting at the bar, so she went straight to the back of the room. I followed behind, even though she'd directed me to stay in the buggy. He was sitting in the back with Ms. Pearl. He was drunk and pulling on her as if she was his wife. She was trying to push him away.

"What's going on here?" Momma asked.

"What the hell do it look like, Mae Lou?" he answered back.

"You still in here running after Pearl, ain't you?" she said, standing in front of their table, "And Pearl, ain't you a married woman?"

Pearl pulled away from his pawing. "I don't want Herman, Mae Lou."

Momma didn't believe her for a second. "You been lying since ya came back here. Let's go, Herman."

"Go on, Herman, with yo' wife," Pearl said sarcastically. "My husband is on his way to get me."

"Yo' husband is a damn fool," Mr. Camm said.

He stumbled behind Momma out into the cold. His breath was heavy with the smell of liquor as he hopped in the buggy beside me. I cringed and slid over so he could get in. Momma didn't say a word and neither did I. When we arrived back home, we all went to bed. I could hear the rumblings of their conversation, though. At one point Momma said, "Get yo' things and go, Herman."

"I'm staying right here," he slurred back at her.

He must have won the argument, because he didn't leave.

CHAPTER 22
CARRIE

It was the middle of April, over a month since it had happened. Physically I was back to normal, but my emotions were wound tight, leaving me always yearning for a reason to explode. Each night before I went to sleep, I bent down on my knees beside my bed and asked God to help me through my horrible nightmares.

Every evening after dinner, I'd finish the dishes fast and get out of the way. I stopped using the chair as a barrier of entry into my bedroom and started pushing my bed up against the door instead before I went to sleep. I felt safe in the understanding that no matter what Mr. Camm tried, he wouldn't be able to get in.

During the day, I had my job to take my mind off of things. I'd followed Mrs. Ferguson's advice and Mrs. Gaines had hired me. I didn't have to worry about Mr. Camm during the summer break, either, because I wouldn't be home.

Mrs. Gaines was nearly seventy years old. She moved slowly, but her mind was sharp. At first she spent most of her day following me around her house, making sure that I did not steal anything. At least, that was how I saw it. Other than her constantly watching me, she was pleasant, and I got used to her. She had been living alone ever since her husband had passed, more than ten years ago. She did the exact same things every day. She was so used to her habits that she even fixed the same breakfast each morning: one egg over easy, a piece of dry toast, and coffee.

She enjoyed her breakfast in one of two places, either on her porch or in her parlor. Both offered a panoramic view of the beautiful Blue Ridge Mountains. "I love the view," she'd told me. "The deep green foliage along the hillside is almost blue. You should come here in the fall when the leaves change and float to the ground. It opens up a perfect view of the mountain peaks. And when it snows, it's like heaven."

She also insisted that her lawn was finely landscaped by a man who performed the duties of gardener and handyman. He almost looked as old as Mrs. Gaines. He was a small, colored man, yet his strength amazed me. "Otis is as strong as a bull," Mrs. Gaines would say. "He never takes a break." And that seemed to worry her.

Her house was not real large but it was comfortable. She could easily entertain twenty-five people without any one of them feeling crowded. I don't think she communicated with too many people in the town because she talked to me all day. Otis rarely came into the house. Most times he was busy pruning trees and fixing up what little there was to do. She seemed to be a real lonely lady. Every afternoon I'd find her sitting in her parlor anxiously waiting for me.

"Come on in," she'd say, and her old weary eyes would light up. She had become attached to me. Each day she looked forward to my visit. That's what it felt like—a visit. There was hardly enough work to keep me busy. A little dusting and an occasional damp mopping was all that was needed. Most of the time she followed me around and talked to me. Being at her home was relaxing for me, too. It gave me a chance to get away from the fear that suffocated me at home. Mrs. Gaines turned out to be quite a pleasant old lady, one who had seen a lot of changes during her years.

"My father owned over one hundred slaves. He was a very wealthy man. He was even the mayor of the township years ago. I never needed folks to take care of me, though. I was too damned independent. Had me a colored suitor one time, but my daddy beat me for that, so I let him go. We still remained friends, but at a distance. I was a rebel in my time, a woman with a purpose. Now I'm all alone," she told me one afternoon after drinking a cup of tea imported from England.

She didn't talk much about her children, and I knew that it was not proper to ask. She did mention that all of them craved the city lights. She talked all day about her youth, about her suitors and Mr. Gaines. I wasn't really interested in some of the things that happened during those times when colored folks suffered. To her it was the height of her life. She'd often say that she wished things were like they used to be. I suppose it was her younger days of love that she longed for, and one afternoon she informed me:

"Now I want you to use the front door. The back door is for people with dirt on their feet. You are my friend."

"Yes, ma'am," I said, enjoying the confidence of a white lady.

I really enjoyed working for myself. Twenty cents a day was not very much money to some, but it was more than some people worked for. In time, I would have money saved up for books and even my journey out of Jefferson County. Hester had found a job also, working at the white lady's house her momma did laundry for.

In the evenings, on the way home from Mrs. Gaines', I'd stop by Hester's. As I tramped through the shortcuts, I couldn't help remembering when we only saw one another at school. Now I was making frequent visits. Hester's parents always welcomed other children in their home, since Hester was an only child. It was a secure and lively place. Her father reminded me of Papa in that he never disrespected women, either.

One evening, instead of going to Hester's, I walked down the road a bit to Ginny's. I hadn't visited her in more than a month. When I walked up on the porch, she was sitting totally still with her eyes shut and her arms hanging by her sides. Even with the sun's help, there was no vigor in her pale bloodless cheeks.

"Ginny, are you all right?" I asked as I stepped up on the porch.

She opened her cloudy eyes and lifted her head. "I'm okay. I's just dozed off a minute. Furst I done seen ya in a time. Come on, gurl, sit down."

I sat down on the porch steps. "Have you been sick?"

"I've been down a spell, but I am getting back up." She took a sip of water out of a Mason jar.

"You taking anything?"

"Yes, I's got some corn liquor in the house, mixed it up with a little sugar and lemon. Yestidy I made a mess of poke salad with onions. All that will knock any sickness out my body."

"You got to take care of yourself."

"You betta do the same, gurl," she said, and smiled. "Been up to Minnie's lately?"

"No, I haven't had time to visit nobody much. I've been too busy working. I got a job."

"Where's ya wo'kin?"

"I'm working for old lady Gaines."

"I knows where that is. It's up yonder road a spell." Clearing her throat, Ginny added, "I know an old lady that used to wo'k for her. She died."

Mrs. Gaines had already told me about the lady getting sick and dying.

"Heard she's all right to wo'k for, she don't mistreat anybody," Ginny went on. "She doesn't keep ya too busy, do she? Have you talked to Minnie since you were here?" It was as if she hadn't heard me the first time.

"I've been busy. I haven't had much time for myself, much less time for anyone else."

She took out a balled-up handkerchief from her apron pocket and patted her forehead. "I told Minnie that I told you what happened, and she didn't take it too good. Told me I talk too much. Now she go and get scared you mad and won't come back up there. You is going to see her again, ain't ya?" she said, as if her role was to bring us together.

"I'm not mad at her. I had to think about things. And a whole lot of things have been going on in my life," I said, idly putting my finger in the corner of the loose plank on her porch.

"Lord, gurl, leaves that 'lone. Ev'rythang around here is falling apart. How's Mae Lou? I heard 'bout that old man she married. Heard he been drinking all over town. You be careful 'round him. He ain't the kind of man that needs to be 'round no young gurl."

"Yes, ma'am," I said, and lowered my head in shame. She was too late.

Ginny didn't seem to have a lot of visitors, but on Sundays after church, she'd stand around gossiping with the other lonely church sisters, needing something to talk about.

She drifted right back to her original question. "Now, you gonna take some time to visit with Minnie? She like to see ya."

"I'll try to stop by one day this week," I said.

She grinned and folded her hands across her bosom.

"Stop by here and take her some of them apples. She can make them chirren a pie or som'thin. I's got plenty, and my trees are hanging full. Get you some 'fore you leave." This was Ginny's way of making sure that I visited Minnie.

"I'll pick up the apples after work."

"I got some a boy picked for me yestidy. She can have 'em all."

The longer my visit lasted, the better she started to look.

"Ginny, did you know my daddy? What kind of man was my real father?"

She cleared her throat. "I ain't know him that well. Ev'rybody say he a fine man. Some of his peoples still 'round here. Some of 'em 'tend church with us." She spat a wad of tobacco in a can. "Maybe one day when you's leave from 'round here, you's run into him. Peoples run into family all the time. I knows Minnie would've been better off with him."

"Do I look like him?" I asked, glad he didn't have a reputation that would cause me embarrassment. When Ginny spoke of him, she smiled like he was a good man.

"Gurl, you look like all of yo' peoples. You are a little of both of them, even Mrs. Mae Lou. You know, folks say if they feed ya long enough, ya look like 'em."

"Ginny, you're something else," I said, blushing.

"Well, yo' papa's name is Jimmy-Jimmy Tucker. You know yo' auntie goes to the church. You come from good stock. They's some hardwo'kin' people. They got a nice-size farm, too."

As Ginny spoke, my heart swelled by her openness with me. Shortly after meeting her for the first time, I'd added her to my prayers. She held nothing sacred when it came to family and love.

"I ain't got no reason to lie to ya, dear. You's got a good family on all sides. Besides, my life's been an open book. Never could keep my own business private. But one thing I don't do is keep up a lot of shit."

Ginny was still a mystery to be solved, the lines around her eyes telling a story of their own. I wondered where she had been and what she had seen. It was easy for me to open my heart to her, but my shame kept me from telling her about the situation with Mr. Camm.

The very next day, I stopped by and picked up the apples on my way to Minnie's. Ginny had packed them in a large brown paper bag, so full I almost couldn't carry them. She smiled.

"Do ya think this is 'nough for all them damn chirren? They's a bunch of greedy-ass chirren," she mumbled while trying to force one more apple into the bag.

The color had come back into her sallow skin. Like everyone else that lived alone, she'd been suffering from lack of company, and my visit had done her good. I was pleased to be able to visit my old aunt and make her day. I felt safe around her. She wasn't judgmental or concerned about changing the habits of others. Her business was her own.

When I arrived at Minnie's house, everyone was mingling outside. She had moved her kitchen chairs outside and was sitting under a tree fanning flies with a church fan. It was hot and everyone, including the goats and chickens, was panting around in the yard searching for water, shade, and a breeze. Anna saw me and headed straight over. It had been weeks since we'd seen one another at school.

She embraced me. "What's in the bag?"

"Ginny sent these to Minnie. They're apples." I handed her the bag.

"What you's been doing all summer? I missed ya. I thought 'bout walking over to yo' place, but didn't know if it was all right."

"I'm working over at Mrs. Gaines'."

"Momma won't let me work. I's got to help with all these chirren. I want a job. I need the money," Anna said sadly.

Minnie signaled for me to come to her. I went over and gave her a warm hug. Her husband watched us from a tree stump, where he was sitting with a cigarette hanging out the side of his mouth. I waved in his direction, but instead of acknowledging me, he rolled his eyes. Minnie saw him and her smile disappeared.

But before she could respond, Anna handed her the bag of apples.

"Ginny said they make the best pies and cobblers," I told Minnie, speaking of the apples.

"I sho' got a taste for a cobbler," Minnie said, smirking.

As soon as she set the paper sack down beside her, the children started begging for apples. Minnie gave each one an apple, including her husband, until only a few were left in the bag.

"It ain't many left. I'll save the rest and fry them for dinner."

"Have you's heard from Simon?" Anna asked.

I gazed off into the woods. "It's been more than a month. I think this is their season to travel. I hope that he writes soon."

Minnie kept her hands folded in her lap. Every time I looked at her she smiled, despite the fact that her husband was never far away. He was always watching Minnie, making her uncomfortable, stealing her joy.

"See, Ma? Carrie is wo'kin'."

"Anna Mae, don't start with me. You's got plenty to do 'round here. I done told you that."

"Yeah. Watch yo' mouth, gal," her daddy commented, and gave her a stern look.

"Yes, sir."

He reminded me of a woman from when I was ten or eleven years old. Mrs. Paige, a regular churchgoer, was always watching Momma. At times she would turn her back or look the other way whenever she was in Momma's presence. And Momma never made eye contact with her. Something about Mrs. Paige got to Momma, made her fidgety. She was around Momma's age and built similar. Petite, with shoulder-length hair and dark skin, overall an attractive lady. She was also bold. She wore cherry-colored lipstick and an excessive amount of rouge. At one of the many church gatherings where Momma and some of the other ladies served the food, I heard someone say, "She look better without all of that."

"Mae Lou, you are the best cook 'round here," the reverend said after he'd tasted Momma's homemade dressing and giblet gravy.

"Thanks, Reverend, but we all some good cooks today."

Mrs. Paige didn't like what she heard. "Well, what about my cooking, Reverend? I can cook, too. You act like Mae Lou is the only cook in this church, and I'm getting tired of hearing her name all the dern time."

Some of the other women turned their heads and kept piling food on the plates, ignoring the comment.

"Well, you right. You can cook, too, Mrs. Paige," the reverend said, and then turned to walk away. Some of the other sisters giggled. One reached over and whispered in another's ear, "This is some mess here, girl."

Everyone knew that Momma was the best cook around.

"Why are you leaving? Did I hit a nerve, Reverend?" Mrs. Paige asked sharply.

Momma kept on stirring her homemade peach punch.

"No, I'm hungry," he replied, and kept on going.

Then Mrs. Paige walked over to Momma and got right in her face. Momma retreated two steps backward, almost tripping over a chair.

Momma finally said, "Mrs. Paige, you's and me are 'bout to come unbenefited if you don't move. Now I suggest you haul tail out of my way so I can get by."

All of the sisters stood there waiting for one of them to back down. Finally, Mrs. Paige moved aside. Momma set a cup of punch on the table and took her hand. Mrs. Paige tried to pull back, but Momma had a strong grip on her arm.

"We need to go outside. I ain't gonna say the wrong thang in church."

Mrs. Paige's eyes opened wide. The coldness eased as Momma coaxed her to the front of the small church. The ladies around the table grinned and whispered.

I stood listening.

"Now, let me tell you one thang. We all bring food to this place, 'cluding you. We gonna respect each other."

"Wait a minute, Mae Lou." Mrs. Paige shook loose from Momma's grip and pointed her finger.

"No, you listen. I know you got a thing for my husband, but he chose me. For years you done talked about me and been jealous of me and it's time to stop. You's a married woman; leave my husband be."

"He chose the wrong one. Don't no man want a woman as holy as you."

"My husband does."

Raindrops had begun to fall. Mrs. Paige held a hand-fan over her head as Momma turned and walked back in the church. "Don't make me lose my religion up in here." Then the clouds roared and opened up; it thundered and melodious rain beat down for a good thirty minutes.

That was the most Momma had said to one person in a long time. Then she went right back to serving food and even instructed me to take a cup of punch to Mrs. Paige, who accepted with her head lowered.

Before I left, I helped Anna do some of her chores. We carried water in the house and filled up the big kettle sitting on the wood-burning stove. We walked to the spring and gathered some drinking water for the night. Her brothers stood around with their hands in their pockets as they watched us carry the water back to the house. None of them bothered to help us.

Minnie hugged me as she'd done the first time we met. This time I could embrace her just as tightly. I didn't want her to worry about me coming to visit; she already had enough on her mind. After hearing my story from Ginny, I'd forgiven her. Yet, during quiet moments, the thoughts of neglect and abuse danced around inside my head and it saddened me. I wondered why she'd given me away instead of dropping the husband she had clung to so closely.

CHAPTER 23
CARRIE

I barely made it to the night chamber pot. My food came right up. I was so weak I had to grab the bedpost to keep from falling. My head was spinning. Ginny had been sick and the last thing I wanted was her virus. I cleaned up and went out to do my morning chores. Momma persuaded me to eat my breakfast, but my stomach would not let me. The sight of food made my mouth water, sending burning sour fumes back in my throat. I ran back into my bedroom and upchucked again before leaving for work. After, I washed my face and took the pot outside to empty it in the outhouse.

When I came back in the door, Momma asked, "Why can't you hold yo' food down?"

I lied, as usual. "Mrs. Gaines has been sick. I think that I have whatever she has. I'll be all right, though." In truth, Ginny had come down with something, said her stomach was upset, and I knew I'd contacted whatever she had.

"Well, you need to eat something. A dose of soda and vinegar water will settle yo' stomach."

It worked, and I felt better during the day.

There was a letter on my bed from Simon when I returned home. I quickly pushed my bed up against the door and opened the letter. He wrote that he would not be home until Christmas. Inside the envelope was a bracelet adorned with pearls. I had never seen anything so beautiful. He signed the letter, *Keep this as a token of my love.*

I put the bracelet on. It was the first piece of jewelry I'd ever received.

"I hope I can last in this house until Christmas," I murmured. The only good thing about the summer was John being home. His presence had kept Mr. Camm in check. I didn't take any risks, though. I made sure that I watched my back and kept a weapon around, in case I needed it. I had a big stick behind my bedroom door and another under my bed. I also stored a kitchen fork under my pillow. The next time he tried anything, he was going to die.

In my diary, I wrote, *Ginny reminds me so much of Mrs. Gaines. Every time I visit her she is sitting in the same place. She is always elated about receiving a visitor.*

"Lord knows I was hoping that you came by today," she said as soon as I walked up on her porch the next day.

"Are you all right?" I asked.

"I'm okay. S'pose I'm used to seeing ya. Now, what did Minnie do with them apples?"

"She gave everybody around there an apple and then she peeled the rest to cook for dinner."

"I'm sho' glad that she used them. Minnie and her chirren ought to come down here. There are plenty on the ground. They need to be picked 'fore they go to waste. I got too many fo' jest me. And Lord knows she got some greedy little chirren running 'round there like heathens."

"It's a lot of 'em."

"She need to keep her legs closed. I ain't against chirren, but she can hardly feed 'em. And her husband is about as smart as a piece of wood."

It was hot that evening and I was sweating profusely. The breeze circulating through the trees was subtle. The leaves swayed, and still I was burning up.

Ginny told a story about Mr. Camm's family. He had lost his mother at a young age. She said his momma was a hardworking church lady. But he was raised by his drinking father. His father was no good and told his children they were sorry pieces of shit.

Mr. Camm had started out differently, moving to Washington and finding work, but since his return to Jefferson, he'd taken on some of the same ways as his father. Instability chief among them. And the work he'd done in Washington went by the wayside once he'd made it back to the country. Now he had nice-looking and self-sufficient women to provide for all of his needs.

"That was 'xactly how he noticed Mae Lou," Ginny said. "He'd only been 'tending the chu'ch for about a year prior to knowing her. She was always busy. Ev'ry chu'ch outing and ev'ry fourth Sunday, she was doing something. Cooking, ushering, cleaning the chu'ch yard. She was perfect for him. She reminded him of his mother. She could do it all."

I understood perfectly.

"So I bet as soon as he hurd 'bout Mr. Robert's dying, he scoped out Mae Lou," Ginny added.

Ginny stared at me all of a sudden in a way that made me uneasy.

"What's wrong?" I asked.

"You ain't with child, is ya?"

"No, Ginny, why did you ask me that?" I brushed down the side of my dress with my hands and crossed my arms over my chest.

"Chile, I done had six chirren of my own, and I know what it look like when a woman 'specting. You got that glow. Yo' skin is simply pretty. Most women with chile is real pretty at furst."

I had to let that settle before I could respond. "Ginny, I'm sorry."

"Sorry 'bout what? You with child or ain't you?"

My heart started to race. I wanted to tell her what had happened to me, but I was ashamed. I didn't want her to look down at me, even though it seemed as if all my high hopes were beginning to fade.

"It must be a coincidence," I struggled to say.

She finally looked away. "I ain't too big on words, but you sho' got that look."

"I'm not having a baby," I said.

"Okay, you ought to know. Now you 'member this, if you's need to talk to me about it, I'll be right here." Then she leaned back in the rocker and started to rock.

Did she hear what I just said? I thought. *She's a stubborn old woman.*

Yet her suggestion continued to gnaw at me.

Was it possible Mr. Camm had made me pregnant? I told myself that it could not be. *I can't be that way, I can't be that way,* I thought, trying to forget what Ginny had said.

I'd heard him in the house, but I hadn't seen his face more than twice in the past two months. One of those times, the end of a long day, I'd stared him down in the kitchen. The other time was pretty much the same thing. Either I came home too late to eat with the family or I wouldn't eat. I could not stand to see his face.

Now, for the first time since the rape, I gazed at him with dark and evil eyes similar to his own. The rape had changed me in so many ways.

"You hypocrite," I mumbled to myself. He was standing in the kitchen with Momma, acting as if he was a dedicated husband, helping her set the table.

"Are you eating at the table with us tonight?" Momma asked sarcastically. As I said, for two months, I had managed to avoid eating with them.

"I'm really not hungry right now. I'll probably eat later," I said.

Momma frowned. "Well, everything is nice and hot now."

I *was* hungry. My stomach had been growling all day. But I'd have to convince myself that Mr. Camm didn't exist to even consider eating with them. I would do anything for Momma, but I couldn't bear the sight of him. But again, I was angry and hurt at the same time. As Momma started serving the plates, John walked in through the kitchen door. I immediately felt the tension lifting. Having John at the table would make it so much easier for me.

"Okay, Momma, I might as well eat now," I said. And her disapproval subsided.

I ignored Mr. Camm the entire meal. The conversation centered on my work and John's reluctant summer work for the Fergusons.

"I am going to make sure that I don't spend my life working for no white person. There is no way that I could do this type of work for a living," John said. "I want to use my mind, not my hands, to make money."

"Me either," I said, even though working with Mrs. Gaines was the best thing that could have happened to me. I could tell that Mr. Camm was just as uncomfortable with me sitting at the table as I was with him. He didn't say much. Guilt was written all over his scrawny face. When I summoned the courage to finally look at him, he quickly lowered his head. A stream of sweat slid down the side of his face. I studied his beady eyes, quivering lips, and receding hairline. He must have been deathly afraid that I would bring up what he'd done to me.

"Well, I hope that both of you will go to college and get a better job than either of us," Momma commented. Mr. Camm shook his head agreeably, then blotted his forehead with a napkin. John and I glanced at one another with narrowed eyes. Neither my brother nor I cared about Mr. Camm or his nod of support for Momma's thought.

After I finished the dishes and swept the floor, Mr. Camm came into the kitchen. He got some water and stood on the other side of the room, gawking at me and licking his lips. Then he put his hand on his crotch. "You better keep yo' mouth closed," he whispered and grinned.

I picked up the butcher knife. "You better leave me alone."

"I ain't scared of you."

"You better be," I said, and stared him down.

Instead of going back to his bedroom, he went into the front room. I stood watching as he gazed out the window at the full moon. After a minute, he noticed me watching but didn't grin in response as he sat down on the Davenport and put his head between his elbows and massaged the temples on the side of his head. His hands trembled.

After sitting there for a few minutes, he fell asleep and snored in the chair until the next morning.

I slid the bed against my bedroom door and pulled out my diary and started to write about the day. The implication of being pregnant worried me, so I counted the days. My journal was also my calendar. And I made a mark to signify the beginning of my cycle. My jaws tightened when I realized I'd actually skipped a couple of months. I crawled in the bed like a baby and hugged my pillow.

After a few days, I managed to put the notion behind me and focus on the money I needed to make in order to get away from Jefferson County. I had saved up nearly ten dollars. It was enough to buy a bus ticket to Richmond or Washington, D.C. and have a little money left over.

That's what I would do, I decided. I would run away and find Simon. I would tell him everything.

CHAPTER 24
PEARL

The old folks might have said that I was a slick woman. I could slide in and out of places as easy as an oiled hinge. I had started a new routine with Herman and it was working like clockwork. When Willie got dressed in overhauls and turned-over boots and put his red handkerchief in his back pocket, I rolled over in the bed. I knew the daywork cutting down trees and clearing land for white folk would keep Willie occupied way into the evening hours. Some days I was saddened he had chosen living in the country over the city and the promised government job for returning soldiers. I got dressed and headed out the house as if I had a job, which, considering my color and the times, would have been slaving in a white woman's kitchen or cleaning her house, while her husband pinned me against the floor at every opportunity.

"You are acting like a damn slut," my momma said as soon as I stepped foot into the kitchen. At my age, living with my parents had been a difficult challenge. Going to bed early and waking even before the cock crowed was something I found hard to get used to. I resented it even more than some because I was a night-club singer at heart. The night was my time.

"Momma, what are you talking about?" I said and picked up the old tin coffee percolator she'd made coffee in for as long as I could remember. I poured myself a cup of coffee and sat down at the kitchen table.

She stood over me, pointing her chubby finger in my face. "You're sleeping with two mens. You might have three, for all I know," she yelled.

"I'm a city girl."

She rolled her eyes. "You a damn slut, that what you is," she repeated. "Going out here every day while yo' husband is working hard like a dog. You ought to be ashamed of yo'self. You are acting like someone with no home training."

I gaped at her. "I'm not going out with any man. I like to be around different types of peoples for a change. Plus, I do work at the joint. I'm a singer, if you can remember."

"You are a woman in her thirties chasing men and acting like a damn fool. That's what you is."

Her anger roared through her voice. She was barely five feet tall, yet she seemed to tower over me.

"I'm not chasing a man, Momma. I want to live my life and have a good time. This is the twenties, not slavery days. We stopped answering to the master," I said sarcastically.

A vein protruded at her temple. "Listen, when you came back here, I thought Willie had been abusing ya up there in Washington. You came to my door with a bruise on yo' eye, looking like someone had treated you wrong, and ya said it had nothing to do with another man. Now I know the truth." She threw her arms up in despair. "I thought you'd gotten over telling stories. What have the city done to you?"

"Oh, Momma, please, everything isn't about a man. I want to live my life. Is that all right with you?"

"Most women yo' age is married with a family. Yo' daddy would be so disappointed if he knew what you've been up to around here."

"See, that's why I know I need to get out of here. Everything is so domestic."

"What does that mean?"

"I'm not like the women around here, spending all of the day cooking, cleaning, minding a garden, serving a man, and getting up at the crack of dawn to empty a chamber pot..."

"Chamber pot?"

"A slop bucket, Momma."

"Now ya think you're better than ev'rybody else."

"What?" I said, incredulous.

"And don't you need to eat, too?"

"Yeah, I do."

"Why can't ya do it for yo'self?" she said and threw the dish-towel irritably across her shoulder.

"I can tell I'm not going to win this argument."

I went to the wash pan and washed my cup, hung it on the drain nail and walked out of the kitchen. From behind me, she called, "You a fool, girl. A damn fool."

I pinned my hair up in a chignon, threw my shawl over my shoulders, and left through the front door.

The joint was empty with the exception of Jake, Earl, and another old man who was there every day, nursing a bottle of corn liquor. Jake was sweeping the scuffed wood floor. On the bar made out of two long slabs of wood, were a few jugs of liquor he'd probably gotten from Mr. Lolly, who had a still hidden back in the woods near the creek. He kept the jugs sealed tight in a fishing net right by the creek. During the day, only a few people partook of the spirits of liquor, but at night, it was the medicine needed to drown their troubles away. So Jake used the daylight hours to get things ready for the evening crowd.

Earl was a handsome man with dark features, thick eyebrows,

long black lashes and a mustache that shadowed his perfectly formed dark brown lips. He sat alone at the table, and smiled when he saw me approaching. I sat down across from him.

"Pearl, the first time I ever saw you, I knew I wanted to meet you," he said, stumbling over the words, "but I knew Herman had his eyes on you."

"Oh, don't worry about him. We're just good friends."

I lied, even though Earl knew the truth. I had become accustomed to the attention of men, but since I'd been back to the country, the attention had dwindled because most of the men were locked up at home.

"I sure wish I wasn't a married man, I'd take you home with me."

I reached over and touched his thick fingers, feeling the thickness of his calluses and dry skin from hard work.

"You better stop flirting with me before Herman comes," he said.

Between sips of water, I whispered, "Herman who?"

We both giggled.

Earl made me happy. He was never too serious for a little fun. And on the days when Herman didn't come by, he and I would sit for hours talking and flirting.

Soon Herman strolled into the joint, wobbly. "Y'all always got y'all heads together," he said.

Herman's eyes were bloodshot. But even drunk he was better dressed than most men. Mae Lou kept him clean. Living with her, however, was taking a toll on him. He was drinking too much.

"We just having a little fun," Earl apologized to Herman.

"Every time I come in here, you up in her face."

"Come on, Herman, don't be jealous. My heart belongs to you," I said, and patted the seat beside me.

"Me, Willie, Earl..."

Earl's eyes were fixed on me, yet he didn't open his mouth. I sensed he didn't like what Herman had said. He rose to his feet. "I've got to get out of here."

"Yo' wife probably miss you," Herman teased.

Earl smiled at me. "You have a good day, Pearl."

When he left, things began to heat up.

"Why is Earl always here with you?"

"Come on, Herman. You've been drinking and the liquor is talking. Earl is your friend. You introduced him to me."

"Yeah, but that nigga want you."

"I came to see you."

Herman was drinking more and more. By the middle of the day, he was usually staggering. All the finesse he used to possess had dwindled since he'd moved to Jefferson. Being a gambler, he made money off of other people. Now he barely had anything, and it showed.

"What is bothering you?" I asked.

"Ain't nothing bothering me," he snapped. "I'm tired of him always smiling up in your face."

I shook my head, and he finally saw that I was annoyed.

"What you want to do, girl?" he asked, rubbing my thigh underneath the table.

"You know," I answered.

He walked over to Jake, whispered in his ear and came back.

The back room contained an iron post bed and a small table, with a door that opened up to the backyard. It was familiar to us in the cold months and we took advantage. More importantly, it was clean. Jake said the sheets were changed daily. Still, we lay on the top of the beautiful patch quilt someone had made.

Herman peeled off my dress and took the pins out of my hair.

He liked it down below my shoulders. Even with the stench of liquor on him, I kissed his neck and ran my tongue across it.

"Girl, you gonna make me a man up in here."

We got butt naked, and he started to run his long tongue over my nipples while his fingers fondled my hot spot. I stroked his manhood and we both started to pant in short breaths. When he rolled over, I straddled him and gyrated up and down and swung my heavy breasts in his face. We both sighed and then grinned when we were done.

I washed off with the wet towel Jake provided, pinned my hair up, and exited out the back door. Like Momma said, crooks know how to come through the front door.

As I walked back to the house, I couldn't get Herman out of my head. Now I needed to refocus on what was in store for me at home.

Momma was still piddling around in the kitchen when I returned. She was just finishing the meal she'd prepared for her husband and mine.

She turned around and shook her head. "You need help."

"Yeah, I know," I agreed, to avoid an argument.

"I want you to talk to the preacher," she said.

"For what?"

"You need the Lord's forgiveness."

"Momma, nobody is perfect," I said breezily.

"I never should've let you go off to Washington."

"Momma, I am who I am."

"You a married woman," she argued.

Ignoring her, I went into the bedroom Willie and I shared. I threw myself across the bed and peered out the window. Yet what she said did not fade away easily. Carrying on this affair was going to catch up to me. I really did need help.

CHAPTER 25
CARRIE

Several weeks went by before I felt the first symptom. I was getting dressed for work when my stomach started fluttering. It scared me at first, but I'd known what to expect. My classmates Anna, Mabel and Purdie had all had babies by the time they'd turned fourteen. Purdie actually had two. The girls shared their experiences with the rest of us, talking about breast-feeding and diaper changes, although at the time I really didn't care to know the details. Now, I was glad for the education. I knew that I was carrying Mr. Camm's baby. What would I tell Simon? The last thing I needed was a baby.

I pulled my dress above my waist and gazed down at my stomach. It was the same size that it had always been. To be sure, I completely undressed and examined my entire body. I stood in front of the dresser looking in the mirror, and checked my breasts to see if they had changed. My eyes panned up and down my frame, making sure that I inspected every part carefully. Then I turned sideways to make certain my profile was the same. I was pleased that there was no real physical evidence of my condition. Ginny was the only person who managed to recognize I was pregnant by looking at my complexion. But she had that old folk wisdom. I supposed that if I lived to be sixty, I would be able to prophesize to others, too.

In a few weeks, the summer would almost be over and I would

have five more dollars saved up. Then I'd go to the old lady who I had been told got rid of babies. I didn't know anything about her personally, but people said she was a witch doctor. They said she'd let one girl bleed to death many years ago. "That woman has been playing God. Peoples ought to leave her alone. She should be locked up," one of the townspeople had said, and then the town gossip, Miss Minerva, added, "You know, Mary Sue's girl was over there just yestidy."

All of the talk frightened me. I didn't want to die. I had to do something, though. I needed a way out. I couldn't be a mother. Not only had Mr. Camm stolen my innocence, but he had robbed Simon of his right to father my firstborn. Simon and I had sat under the tree at the schoolhouse and discussed our plans to get married and have a family of our own. I took a deep breath and wiped away the tears streaming down my face.

That night I tossed and turned in bed. I balled up in a knot and snuggled close to my pillow and held on to it all night. I closed my eyes but could not fall asleep. I thought endlessly about what I could've done differently. I could have fought harder against Mr. Camm, and then there would be no baby, and my plans wouldn't be floating away like the wind carries a leaf. I pulled my bed sheet over my head and finally drifted to sleep as the sky started turning blue again.

I woke up with a pounding headache. When I stepped on the floor to get up, my stomach started turning. I ran to the pot and threw up the meal I had eaten the night before. I struggled to get myself together before leaving my room. I didn't dare awake any suspicions in Momma. I wasn't feeling good at all, but I couldn't stay home. After I bathed and combed my hair, I checked my body and reassured myself that I hadn't gained weight overnight. I pulled my journal from under the pillow and glanced through the pages to try and judge how many months along I was. Four months had passed since it happened.

It took me over an hour to reach Mrs. Gaines. I took my time, since any movement made me nauseous. As usual, Mrs. Gaines was waiting for me. She opened the door even before I knocked.

"Come on in," she said.

"I don't feel good this morning. I have an upset stomach."

"Sit down, I'll make some tea. You see, good tea can settle the stomach."

She soon handed me the cup. "This will settle your stomach," she assured me.

Steam escaped from the cup and left a vapor in front of me. I slowly sipped the tea and immediately felt warm as it went down.

"Now sit for a minute, I guarantee you'll start to feel better," she said, gazing at me. "What do you think is wrong?"

"I'm not sure. Maybe I'm coming down with something."

"Well, whenever I am sick, tea is always..."

She went on and on about her family, and my mind floated back to my own state of affairs. Who would understand? Hester came to mind. She had been my friend for years and had kept most of my secrets, except for telling John about Simon's interest in me. When I confronted her about that, she vowed that she would never do anything like that again without my permission. I believed her. Anyone could make a mistake, and she was the only person I trusted. We had shared every eventful moment in our lives. It had started with the crushes we had on two brothers in our classroom. We were about nine years old. Both of the boys were dark and handsome, with thick hair and straight teeth. Neither of them gave us a second thought, though. Together we wrote a love letter to each of them, asking them to be our boy-friends. They sent back the same note to us with a big fat "No" written across the page. We laughed and decided to beat them up instead.

I pondered my dilemma for over two weeks. I had to do something. I was exploding inside with all of this misery. School would be starting soon and I needed to make a fresh start, put away the past and focus on the future. I stopped by Hester's when I left Mrs. Gaines' house after work one day. She had just gotten home from work and was in the kitchen helping her momma prepare supper, picking string beans and peeling potatoes.

"I was just planning to come see you," she said, hugging me when she opened the door.

"I dropped by to see if you and my brother are still an item." I nudged her and smiled.

Her mother said, "She needs to concentrate on getting out of school instead of John," which made us all giggle.

"I guess we are," Hester said. "Soon he will be heading off again to the big city. I can't wait to get from around here myself. Washington, here I come."

I enjoyed the kind of love that Hester's parents showed me whenever I visited. They treated me like family. They were not the ordinary colored folk in our community who all seemed to farm. They practiced a trade they'd learned from their parents and grandparents. Hester's daddy made furniture on the side. On Saturdays when everyone had finished sowing seeds and bringing in wood, cutting and shucking, he would cut timber. Then he shaved it down and sanded the logs and whittled them into chairs and tables. His only equipment was his hands, an axe, a saw, and his carving knife. He didn't make a lot of money in his business, but to everyone around Jefferson, he was making something of his life. He was a craftsman.

And on occasions, especially in the spring, he would clear pretty good money. Some people, mainly whites, paid him to build picnic tables or even whittle the detail in the gazebos that those who had money could afford. Mr. Taylor was always expanding, adding chairs, and building shelves. He loved his craft and shared his skills with the community.

Hester and I went to her room. On the way, she asked, "How are things with you and Simon?"

"I heard from him a few weeks ago, and he is doing all right, but he won't be home until Christmas." I slumped down on her bed as if it was mine.

"What's wrong with you? Why do you look so sad?" she asked, puzzled. "You usually blush when you talk about Simon. You've been holding back on me, girl. What the heck is wrong? Whatever is bothering you, you need to talk about it." Immediately my eyes watered, and she closed her bedroom door.

"Carrie, it's gonna be all right, I promise," she said, and put her arms around my shoulders.

"I've got things going on in my life that are too painful to talk about."

"Release the pain to the ears of an old friend," she said softly. "Remember our dreams of leaving Jefferson, going away to school and becoming teachers."

"Yep, and I can't wait any longer," I said, still miserable. "I think it may never happen for me."

Hester put her arm around my shoulders and stroked my back. Then it all spilled out, everything that I'd been holding inside for months.

"I was raped," I said. Tears flowed silently down my cheeks.

"What?" Hester said, startled. "Why haven't you said anything? Now, you know we've got to do something about it, Carrie. When did it happen?"

I cleared my throat and wiped the teardrops rolling down my cheeks with the back of my hand. "Remember when I came to visit you a couple of months ago, and you weren't feeling well because of your cycle...It happened around that time."

"I barely remember the stuff we talked about that day. But I thought we could talk about everything. That's what friends do, right?" Hester was gazing at my face. I still couldn't explain why I had been such a coward.

I hung my head low and whispered, as if I still had a secret, "I'm scared. I'm expecting."

"Oh, my God, you were holding that back, too?" Hester threw a hand over her mouth. "I don't know what to do."

She tried to think, but had no more idea of what to do than I did. "Look, let's talk to Momma. She can at least tell us where to start, because I don't know how to help ya."

I grabbed her arm hard. "Oh no, please don't tell your momma. I've got to fix it and get rid of it. I don't want anyone to know."

"Did you tell yo' momma?"

A wary look covered my face. "No, she's not like your momma. I can't talk to her. She's got the morals of a saint. And how can I tell her that the son of a bitch who raped me is her husband?"

"What? Mr. Camm is the one raped you?"

"Yes," I managed. "What do I do?"

Hester shook her head. She didn't know how to answer me.

"Listen, what is that lady's name who lives around here that helps young ladies out?" I asked.

Her eyes grew wide with fear. "I don't know, but I've heard horror stories about her. You know how country folk talk. You might not want to do that."

"Yes, I do."

"I do know where she stays, though. It's not too far from here, just up past the church. Momma knew someone she took care of. They say she's a witch, something like a voodoo doctor."

"Will you go with me to see her?"

Hester inhaled deeply. "Yeah, I'll go, but you should think about it first."

"I'll think about it, but right now I'm running out of time."

We both sat in glum silence for a while. Then she asked, "Are you gonna tell Simon what happened?"

"I can't put that in a note to him. I'll tell him everything when he comes home for Christmas."

"Okay, but promise me that you'll take care of yourself."

I spent most of my evening at Hester's house. I ate there before going home. At the dinner table, her daddy told a joke that was so funny, my belly shook. For that one moment, I forgot about my troubles. The sounds of laughter reminded me of my family when Papa was living. Before I left, I made Hester agree to keep my secret and to go with me to see the lady.

CHAPTER 26
CARRIE

I had tried all the things the old folks tell you not to do when expecting. I'd swallowed large doses of castor oil. I'd lifted heavy objects. I'd run until I'd lost my breath. I'd prayed, yet the frequent flutters in my stomach wouldn't go away.

Mrs. Gaines had given me permission to leave early to visit a sick friend. She'd warned me, "Now don't get too close to her; you don't want to get sick again."

When I arrived at Hester's house, she was waiting for me. She had lied to her mother, saying we were going to visit a friend from school, and she'd even managed to get the buggy to take us there. Her mother's eyes were filled with suspicion. She didn't ask any questions, though, but stood with her arms folded, watching me closely. Hester always thought things through. She had been blessed with the ability to remain calm in tight situations. She said that taking the buggy would get us there faster and she wasn't sure how well I'd feel afterward. I was frightened and peeing every fifteen minutes. My head had been spinning for months as I wondered how to handle everything going on in my life.

We both climbed into the old buggy hitched to a stubborn-looking mule, that was twice the size of any normal horse. He was no more excited about this trip than I, bucking at first, until Hester rubbed his coat and reassured him.

"You gonna be all right?" Hester asked me as she coaxed the mule down the road.

My jaws were tight. "I guess so," I said. "I've made my decision."

"You got to make sure that you're comfortable with it, though. Think it over. You can't undo it once it's done," Hester said. "That's the only advice I can give you."

"I know. I thought about it all last night. I even prayed about it," I said. "Even asked God to forgive me."

I held my hand over my brow to block out the sun's fierce rays. The sun was high, even though it would soon be overcast by the rain clouds visible over the hills west of us. I took mini breaths to keep from hyperventilating. A frown had taken over Hester's face, her eyes dark with worry, like mine. She concentrated on the reins, making sure that the mule trotted in a straight line.

After a few minutes of silence, Hester patted my arm. "I don't want anything to happen to you."

"I'm scared," I said in a small voice.

"Me, too."

When we turned down the familiar path that led to Ginny's house, my heart started to race. I was overcome with heat flashes.

"You sure this is the right way? Is this the place we need to go to?" I thought that maybe the directions weren't good or that Hester didn't remember the turn, since it had been some time since her mother had mentioned the woman to her. So many paths led to houses in the country. Most of them were so far away from the main road that neighbors didn't know that they existed.

"Yeah, this is it. Momma said that she used to do that kind of thing years ago. She is an old lady now. I don't know if she is still doing it."

Beads of sweat started popping out on my forehead. I was flustered. I couldn't believe that we were headed to Ginny's. This was not the way I wanted Ginny to find out about my condition. She had already realized that I was expecting. What could I say to her? *I couldn't do it.* I told Hester to slow down until I could calm my nerves. I inhaled deeply a few times and blew the air out of my mouth. I could hear Ginny saying, "I told you so."

"Hester, are you sure this is the place?" I asked again, doubting if she really knew the way.

"This is the place. Momma knew of somebody that she took care of. She was a close friend of hers."

Anna had called Ginny crazy on more than one occasion, and now I understood why. Ginny was helping women undo acts of nature. I didn't agree with what she did, but I was one of those women seeking her help for the same purpose.

I trembled violently.

Why did it have to be my aunt? I thought.

"We've got to go back," I ordered Hester.

"What are you gonna do about the baby?"

My plan was beginning to turn sour. The only other thing I could do was give the baby away once it was born, because the Lord knew I had no intentions of raising an unwanted child. I sat rocking back and forth, trying to think of a way out.

"I'll give it away, leave it on the church steps. I'm sure that someone will want it." All of a sudden a chill went through my limbs, as I remembered my own beginnings. I was an unwanted child. It was a different circumstance, but was I as cold as my birth mother was? Was this my only option?

"I wish I could answer that question, but I was lost in thoughts and didn't know what to do." Hester backed the mule up and turned around. We both had tears in our eyes. We didn't know what to do.

"You want to do something else today?" Hester asked after she'd recovered.

"I want to go to sleep. I want to go somewhere and lay my head down."

"Why don't you come over to my house? You can get all the rest you need. My parents won't mind. Carrie, you know, this is the first summer we've been able to visit one another…and it is a good thing. I wouldn't want you to go through this alone."

All the while I was shaking my head. "I'm going home."

"You sure you want to do that?"

"I want to lie down in my own bed."

"Be careful."

My intentions were to go home, but I felt compelled to visit Ginny.

Ginny had been forthright with me from the very beginning, and now I was forced to do the same. Besides Hester, Ginny was the only other person that I felt comfortable talking to, and now I needed her. I was still too embarrassed to tell Hester that the voodoo lady was my aunt. I sat there wondering when I would gather enough nerve to tell Hester the rest of my story.

I left Hester's house and headed straight back in the direction from where we'd come. The haze lifted and the sun crept out from behind the clouds. I could barely place one foot in front of the other. I felt beat, both disturbed and bothered about what I was about to do. Ginny was not in her usual place, but her chair was still rocking as if she had just gotten out of it.

I tapped on her front door and stuck my head in. "House keeps," I yelled, and then proceeded to walk in.

"Come on in, I'm back here in the kitchen getting me som'thin to drink."

"Are you coming back on the porch?" I yelled.

"Uh-huh. I'm coming back outside, was getting me a glass of ice water. Want some?"

"No, thank you. Do you need any help?"

"No, I'll be right out."

I flopped down in a chair on the porch and waited for Ginny to return. A moment later she slid herself into the rocker and set her glass of water on the porch rail.

She gazed at me with those mysterious hazel eyes.

"Lordy, what's on your mind? You look like you got som'thin' you want to say. G'won, speak up." It was like she could see and predict the future. I could understand why others said she knew voodoo.

"I wanted to talk to you about something." She kept rocking as if she knew what was on my mind. "It's about what you said," I murmured.

I didn't look at her. I lowered my head as I'd rehearsed in my mind on the way to her house.

"Now I can see in yo' face som'thin' is bothering you. Now, g'won and spit it out. I can't read yo' mind."

"I'm expecting a baby."

"Okay," she said with slits for eyes.

She intently listened to me tell her all about the day Mr. Camm raped me, leaving out the details that were too painful to mention. Then she took her handkerchief and dotted her face, bent over in the rocker, grabbed my chin and stared into my eyes. "Ain't nothing to be sorry 'bout, unless you ain't telling the truth now."

Ginny had seen many a young girl in her day, violated by white men, colored men, fathers, and boyfriends. She'd always been a strong woman. She could remember taking a frying pan to a couple of heads in her day. What she didn't understand was why women today were still resigned to serve in the role of victims.

"Don't ya know that when shit happens, ev'rybody says it ain't their fault. Whose fault is it then?"

"I didn't want it to happen."

"Uh-huh, you got to learn to fight fo' yo'self. Don't take no shit. If you can't whip 'em, tell som'body. If ya scared, tell som'body. It's folks badder than Mr. Camm," she said, sipping her glass of ice water.

"Yes, ma'am."

"I ought to get my shotgun and blow his head off my damn self. That nigga reminds me of John Robert," she said, shaking her head. Then she told me the whole story:

"He was built like a ho'se, and folks always told me I had pretty legs. And I must admit I had budding breasts and a good build. He'd called me 'sweet-thang' for as long as I could 'member. I didn't mind at furst, 'cause he was a boy. But one Thu'sday, since I's be the oldest, I fixed peas, rice and biscuits. Ev'rybody else was wo'kin' in the field. John Robert knocked on the door. Momma tole me to don't let folks in while they's wo'kin'. John Robert pushed his way in and started to get the best of me. He was strong but he didn't get far 'nough to put his self on me. I grabbed the butcher knife and carved a hole in 'im. He ain't die, though," she said. Then added, "Ain't no man gonna take advantage of me."

Ginny touched my arm. "I told ya to watch him. Ev'rybody been wondering why Mae Lou married him. He ain't no good and never has been no good."

"I didn't tell Momma. I couldn't. She probably wouldn't believe me no way."

"That's all right, som'body else ought to wake her up. Do you wants the baby?"

"No, ma'am."

I started shaking my leg. It was a habit I took up whenever I was nervous. The fierce sun was beaming directly down on my back, making me hot.

"What do you plan to do? If ya don't want it, are ya gonna give it up to somebody else to raise?" Before I answered, I reminded myself of the trip that I had taken earlier to Ginny's with Hester. She was supposed to have the answer. That's what Hester thought.

"I don't want this baby. I can't take care of his baby. I want to get rid of it," I said, worried and waiting for her comment.

"Listen here, chile. You need to give the baby to someone who want one. Don't get rid of yo' baby." Ginny's hazel-brown eyes narrowed when she spoke. "There are some thangs you don't do."

I was confused because I'd thought she was the lady Hester had told me about. Trying hard not to hurt her feelings, I asked her, "Are you the lady that gets rid of babies?"

She stopped rocking and regarded me with cold eyes. "There are thangs you don't need to know 'bout. I've made my share of mistakes, but I'm gonna try to live right for the remaining of my time here on Earth." She scowled. "You sho' got some damn nerve."

"Ginny, I am sorry!"

She saw how upset I was. My moods were strong enough to move the sun from behind the clouds. "That's quite all right," she said calmly. "Say, was that you up yonder I saw earlier in a buggy out in front of the house?"

I confessed that I'd wanted to get rid of the baby, but I couldn't come to her with Hester, so we'd turned around and left. At the time I felt as if there was no way I could ask her to help me after I had lied about being pregnant.

"Chile, pay close 'tention to what I am 'bout to say. I want you to thank 'bout all of this with a clean heart. 'Member yo' momma gave you away. She could have gotten rid of you but she didn't. Minnie was in the same sit'ation that you are in, a long time ago. She wasn't raped, though. She chose to keep you in spite of the peoples around her. I know what happened is wrong, but keep yo' baby."

Ginny told me that she understood, but knew that if she performed the procedure, she'd end up regretting it like so many other young girls that she had serviced. That is why she'd stopped. She had started doing it back in her twenties because she always hated it when a young girl would be expecting and wasn't married, how most of the townspeople would gossip and whisper. They would condemn the girls to shame. When the children grew up, they'd be treated differently, too, because they didn't have a daddy. Then she realized that she wasn't God and couldn't save the young girls, so she asked for forgiveness and quit. But in spite of her efforts, the girls, once they became women, would eventually blame her for what they asked her to do in the first place.

"That baby is gonna bring you some good blessings one day." Clearing her throat, she added, "I know this is not what ya want to hear but I'm telling you, it's the best for you. God will punish that no-good piece of shit in due time."

"Did you hear me? I don't want this baby."

"Calm down, gurl. You's a woman now, be strong. Now, you know Mae Lou gonna come undone 'bout this. If you needs a place to stay, my house is yours. I got a room in the back, been empty since the chirren left."

I got up and hugged Ginny for the kind offer and dusted off my dress. "I don't know what I'll do; I've got to think about it. Right now, I wish that I could die."

"Ev'rybody done dealt with hard times. None of this is yo' fault. If you needs me to talk to Mae Lou, let me know. Now, hold yo'self together. This ain't the end of the world."

CHAPTER 27
PEARL

The Christmas holiday was only days away and the Northern wind had swept in chilly temperatures, causing people to migrate indoors and hover around their fireplaces. Outside, the snow clouds remained high. The moist smell of the earth drifted through the air. Willie was gone. He had caught the one o'clock train to Washington, D.C., to retrieve some of the things he swore he'd left behind. When I learned he would be staying overnight, I fought the wind and dodged through the bare trees to see Herman one last time.

Autumn had come and gone. I'd seen Herman a lot less, mindful of what Momma had said to me. Yet, I hadn't stopped altogether. In a strange way, I felt as if he needed me.

Jake, the bartender, had come to me the last time I was at the club. "Herman is drinking a lot. Something strange is going on with him, Miz Pearl."

I was worried, but I knew the story all too well, so I didn't respond.

"He acting like a complete fool. Yeah, he crazy," Jake said, wiping down the bar as if he'd said too much. "I don't care for the man, Miz Pearl. Don't tell him I told you. He is a crazy son of a bitch."

"I won't," I said, and tapped his shoulder to assure him.

When Herman finally stumbled into the joint, I hardly recognized him. His skin was dull, and growing on his face was a wiry beard that almost covered his lips completely. His eyes were pink from drinking, and he was moving like an unbalanced toddler. My desire to hold him in my arms and make passionate love diminished in an instant. All I wanted to do was care for him, get inside his head and make it all better.

It was warm in the joint. I took off my coat and hung it on the back of the chair. The potbelly cast iron stove was filled with wood and was shooting sparks of fire out to the flue. I put my arms around Herman. "What's wrong with you?" I asked. "You don't seem yourself."

He peered at me as if he had seen a ghost. "Where's your big, bad-ass husband?" Beads of sweat dripped down the side of his face. He pulled a handkerchief from his side pocket and patted his forehead.

"He's out of town. We don't have to worry about him."

"You sure big Willie's gone?" he asked, his speech slurred. "That motherfucker threatened me, said he gonna kill me if I don't leave you alone."

"Herman, Willie's out of town, I told you."

He gazed at me and sucked his teeth. "Well, he was here last night at the joint. Sat right where you are and told me your ass done confessed to him about us. What the hell were you thinking, girl?"

I drew back, shocked. "I didn't tell Willie anything. You sure he came in here?"

"Hell, can't you hear, woman? He was sitting right there." He pointed at a seat just beyond me. "He said he was gonna make sure Mae Lou found out, too. That nigger is stone crazy."

The heat was starting to get to me. "Can I have some water, please?" I asked Jake, who was pretending to be busy while listening to our entire conversation.

Jake dipped out a glass of water from the pail of water he'd gathered from the well out back while I had been waiting for Herman.

I said, "Willie told me he had some business in Washington, D.C."

"That nigger's around here. He's probably watching us right now."

"He left, I tell you. He won't be back until tomorrow."

He gazed at me with rage in his eyes. "I got something for his ass if he threatens me one mo' time."

That didn't sound good. Herman wasn't a natural fighter. He was a gambler, a smooth man that understood women better than most. But he was streetwise as well, and used to handling business.

"I'll take care of it. He was just talking," I said, knowing Willie had a bad-ass temper.

"You can't talk to a fool. He caught me off guard. Stood in my face and insulted me and my wife."

"Your wife…"

He glanced over at me. "Yeah, I told you he said he gonna go and tell Mae Lou. Then he had the nerve to say that a good woman like Mae Lou deserves a man like him, somebody who will take care of her."

I pulled out my compact, took out my powder puff and blotted my nose. "I can't believe this. None of it makes any sense."

"I tell you this: if he goes anywhere near Mae Lou, I'm gonna kill him."

"He was just talking," I assured him. "He's upset about us. I'm going to come clean, leave him, and then we can be together with no problems."

He gazed at me in discontent, head wobbling. "Pearl, you are a beautiful lady. I enjoy spending time with ya, but I need someone to cook and take care of me."

I cringed. "What are you saying?"

"Pearl, you are not the type of woman that wants to settle down. Your heart is in the nightclub. You like the lights and glitter. You want to be like Bessie Smith and that old Ma Rainey. One man can't please you."

"I love you," I pleaded. "I thought what we share is special."

"I love you, too, but you are not the only one." His eyes clouded over, and a strange tone came into his voice. "There's this young girl…"

"You bastard," I said.

With the stench of liquor on his breath, he slurred, "I thought you knew me, girl."

I was quick to come back. "Knew what? That you are a drunk with a thing for young girls?"

"Naw," he interrupted, laughing, "that I like how you make me feel in bed…grinding them big hips up against me, making me feel real good." He tooted his lips to kiss me.

I slapped his face so hard that Jake heard it and came running toward us.

"Is everything all right over here?" he asked, inserting himself between Herman and me.

"Calm down, girl. What's wrong with you?" Herman bellowed as if he'd had his senses awakened.

"I don't like what you said to me," I cried. "You need to stop all that damn drinking. You are a fool when you drink, thinking that Mae Lou is gonna take care of you."

"You can't take the damn truth," he said, riled up.

The longer I stood staring him down, the hotter I got. With every word Herman expelled from his turned-up lips, the tighter I balled my fists.

I couldn't stand to hear any more of his rotten words. I stood to my feet, ready to leave.

"Come on, sit back down," Herman pleaded, pulling on my dress.

"Take your hands off me."

Then I walked out before I slapped his disrespectful ass again.

When I got back to my parents' house, I was still fired up. I went straight to bed, but my rage at Herman didn't die down for hours.

Around 2:30 the next day, Willie returned.

He came back with an army bag. Inside was one pair of trousers, a flannel shirt, a jacket, and a new shiny revolver.

"What's that?" I asked when I saw the metal barrel gleaming.

"Nothing," he said, trying to cover it up with his hands.

"Willie, when did you get that gun?"

"Everybody's got a gun, Pearl."

"Where did you get the gun from?" I asked.

"I had it. I brought it home with me from the service," he answered as he held it up. It was clean, so shiny it didn't look like it had ever been fired.

"She pretty, ain't she?"

"Guns kill—makes me shake to look at it."

"People kill."

He made sure I saw the revolver. However, I wasn't sure if he had been back to Washington, D.C. or purchased the things he returned with from the seed and feed store in town. It had farm goods, groceries, and clothes. I wasn't sure of anything. Willie was acting strange, holding up the gun for me to see.

"Willie, I don't like guns."

"Yo' daddy got two of 'em, a shotgun and a revolver."

"I still don't like them."

"This gun is for our protection," he remarked. He spun the chamber around and checked for bullets, then cocked the trigger and released it.

I jumped. The hairs stood straight up on my neck. I felt a chill all the way down to the marrow in my bones.

"Put it away, please."

Afraid the mention of Herman would set him off, I closely watched him pack the weapon in the box and put it away, sliding it under the bed. I wondered whose name he had engraved on the bullets he also stuffed in the box. He never mumbled a word about Herman. So all day we both pretended as if nothing had happened.

Momma and I sat at the kitchen table and cut up turnip greens and washed them twice in the tub. She'd poured flour in a ceramic bowl and checked to make sure no flour mice were in it before she added it to the hen eggs and sugar and butter. She put in baking powder, nutmeg, allspice and cloves, and beat the mixture for two minutes before stuffing the batter in the wood-burning oven. The mixture of the aroma of the cake baking, greens cooking, and meat simmering wafted throughout the house. We were busy, but not too much for me to keep a keen eye on Willie.

He went in the woods with my daddy, found a stout knotty pine tree, and cut it down. Willie was mysteriously quiet while we decorated the small tree with pinecones, newspaper, and popcorn. Momma made eggnog from the eggs, cream, and nutmeg. Twice Willie took his eggnog to the back bedroom and spiked it with corn liquor. Each time I followed him to make sure he was not going for his gun.

That Christmas Eve night I lay in bed struggling to keep my eyelids shut. My mind still racing with the things Herman had told me about Willie. And now Willie had a gun kept right under our bed. He started to snore and soon was sleeping as sound as a baby. And I kept telling myself, if I made it through the holiday without Herman, I could make it from then on.

CHAPTER 28
CARRIE

Each morning I peeled my body out of the bed, limb by limb. I'd stand in front of the mirror naked, noticing the rise that was developing in my belly. No one noticed the heaviness of my chest, and my pooch vanished once I'd hooked all the notches of my corset. The tightness and discomfort of the corset stretched against my bulging belly. But I refused to loosen it. Even Anna hadn't noticed the changes to my body.

One person noticed, though. "You look different, Carrie," Mary said when she walked into the house. "Did you change your hair?"

"No," I said, alarmed. "Maybe it's because you haven't seen me in a few days."

"Maybe, but…You heard from my brother?" Mary gazed at me, her eyes roving over me like she'd missed something.

"Yeah, he should be here around Christmas. He writes every now and then."

"That's what I heard, too. We all can't wait to see him. He's been gone for months." She chuckled. "I want to know if he's grown up any more, since he's a world traveler now."

I also had things I wanted to say to him, and Christmas was coming. My conscience was eating at me, and I wanted to tell him everything. Inside, I knew that no one could really understand the hell the last seven months of my life had been.

"What are you gonna do when he gets here?" Hester asked.

"I don't know. I don't want to think about it. I wish I could go somewhere and come back the same way I was before he left."

"That's nonsense, Carrie. You can't think like that. You got to say som'thin'."

I'd always been good at keeping secrets, except this time I was trying to protect myself from disappointment. Simon was as human as any other man. He wasn't going to want me. He always had high expectations for us. The thought of him trying out for the Negro Leagues made people whisper, "Do that boy really think he is that good? Ain't no coloreds 'round here can play good like them boys." Simon didn't let anything compromise his ambitions. I feared he would leave me and go on about his business. The thought of that made me feel awful. I'd written to him and mentioned Anna and Minnie, but the rape was too much.

Hester tugged at my arm. "You all right?"

"Just so much to think about," I said.

Standing, looking out of the window at the end of the day, Mrs. Miller cautioned us about the gray clouds hanging low in the sky. "I think we may get some snow here tonight. Make sure that you study your words and practice writing at home. No telling when the schoolhouse will open again."

I grabbed my books. Hester, Anna, and I headed for the door. When I placed my foot down on the first step, I discovered Simon standing underneath the pine tree. Anna noticed him at the same time, and she nudged me with her elbow. My heart started racing.

Hester moved closer, almost causing me to trip, and whispered in my ear, "On second thought, don't say a word today. Why don't you wait until tomorrow?"

"Okay," I mumbled, keeping my eyes planted on Simon.

I inhaled deeply and stopped to gather myself. Then I carefully placed one foot at a time in front of me. My bosom was rising and falling fast. His smile extended across his entire face. My eyes watered. I batted each tear away. I wasn't sure if the tears were of happiness or shame. I walked over to Simon and threw my arms around his neck. I laid my head on his chest and buried my face in his chest.

"When did you get home?" I asked with my face still against his chest.

"I got home about ten-thirty this morning. Did you think I'd come to town and not come see ya? Girl, after Momma, you were the next person I wanted to see."

He made me feel so much better. "I didn't expect you today."

"Yeah, but it is only a few days before the holiday. Right now ev'rybody is trying to beat the snow home."

"Mrs. Miller was warning us about the clouds."

"Yeah, it's gonna snow." He tried to pull away, but I still had my head laying on his chest. Finally he got a good look at me. "What's been happening with you?"

"I've been trying to get through school. It's been pretty rough this year. Everything seems a little harder."

"Oh come on, I thought you liked school. It couldn't be that bad."

My life is so screwed up, I thought.

Everybody was gone except Mrs. Miller. As she was leaving she came over to us. "Y'all need to go on home now. Looks like we are in for a snowstorm."

"Yes, ma'am," we both answered.

The fierce wind was whipping around my ears. The branches on the trees were swaying, and their last leaves were falling to the ground and carried across the schoolyard by the wind. Nothing seemed to matter when I was with Simon—not the wind or even the snow.

"Well, everybody is still the same at home. There is nothing new to report," I said. We walked to his car together, and hopped in on our separate sides.

He waited for more, but when I didn't keep going, he remarked, "This is not like you. You're usually full of words. You have got to bring me up to date. You're not seeing anyone else, are you?" he asked with a nervous smile.

"Simon, no, it's not that," I said in a rush. "I have a few things on my mind right now."

"Tell me what's bothering you." He snuggled close in the seat.

"Oh, it's nothing," I said, looking away.

Simon pulled me closer and the hollowness inside disappeared. He gave me a smothering kiss and eased his tongue in my mouth. A warm sensation traveled over my body. I felt the tension rise from my shoulders and my legs buckled. For that moment all I thought about was us.

Then we sat in the car for another few minutes, cuddling as lovers do.

Simon held my hand the entire whole way home. He got out of the car and escorted me inside. The air seemed to get thicker by the second. The mood changed.

Momma and Mr. Camm were sitting at the kitchen table sipping coffee.

"Good evening," Simon said.

"Lordy, Simon," Momma exclaimed, and her joyful response surprised me. "It's nice to see you again. Sit down and tell me about playing ball with the best colored boys in the nation. I love baseball." Simon proudly stuck out his chest and took a seat. Mr. Camm eyed him hard and nodded his head, interested in Simon's stories, too.

After a spell, Simon and I went into the front room and I listened to him go on and on about his playing. He really loved what he did. I snuggled closer, feeling as if I was wrapped up in a bed of quilts, sheltered from all hurt. I cherished the moment as if it was our last. I suspected things would change once I told him the truth.

It didn't snow like Mrs. Miller thought it would, so we returned to school the next day. Hester didn't wait for me to start speaking. "Did you tell him? Did you tell him the truth?"

I turned to her and shook my head. "I couldn't tell him; it wasn't the right time. Besides, didn't you say to wait? Wasn't you the one that said to have fun?"

She smiled, seeing that I was happy for once. "So did you enjoy him kissing and hugging all over you?"

"We tried to do some of the things you and John do, but we didn't have enough time."

"Girl, you're crazy." And we both giggled. "What I meant was to have fun, but don't run from the truth." The tone of her voice was as stern as Momma's. "But you gonna have to tell him soon. There comes a time, Carrie, when you have to say it, no matter how hard it is. You can't keep him in the dark. He'll never forgive you."

"I know, but I'm scared."

"Pretty soon everybody is going to know. Your cheeks are plumper and you're wearing dresses large enough for two people to get into. I don't know how you've kept it a secret in that house for this long. Do you want someone else to tell him?"

"No but..." Mrs. Miller started class and interrupted my train of thought.

Hester was right. I had been running from the truth for too

long. I had thought about telling Simon last night and deliberately avoided it by changing the subject. I'd had over seven months to think about what happened. Now all I wanted to do was enjoy the time we were spending with one another. He was home for the holidays, and he didn't need to be concerned with my troubles.

Simon was standing outside waiting for me when school let out. I felt overjoyed, scared, and confused, all at the same time. How could I knowingly lie to him? Eventually, the corset was not going to hold me in and everyone would know my secret. Already people were asking me if I'd gained weight. I couldn't afford to let Simon find out from gossip.

I loved the way he embraced me. I wanted to sit in the car and cuddle for one last time before I told him the truth.

"Wait," I said, before he eased his tongue in my mouth.

"What's wrong?"

I smiled and gave in to a kiss that mellowed me enough to want more.

He pulled me close and rubbed against my full breasts.

"I love you," I said as he planted a kiss on my neck.

When I thought I might melt, he said, "We better stop. It won't be long. We can wait until we're married."

The moment of truth had come. "Simon, there is something I need to say to you." I reached over to grab his hand before continuing, "I have been in a great deal of pain since you were here last."

He let go of my hand and slid closer to hug me, putting his arm around my shoulder. "I know that it must be hard wanting to leave, and waiting until we can be together."

"Simon, yes, that has been hard, but that's not what I mean." I closed my eyes and tilted my head back to think. How was I going to say this? How could I say it in a way that would not make him hate me?

"Calm down. Your heart is beating a mile a minute. You can tell me anything," he said, massaging my hand.

I snuggled closer to him. "Promise you won't hate me. Simon, something terrible happened to me some months ago. I should have written you, but I couldn't." Tears were forming in the corners of my eyes and my knees started shaking.

"Tell me."

I pulled free and told him straight out. "My stepfather took advantage of me."

There was complete silence in the car. Tears continued to stream down my face. I couldn't hold them back. Then I gained control and wiped my face with the back of my hand.

"What do you mean, 'took advantage'?"

I raised my voice. "Didn't you hear me? I was raped!"

"What?" He was shocked and instinctively shrank away from me in reaction.

"Say something," I said, clenching his hand.

He finally came out of his stupor. "I don't know what to say. Sorry? What good is that? Why you didn't write me?" he said, shaking his head in disgust.

"I was scared. I wanted to," I mumbled, too timid to turn and look at his face.

Sliding closer to the door, he shouted, "Why did this happen? *Why?* I am going to kill that bastard." Then he snapped at me, "You should have told me. Why didn't you say something?"

"Simon, please listen to me. I couldn't tell you that way. It was too much to put in a letter."

"I can't believe that you've kept this to yo'self for all these months. I thought we didn't have any secrets. I thought we could talk about anything and especially something as important as this."

Finally, I dared to look up. "Simon. Why are you making this so hard for me? It's been a nightmare." Tears rolled from my eyes. Simon shook his head and bit his bottom lip.

I quietly continued talking, resigned to telling him everything. "It's not over, Simon. I'm having a baby."

He didn't react at all this time, and my worst fears swept over me.

"I am so sorry. I am so sorry," I said dully.

"Tell me the whole story," he demanded. He crossed his arms over his chest.

I sighed. "Mr. Camm, he was always looking at me. He scared me."

Simon hit the dashboard of the car so hard, I jumped.

"I can't believe that this shit happened. You can't have this baby! No way can you have this baby! You got to do something." He looked down at my stomach, looking for signs of my pregnancy. "You don't look like it. I thought you'd just put on a few pounds," he said.

I had gone to great lengths to keep my pregnancy hidden. I had taken out the waist in all of my skirts and in some cases the entire seam, and then sewn them again with enough room for me to feel comfortable. The corset was uncomfortable and binding. My stomach still bulged outward, but no one had paid me that much attention.

Simon was enraged. As I explained what happened, he banged his fist on the dashboard in frustration over and over. He wanted to know all the details, but not even for him would I relive that terror all over again. I told him as much as I could get out without totally breaking down.

"Simon, it's too late. I can't get rid of the baby. I'll give it to someone else who wants children."

"Do you realize what the people will say when they find this out? They're going to laugh at you, no matter what the circumstances are concerning the rape. You have got to leave."

"I don't have anywhere to go. Where am I going to go?"

I was hoping he'd say, "Richmond," but instead he groaned. "I don't know where you'll go. I don't have a clue. All I know is that son of a bitch is going to pay. I know his type, preying on young girls and helpless women."

I had been forgotten. I was the girl who'd gotten knocked up.

Tears started flowing uncontrollably, and I broke down completely.

He watched me for a while, and then said, "Stop crying, please." He handed me a handkerchief from his coat pocket.

"I know. I know," I whispered. The sun had started to set and the sky was a radiant orange. "I've got to go home."

Simon started the car and drove out of the schoolyard. Before he got to the end of the road, he stopped. "Do you want this baby?"

"No! How could I want my stepfather's child? Who would want what I'm going through? But I can't throw the baby away."

"What about school? What about our plans?"

"I was the one raped, not you! I didn't ask for it. I was waiting for you! Can't you understand that? I'm adopted myself. I want the baby to be with a good, loving family, one who cares. Is that too much to ask for an innocent baby?"

My outburst had a calming effect on him. "Are there any other things that you haven't told me? You seem to be full of secrets," he said sarcastically. "For one, what do you mean, you're adopted?"

I was lower than I'd been in all these months. "I found out that I'm adopted. Anna is my real sister. I don't know who I really am." His face was like stone, and I slumped in the seat. "I did not ask to be adopted nor did I ask to be raped. What more do you want me to say? I was not hiding anything from you. I wanted to tell you to your face."

My eyes were red and swollen, but I had no more tears left to cry. I knew that Simon would be mad, but I couldn't handle him lashing out at me. I apologized to him for the pain that I'd caused, even knowing that none of it was actually my fault. Yet all the way home he seemed far, far away.

I had destroyed everything.

CHAPTER 29
PEARL

Christmas was a special time in our community. Everyone, no matter where they lived, packed their things and traveled to a relative's place. Many walked miles on foot and others rode in horse and buggies. My sister and brother arrived at our house early, wrapped up in hand-knitted scarves and hats. The snow had slowed them down, but nothing could keep them away. Momma had prepared all the fixings, turkey, dressing, and cranberry sauce. Since cooking wasn't my thing, I helped where I could and cleaned up the mess after she was done.

Willie had been acting strange all morning. He had gotten up when the sky was still dark, sat on the side of the bed for the longest time, and eventually had gone back to sleep. When he woke up again, he dressed, and instead of going into the kitchen for a cup of dark coffee—he liked his black—he went straight outside and started chopping up kindling. A bit later, when I checked out the window, he was gone. He stayed gone for more than an hour without coming in from the cold weather.

"Where were you?" I asked when he came back in, rubbing his hands together in front of the fireplace.

"I went out, to grab a few logs of firewood."

"We got plenty in here already. Rest, man, it's Christmas," my daddy said to him.

He'd sit for a few minutes and then stand up. He was biting his fingernails, and leaving shoe scuff marks as he paced back and forth. I tugged his pants leg.

"Please sit down. Come help me sing this song, Willie."

He sat down, still on edge, rubbing his hands together and shifting around as if he had somewhere else to be. He joined me with his deep baritone voice, but he gazed off into nowhere, moving his lips but removed from the spirit.

We all sat around the fire singing Christmas songs. "O Holy Night" and "Away in a Manger." My momma had a great singing voice and used to sing in the choir. Inside, she had yearned for the glitter of the nightclub as I'd done, but Daddy had kept her close to him.

We opened the gifts of horehound candy, lemon drops, a blanket spread, and the gloves Momma knitted. I had ordered a hair curling iron for myself at the cost of a dollar from the Ellis Rand Co. in Chicago. The giving was customary for us and Willie had said his family did the same, yet by the look in his hollow eyes, he wasn't getting any pleasure from it at all.

After dinner, he announced, "I need to take a little walk. All this food done nearly put me to sleep." He did that sometimes after a big meal, when it was still early enough to see the sun, so I didn't think much of it. He put on his coat and hat. I watched him out of the family room window, watched him trample out of the yard, planting his brogan boots carefully in the snow. I must admit I was worried.

Ten minutes passed, and a strange feeling came over me, like a ghost trying to tell me something. I was drawn into the bedroom. I pulled out the wooden box from under the bed and removed the towel on top and looked for the revolver. Along with Willie, it had disappeared. The bullets were missing, too.

I panicked.

I hastily put on my galoshes and coat.

"Where are you going?" my momma asked.

"I'm going to catch up with Willie," I said, forcing a smile.

"It's cold out there, girl. It's Christmas. Y'all ought to be in the house with the family."

"I'll be all right."

I dodged the scratches of the barren twigs, trees, and brush. Snow was still piled on the ground, but no footprints could be seen. All the way I prayed that I would find Herman before Willie did.

The holiday had enticed folks out of their houses to the joint, where everyone found spirits and cheer. For the first time since I'd been back in town, the place was packed. Folks were sitting around, others standing, everyone drinking homemade liquor and cheering in the season. One woman was drunk and still shedding tears about the death of Madame C. J. Walker, who had passed away back in August. "I'll never learn how to do hair," she cried.

People around her laughed.

"She's crazy," someone said.

The bar was crowded. Jake was going to go home happy and with more money than places to spend it.

"Jake, have you seen Herman, or Willie?"

He heard the concern in my voice. "What's going on 'round here, Miz Pearl?"

"Have you seen them?" I asked impatiently.

"Tonight, everybody is looking for Herman."

Alarmed, I asked, "What does that mean?"

"Ms. Mae Lou came looking for him, then Willie, some old lady, and now you. What the hell is going on 'round here?"

"Come on, Jake, did Herman come in here today?" I asked, pushing him for a reply.

"Yeah, he was here a few minutes before they showed up, all lightheaded and loose. He wasn't feeling no pain. He took off a while after that, said he was going home."

"Which way did he go?"

He scratched his head. "Well, there's a shortcut Herman always take."

"Where? Which way?"

He came from behind the bar. "Let me show ya where it is."

One of the patrons asked, "You singing tonight, Pearl?"

"No, not tonight," I said, and kept walking.

I followed Jake through the crowd to the door. He pointed out into the snow. "Now, if you go down yonder, it will lead to Herman's place."

"Thanks."

"You be careful. Snow clouds are in the air."

The path had been trampled down, as the one I'd taken to the joint. The bushes had been torn back, leaving a straight way through the barren trees. I had my hands down deep in my coat pocket, my fingers clenching Willie's switchblade. I'd taken that out of his pants' pocket before I left.

As I walked down the path, all sorts of thoughts raced through my head.

It was getting dark and the last thing I needed was to get lost in an unfamiliar path in the dark. The farther I traveled along the route, the more I began to hear voices in the distance. I started to run when I recognized Willie's baritone pitch.

Willie was on his knees, and Herman was standing over him. As I walked up, he had a gun pointed to Willie's temple.

"Please, Herman, what's going on?"

"This mutha-fucker wants to kill me. Well, look at big Willie now."

Willie was on his knees panting like a dog, so scared he didn't move.

"Pearl, take a look at yo' boy. He ain't the big-time soldier now."

"Don't shoot him, Herman."

"He threatened me," he slurred.

"Please, Herman," I said, trying to edge close enough to knock the gun out of his hand.

He turned toward me.

"You take another step and I will blow his damn head off."

Herman had an enormous amount of street in him, but I didn't think he could be so brutal. But he was not intimidated by anyone, no matter how big they were.

"Herman, let him go."

"Didn't I tell you to shut up?" he yelled.

"Sorry," I said, trying to gauge the best way to handle him.

Then I couldn't help it. "Herman, we can be together. Don't do anything you will regret."

He turned toward me. "You ain't nothing but a washed-up singer with a pretty face."

"Don't, Herman," I pleaded.

"Don't talk to her like that," Willie said.

Herman stepped closer to him, and pushed the nozzle of the pistol in his ear.

I was helpless. "Please don't..." I begged. "I love you, Herman."

He kept the pistol impressed against Willie's ear. He turned his head toward me, and with a penetrating gaze, he said, "I don't want no ho. This mutha-fucker told Mae Lou about us. Now he's gonna pay."

When he cocked the gun, fear rushed over me like a gust of wind. I pulled the switchblade out of my pocket and lunged at Herman and stabbed him in the shoulder.

With a shriek of pain, he fell face forward in the snow with Willie's switchblade still stuck in his right shoulder.

Willie sprang to his feet.

With a quick tug, he pulled the blade out of Herman. Herman was moving, scrabbling around on the ground.

Willie grabbed my hand.

"Come on, gurl, let's go."

I roughly pulled away from him and bent down to help Herman.

"Help me," he mumbled.

Willie put his arms around me and pulled me back. "Leave him there. Let's get out of here."

I didn't want to leave Herman lying helpless in the snow, but I had no choice.

It was dark by the time we returned to the house. Everyone had gone to bed. The coals of fire were still hot in the fireplace, and the flames in the cast iron stove in the kitchen were dying down.

Willie lit the lamp. We crawled onto the bed, both of us trembling. He put his thick arms around my shoulders. I laid my head on his chest as we pondered what was next.

"Do you think he's still alive?" I asked.

Willie kissed me on the forehead.

"See how this turned out? He was gonna kill me."

I turned partway to look at him. "I hope he doesn't die. I didn't mean to kill him. I wanted him to stop."

Willie remained calm. "We gonna ride this one through."

"You had a gun, Willie."

I could feel him shaking his head. "I was trying to scare him, make 'im leave you alone."

Why did this have to happen, I thought.

"I killed him," I said, and the tears started to roll down my cheeks.

"You stopped him from blowing my head off. He's a crazy fool."

"I'm scared, Willie."

"Don't be. It's self-defense. Besides, I don't think he was dead. The knife was in his shoulder, not his heart."

Willie comforted me, wiping away my tears and rubbing my head.

After a time, he blew out the oil lantern. I fell asleep wrapped in his thick arms and didn't move all night. Willie held me close, even though I was the center of all the confusion.

CHAPTER 30
CARRIE

Momma and I stayed up decorating the house with streamers of popcorn and ribbon. We lit candles around the house to aid in the Christmas Eve celebration. Carl and Mary were celebrating their first Christmas as a married couple. Everyone gathered in the kitchen for roast turkey, ham, dressing and all the fixings. Aunt Bessie and Uncle Bill both took a turkey drumstick. In between bites, Uncle Bill licked his fingers and smacked his mouth. "Bessie, don't take this the wrong way, but Mae Lou is as good as they come with cooking."

I spent most of the day in my room waiting for Simon to arrive, hoping that he'd decided to forgive me. I had just finished eating Hermit cake and drinking eggnog when he finally walked through the door.

We went into the front room, where two of Aunt Bessie's children were finishing their food, licking their plates and hands as if they'd been starving. As soon as we sat down on the Davenport in front of the fireplace, Simon pulled a small, unwrapped box out of his pocket and handed it to me. Inside I found a necklace with a small cross on it. However, when I reached over to hug Simon's neck, he recoiled. Obviously, he didn't want to be touched.

"When are you going back?" I asked, sadly.

"I'm leaving tomorrow afternoon, right after dinner is served. I don't want to hang around too long."

"Will I hear from you? Will you write me?" I asked.

"You know how I am about writing. I'll do my best, though." Aunt Bessie's two children were listening as intently as me, until I rolled my eyes at the both of them and they ran back into the kitchen.

Simon seemed to be too upset to make any commitments. "We can't talk in here," he said.

"Sorry, Aunt Bessie and her children are staying the night with us."

"Let's go outside."

He helped me put on my coat and we walked out the front door. We sat in his car, neither of us saying a word. I slid closer to him, and thankfully, he didn't move away. But he didn't hug me or touch me, either.

I asked, "What's gonna happen with us? Have you changed your mind about the plans we made?"

"I don't know right now." He was bitter, short. Then he rubbed his forehead. "Carrie, where's your stepfather? I didn't see him nowhere."

"Why are you asking me about him? I don't know where he is. I don't care if he never comes home. What about us, Simon?" I insisted.

"You dropped this stuff on me and I can't think right now. I don't know. When will he be coming home?"

"Simon, stop it. I don't want to talk about Mr. Camm. I've had enough of him for all eternity. I want to know about us. Tell me, do you still love me?"

"You can't stop loving someone overnight, can you?" He slammed his hand down on the steering wheel and the horn accidentally blew. I glanced at the front room window and Aunt Bessie's children had their faces glued to the pane. Simon acted as if he'd been the one who was violated, as if he'd been raped, not me. I had never known him to be filled with so much rage.

"Are you gonna write me?" I asked again.

"I'll try," he said, sighing.

"You'll *try*?"

He relented. "Listen, I don't know about that right now. There is so much to consider. I can't get all this off my mind." He softly whispered, "But I do love you."

"Simon, you know I didn't want this to happen. Try to understand how I feel," I pleaded with him.

The moment had passed, though. He sat up ramrod straight. "It's getting late. I've got to go now, need to pull out tomorrow afternoon. I don't want to be tired."

"Don't you want some dessert? You have to say good-bye to your sister."

He looked horrified by the idea of going back inside. "Nah, I'm not hungry, and I'll see my sister at the house in the morning, for Christmas breakfast." He turned and looked at me with troubled eyes. "I really have to go."

"I really don't want you to leave, Simon."

He leaned over and kissed me on the lips. It was emotionless and dry. It made me wonder if I'd ever see him again. He didn't even walk me to the door. He pulled off before I made it to the porch.

Simon pulled the car out of our yard, his tires growling and skidding through the muddy road from the fallen snow. He was furious; the veins in his neck protruding like those of a wild man. I held up my hand to wave, but all I could see was the fire in his eyes. Before making the left turn off the property, he stopped as if he wanted to stay, but then he sped off, dirt flying from underneath his tires. I watched him until he was out of sight. That was strange. He'd made a left, in the opposite direction of his house.

I stayed outside for a while after he'd left, making sure my eyes were dry before going back in the house. The snow had stopped falling but the wind was blowing flurries. The dim moon behind the snow-filled clouds lit up the heavens.

I didn't know where he might be going. He'd left with rage in his eyes. I felt as if he'd wanted to caress me and comfort me, but he'd held back. He was confused. He loved me, but he couldn't *love* me. It was an awful feeling for me, because now I really needed him.

After I had gone back in the house and the children lay down to sleep, I suddenly realized where Simon was going.

I had been riding horses all my life, had learned when I was four years old. I put the saddle on the mule and pulled him out of the barn. One of the horses was already missing, and I wondered where he was.

I took the shortcut toward the juke joint. Simon already had a thirty-minute jump on me, and I hoped I wasn't too late.

The wind was fierce going through the path. The bareness of the forest opened into an entry Mr. Camm frequently traveled. I was afraid, scared for my life and Simon's. As I got closer to the joint, I could hear gay voices of laughter and celebration. As I took the last curve and caught a glimpse of the lights, the mule came to a halt.

Directly in front of me was the body of Mr. Camm crawling in the snow, struggling for help.

"Help me, please," he said, not knowing who I was.

I couldn't get off the mule. And my conscience wouldn't let him die.

"Hold on, I'll get some help," I said.

"Carrie, is that you?"

"Yes, I'll be right back."

I coaxed the mule around Mr. Camm and hurried to the joint. I jumped down off the mule and ran toward the door, and the fire of a shotgun sound off in the distance pierced my eardrum. The boom echoed in the stillness of the night

"Oh my God!" I screamed.

I saw a man entering the shack.

"A man is dying in the path!" I exclaimed. I pointed in the direction where Mr. Camm lay. The man took off down the path at a run.

I surveyed the yard and there were no signs of Simon. The only car parked in the yard was the one Mr. Camm had gotten from the white man down the road. He rarely drove to the joint. I didn't stick around to find out what was happening. Instead I took the open road back to the house, my chest heaving and my breath short.

When I put the mule back in the barn, our other horse was back and lying down on the hay. Someone had beaten me home.

CHAPTER 31
CARRIE

I couldn't stop thinking about Mr. Camm lying on the ground, and Simon's involvement. I had seen him make the left turn to the joint. It was around two miles from us, hidden back in the deep woods at least two hundred feet from the road. The Shack was lit up with regulars and churchgoers celebrating the holiday. One of the deacons was talking to Momma when I walked in. Momma waved me over. The deacon told me Simon had walked in and taken a seat right beside him at the joint earlier that night.

Momma was listening closely, though the deacon's voice was so loud, it was easy to hear.

"That boy walked over to the bar, and asked if anyone seen a fellow named Camm 'round tonight?"

I didn't say anything and he kept talking, mostly to Momma.

"You know the bartender, Mae Lou? He's that tall, handsome man with thick, curly black hair who almost looks white. He lives down the road a bit."

"No, I don't think I do." Momma didn't go to the joint and she cut her eyes down at the deacon and smacked her lips in embarrassment when he asked if she knew the bartender.

"He stopped in the middle of serving a customer, Mae Lou. Told Simon that Camm usually come in 'round eight o'clock. He poured the boy a beer. And then he told him, he look like a stranger, ain't never seen him before."

Momma listened. "Uh-huh."

"He said it was his first time in the joint," the deacon continued. "Now I don't go there much myself." Momma looked at him skeptically.

"The boy was upset, Mae Lou. He had fire in his eyes," he said with conviction.

I left them in the kitchen and I listened in my room as the deacon's mouth overflowed with gossip.

"You could tell he wasn't a beer drinker, but he needed something to relax him. I need to relax myself sometimes, too, Mae Lou," he said, chuckling softly.

I knew about the place, everyone did. It was a barn that had been turned into a joint. There were tables and chairs set up for the sitting customers and a large area reserved for dancing. Women sashayed around the bar with red lipstick and bosoms way high, looking for men to carry them home. Floozies, Momma called them.

"Peoples were eating fried chicken, 'tato salad and homemade rolls, and listening to the beats of the musicians when Camm walked in the door."

"Who did you say?" Momma asked, as if she hadn't been listening.

"Yo' husband," he blurted, louder.

"He walked through the door with another fellow. Now, I ain't trying to tell on him, but he need to be home with you," he said. "Simon's eyes grew big, looked like he could hurt someone. He downed his beer. After a few minutes, Camm walked over to the bar. Told Jake to give him the same ole' same ole'."

I imagined Momma's face turning sour. "The same what?" she asked.

"Mae Lou, the bartender looked at him, then cut his eyes

toward Simon, trying to warn him. He was sitting two feet away. I watched it all."

"Oh yeah?" Momma dully remarked.

"Camm walked up on the guy, said he heard he was looking for him. He looked Simon square in the eyes, told him to step outside. Now, I followed them to the door. The snow had started to fall again. I stood there peeking out the door. After a few words, Simon grabbed Camm by the collar, but that fellow Camm was with, he stepped in to stop it. He got control after pulling out a switchblade."

"Why would Simon be mad at my husband? Deacon, I hope you ain't had too much to drink."

As if to underscore her point, he slurred, "Mae Lou, you know I ain't a drinker. I take a drink every now and then for medical reasons. It helps get my bones to stirring."

She warned him. "Now don't make up things on people, deacon."

"All I can tell you is that boy was mad, called your husband a no-good bastard. He put his hands around Camm's neck, Mae Lou. Simon is strong and the veins in his own neck were pulsing. I couldn't believe my eyes. Camm was suspended in the air."

Momma was grunting and saying, "Uh-huh," but I could tell from her voice that she didn't believe everything he was saying.

"The bartender had to kick him out," the deacon said, pausing to take what sounded like a sip of the last bit of coffee out of his cup.

"The boy was mad, Mae Lou. He said curse words I wouldn't dare think about. If it hadn't been for that fellow, Camm might've been killed."

Momma listened to him go on and on about this and that. The deacon was like any woman who gossiped. I knew Simon had to restrain himself. He had to cool off. He'd never been hot-headed, but Mr. Camm had that effect on people. He worked everyone's nerves.

The deacon left shortly afterward with a piece of cake in his hands. I heard Momma say, "Lord, I hope he makes it home, drunk as he is."

CHAPTER 32
CARRIE

All of the stress, from the months before and that horrible night, made my insides cave in. It was too much for any young girl to bear.

My fatigued eyes finally closed around two in the morning. Dried tears glued my lids shut. Around four, after only a couple hours of sleep, pains started shooting through my lower tummy. The intensity increased, until it pierced my entire torso. Excruciating pain stabbed me from my legs to my stomach to my lower back. I rolled from one side of the bed to the other, trying to find a comfortable position. The pains grew closer together, only minutes apart.

It can't be time for the baby, I thought. I had a month to go. I had been cautioned about labor pains, but no one had explained them the way they actually felt. It felt as if I was being torn apart. I swung my legs over the side of the bed and inched myself up. I sat on the side of the bed and waited for each sharp twinge to come and then ripple across my belly and then subside. During each crest, I prayed, inhaled, swore and cried. All of a sudden, a gush of water trickled down my thighs. Then the twinges became thrashes of whip-like pain gnawing from my inner thighs to my chest.

I had trouble pushing the bed away from behind the door. When I stood, I required the help of the wall and the bed for support.

I cracked the door open and yelled, "Momma, Momma, please help me!"

Her door opened and Momma peeked out. The pains were so sharp that I slid down to the floor and balled up in a knot. She hurried down the hall to me. She put her arms around my waist and lifted me up on my feet. She put my arm over her shoulder and helped me to my bed.

"I think it's coming…it's coming!" I screamed, short of breath.

"What, Chile? What is wrong with you?" She could tell, but she wanted to hear me say it.

"I'm having a baby, Momma."

She ran into the kitchen and started a pot of boiling water. She brought back an old stained sheet from her trunk and laid it on the floor beside my bed.

She examined me like a doctor, feeling my stomach and looking between my thighs. "When it's time, I want you to stoop down beside the bed. It'll be easier for you."

I rolled over, trying to find a comfortable spot on the lumpy goose-feather and quilt-piece mattress. The pain was too unbearable. She brought a sharp knife and a pail of boiling water bursting with steam into the bedroom. She put the knife in the water. I screamed as loud as I could. She told me to concentrate on a picture of my grandmother hanging crooked on the wall. She checked between my legs one last time and asked me to squat as low as I could beside the bed. I held onto the side of the bed and pushed as hard as I could. Beads of sweat dripped from my face and dampened my gown.

She caught the baby before its head hit the floor, then cut the umbilical cord and helped me back to the bed. She washed the baby off with a warm cloth before wrapping it in one of her quilts and then handed it to me.

"It's a boy, a fine boy." She smiled at the baby, but when she looked at me, she was frowning in anger.

I forgot about Mr. Camm when I saw my baby. He was tiny, innocent and helpless, and he was normal. He had ten fingers and toes. He was bright, lighter than anyone I knew.

Deep inside, I knew Mr. Camm would not be coming home.

Momma practically ignored me for the next day. She brought me Birdseye for the baby that had been torn into pieces for diapers. I didn't know anything about caring for a baby. I felt embarrassed about feeding the baby from my breast. Whenever I'd seen someone else doing it, I'd turn my nose up and mumble to myself, "I'm not gonna be sitting around with a baby sucking on me." Now I was like all the other girls in Jefferson. Most of them were locked into caring for children with men whose only ambition was farming. But I was worse. I was all alone.

Later, I heard whispers in the kitchen. "She what?" Carl said.

"I knew som'thin' was wrong with her. She didn't say a word. Simon didn't open his mouth, either," Mary whispered to Carl.

"Yeah, I told Mae Lou to watch her. She always was a little sneaky," Aunt Bessie added.

Momma hummed one of her spirituals while they whispered in the background. Mary came to the door once and knocked. I pretended to be asleep. Then I heard her say, "I hope she knows what to do with a baby without a husband."

Momma sent Aunt Bessie and her family next door to Carl's. She didn't think that a lot of people needed to be around a newborn. "They can catch ev'rything," I heard her tell Aunt Bessie before closing the door behind them on Christmas morning after everybody had stuffed themselves for brunch on the leftovers from Christmas Eve. The sounds of wood popping in the stove and Momma's occasional hum echoed throughout the house. The near quiet silence drove me crazy. I wanted to tell Momma the whole story and I could tell that she wanted to hear it, but I kept my lips sealed. After all of this, I was still afraid to talk to her. I'd figured out many things, but not how to approach my own momma. The only thing that I was happy about was that Mr. Camm had not come home.

That afternoon, Momma came into the bedroom. She pulled up a chair close to the bed. "Does Simon know about the baby?"

"Yes, ma'am."

"Well, why didn't he do the right thang and marry you? He was just here yestidy and he didn't have the courage to be a man and take on responsibilities?" She looked at me with pity. "I told you to get yo' education."

"Momma, we need to talk. It's more to it than you think," I said, wondering why she was jumping to conclusions before she knew the whole story. I wasn't naïve, though; she'd always been that way. She was quick to look down her nose at people that did not live up to her standards.

"Seems like to me, it's too late for talking," she said, keeping her eyes on the baby.

I sat up in the bed. "Momma, this baby is not Simon's. Simon is not the kind of man you think he is."

She drew back in surprise. "Whose is it, then? Look like all that sneaking done caught up with ya," she said, her voice hardening.

The baby started whimpering. Embarrassed, I put a diaper over my shoulder, and then put my nipple in the baby's mouth.

I was tired of being accused of doing something wrong. I had done everything she'd asked of me and more. I'd never missed a day of school. I'd read like she had insisted until it became my passion and now, when I needed her most, she was thinking bad of me and believing the worst.

"Momma, Mr. Camm is the one that did it. Your husband raped me when you were working at the Fergusons'."

She pulled herself up, and pointed a finger at me. "You hush yo' mouth. Don't make up lies to cover up your own faults. You've been running around with that boy for a long time. You have been sneaking around with him, now you done ruined your own life. Blame yo'self."

She had reacted exactly like Mr. Camm said she would. He'd warned me that she would think that I'd been sneaking with Simon. It was true, but we never even came close to making a baby.

"Momma, Mr. Camm raped me," I protested. "You just don't want it to be him. You know he ain't right!" I shouted, though I still felt weak.

"I don't want to hear another lie from you," she growled. "You have to get out of here. You got to find you and your baby someplace else to live. You are not welcome here."

My ears burned from her hateful words. He'd brainwashed her. She was standing up for a man she didn't really know. He lived here, but no one knew him like I did. He was as low down as they came. His suave talk had turned her against her own family. Now I was as much ashamed of her as she was of me.

"Momma, I have not been with Simon or anyone else," I insisted. "Mr. Camm, he took advantage of me right here on this bed."

Her voice became weaker. "You have got to go, gurl…you gotta go. I will give you a week to get your things and leave." She threw her hands up in the air and disowned me as if I was a stranger.

When she walked out the door, though, the tension around my neck went away. I suddenly felt light as a feather. Holding all that in for all those months had been a burden on me. I only regretted that I hadn't told her sooner. But she wouldn't have believed me then, as she didn't believe me now.

I knew what I was going to do. I would go stay with Ginny. And when the baby was old enough, I would say good-bye to Jefferson forever.

CHAPTER 33
CARRIE

Rumors were circulating all over town about Mr. Camm's murder. With a killer at large, everyone was afraid for their lives. They didn't go far from home, and in the case where they had to, they traveled in threes and fours. Nobody knew for sure who'd killed Mr. Camm, but speculation traveled throughout the county. Some said it was Momma. Others said it was Simon, and one even said that she'd heard Mr. Camm had a young girl expecting and the girl was angry enough to take him out of his misery. "I know someone who heard 'im," this last one said.

The gossip was no surprise to me. Jefferson was a small town and everyone knew one another. That was one of the reasons why I was so determined to leave. The place was so barren one murder was the most interesting subject for discussion at the dinner table. "There's a killer loose 'round here and we need to be cautious," were the words spoken in most homes.

Yet everyone knew that Mr. Camm had too many women and he'd made his share of enemies.

I was one of the people he violated and I didn't feel sorry about what happened.

"He got what he deserved," someone had said to me.

"Sho-nuff did," I fired back.

Jefferson had a sheriff, but most of the coloreds avoided him.

He never minded seeing a colored lying dead. That's what he'd said when he investigated the last killing in Jefferson. He'd even let the young man hang from the tree, where he'd been lynched, for an entire day before he'd allow anyone to cut him loose. He was the last person anybody in Jefferson would seek out for help. But when Mr. Camm was found, Mr. Perkins panicked. He ran straight to the sheriff. The sheriff didn't have too much compassion for anyone. He believed that most people created their own problems. The first thing he said when given the details of the discovery was, "Let 'em kill themselves off; I don't give a damn." Mr. Perkins was immediately sorry that he'd even gone to report the crime.

Soon enough, the sheriff pulled up to Momma's and knocked on the door. The knock caught her off guard, and she dropped the glass that she'd been washing in the sink. It broke into what seemed like a hundred pieces.

"Yes, Sheriff?" she said when she opened the door and saw the sheriff's piercing blue eyes gazing at her. I watched from the living room.

"Let me in, Ms. Mae Lou," he said. The sheriff respected Momma above most of the coloreds in town. She was the kind of person he could get along with. She minded her own business and she never disrespected anyone, especially whites.

"Yes, sir. Come on in." Momma invited him into the kitchen.

"Want something to drink, some food?" Momma offered, and then hung his coat up on the nail behind the kitchen door.

"I don't mind if I do. Coffee?"

Momma poured him a cup. "Cream or sugar?"

"A little sugar to take the bite off."

Momma put a cube of sugar in his coffee and set the sugar bowl nearby on the table. She scooped up a ladle of soup and poured it in a bowl and offered a piece of cornbread.

The sheriff waited for her to sit before he started his questioning. "Ms. Mae Lou, what you know about the murder?"

Momma was nervous. She had been ever since it happened. She'd poured herself some coffee, too.

"I don't know much, Sheriff. I only know what the peoples tell me."

The sheriff talked with his mouth full. "What are they saying, Ms. Mae Lou?"

She twiddled her fingers and bit her bottom lip as she searched for the appropriate words. Over the past few days, she'd heard more stories than she was willing to mention. Most of them were stories she'd been hearing and had tried to erase out of her head the entire time she'd been married. She never saw any of what the people gossiped about and despised those people who spoke badly about her family, in any manner. She felt that outsiders had no right.

"They say my husband had a woman outside of the marriage."

"How did it make you feel, hearing all this about the man ya loved?"

"Not so good," she mumbled.

"When did you furst hear this?"

Momma had always been a cautious woman. She rose from the table and steadied her trembling hands while she poured the sheriff a refill of coffee.

"Why you so nervous, Ms. Mae Lou? You ain't got nothing to hide, do ya?"

"No, sir. It's hard talking about it. I ain't never had no trouble. I abide by the law. This questioning is making me nervous."

Before she could finish what she was saying, Carl came through the door. When Carl saw the sheriff sitting at the table, eating, his face darkened.

"Sheriff," he said, and removed his hat.

"Why don't you join us, boy?"

When the sheriff called Carl a boy, I knew my brother wanted to bash his face in. He was long tired of people calling him a boy. He was a grown man, towering over six feet three inches tall. He wasn't the redneck sheriff's boy sitting in his momma's house.

Carl took off his coat and hung it on the back of the chair. "What can I do fo' ya, Sheriff?"

"I need to know what y'all know 'bout the murder."

Momma peered at Carl from across the table. She waited for him to answer the sheriff.

"All we know is he dead and he had a lot of woman friends," Carl said with a straight face.

The sheriff turned toward Momma. She lowered her head.

"Now, Ms. Mae Lou, I ask ya again, how's that make ya feel?"

"Not good, Sheriff, but I didn't know this until after the murder. I didn't know my husband had other women."

"Did he always come home on time? Did he ever give you any clues?"

Momma was fidgety again, rubbing her hands together. "No," she answered, but this time dropping the "sir."

"He drank whiskey, that's all he did," she stressed.

The sheriff had downed the last spoonful of soup and was finishing off his coffee.

"Look, if ya think of som'thin', drop by the house." He got up, put on his coat and left.

Carl told Momma, "He really doesn't care because it wasn't a white man. I don't like it."

CHAPTER 34
PEARL

I remained close to the house, anticipating the sheriff's visit each day. It was rumored that he was a member of the Klan. Some had even heard a story about him lynching a colored man for being out late one night. Because of these rumors the coloreds never willingly asked for help from the law, only when it was forced upon them.

"When the authorities come down here, keep your mouth shut, gurl," Willie said, sitting on the side of the bed.

"We need to go see the sheriff and turn ourselves in," I pleaded with him.

"No, wait."

"They're going to know it was us. Somebody is going to say something."

"That joker had a lot of folks after him. If the sheriff comes down here, let me do the talking. I'm a United States soldier. My word means something."

Most times lying was easy for me, but not in a case where a man had been killed.

"We can't lie. Let's tell the truth and get it over with," I said.

"He had a gun in my ear."

"I know."

"He wanted to kill me. He little, but he's quick." Willie was bitter about being taken by surprise. "He came up behind me and took my gun right out of my belt. He had been drinking, but he was strong as an ox."

"I'm sorry, Willie. He ain't right," I said, shaking my head because I was tired. I waited for him to lash out at me, but he didn't. For some strange reason, he was ready to forgive me now that Herman was dead.

The corn liquor Willie kept under the bed had been the best medicine for my nerves. Willie snuck a shot of liquor each night before he blew the wick out on the lantern, a habit he had brought across the sea after the war. For me it had been a refuge, used every time I reflected back on the night I'd stuck a knife in the back of the man I loved.

"Pearl, he didn't mean you no damn good. I done seen men like that. They come in and take what don't belong to them. Look what he did to Mae Lou, and she's a good woman."

My eyes became slits when I heard him refer to Ms. Mae Lou. I couldn't believe Willie was pouring salt in my wounds.

"That son of a bitch took advantage of her like he did you. He was nothing but a small-time gambler with a lot of street wit." He raised his voice. "He nearly killed me. If you hadn't come, I's be the one in the ground. Forget about him, I'm yo' husband."

Honestly, I was bewildered. For the first time ever, I regretted meeting Herman. I wished I could turn back the hands of time. I had been much happier before getting involved with either Herman or Willie.

That same day the sheriff paid us a visit.

Momma knocked on the bedroom door, and stuck her head in. "The sheriff's out yonder."

Fear flashed across my face as I shifted my gaze over to Willie.

"Let's see what he wants," he said, and stood up.

Momma eased the door closed behind her. "Lord, are you in some sort of trouble, Pearl?" she whispered.

"No, Momma, we're coming. We'll talk to him."

"You're lying again. And you ought to know ain't no white sheriff gonna be fair with coloreds. They mean to us, mean as hell," she warned me.

"It'll be all right, Mrs. Annie May," Willie said, and tapped her on the back as he moved past her.

I remained sitting on the bed.

After he left the bedroom, she said, "Go on in there with him. He yo' husband, not that damn Herman."

I didn't want to, but I got up and followed Willie into the parlor.

The sheriff was a man of medium height with mixed gray hair around his temples. He had the bluest eyes I had ever seen, and peered at me with a stern look of authority. He didn't have on a uniform or any type of regalia that signified his position as an official of the law, other than the badge pinned to the wide lapel of his jacket.

He spoke with a Southern drawl. "Pearl, I need to ask you a few questions."

"Yes, Sheriff," I mumbled.

Before he could ask me anything, Willie interjected. "I'll speak for her, Sheriff."

The sheriff's face flushed pink, and he shot a look at Willie. "Did I ask you anything, boy?"

"I'm a soldier. I just came home from the Great War."

He stared at Willie, and Willie dropped his head. He didn't want to piss the sheriff off by looking him square in the eye.

"I don't give a damn about the war. This is my jurisdiction. I came to talk to Pearl, ya hear? You can leave."

Willie took a deep breath, and held his ground.

"Now, back to my questioning," the sheriff said. "When was the last time you saw Herman Camm?"

"I haven't seen him in a while," I replied nervously.

The sheriff grunted. "What is he to you?"

"He's a friend."

"What kind of darn friend?"

"Why are you asking me these questions?" I asked, my breathing short and my heart racing.

"He's dead. Been murdered..."

"What?" Momma blurted out.

The sheriff pulled his shoulders back and jacked up his pants by the waistline. "The boy was shot with a rifle right square in the forehead. Had a stab wound in his back, too. Somebody meant to kill him cold."

"Sorry, Sheriff," Momma apologized, apparently feeling obligated to the white lawman.

"What about you, Pearl? You mighty calm, after hearing a friend is dead."

Tears welled up in my eyes, even though I was not one for crying. I knew how to put on a good act and tell a good story if I had to, though. I also knew Willie would go along with whatever I said.

"I don't know what to say. He *was* a good friend," I muttered, and tears slid down my cheeks.

"From what I was told, you more than a friend to the boy, he yo' lover. Any truth to that rumor, Pearl?"

"No, sir. We've been friends for years."

"Do you know anything that will help me with this case?"

"No, sir. Herman was a good person. Don't know anybody that would want him dead."

My momma stood in the corner, frowning. Daddy knew to keep his mouth shut. It was much better for a colored woman to speak than a colored man.

"I may have some mo' questions for you later, Pearl. Seems like being a singing star done gone to yo' head. You can't tell the truth no mo'." He put his hat and coat on and left.

He was an incompetent sheriff. He hadn't asked me where I was the night Herman died, or questioned Willie. He was doing what the law normally did when the killer was colored: harass folk for the hell of it.

No one said anything until the sheriff had left the yard.

"Do you know anything, Pearl?" Momma asked.

"I do," I admitted, "but I didn't kill him."

She saw how upset I was, and bowed her head. "I believe you this time, Pearl. I believe you."

Willie and I slept a little sounder after learning about the gunshot to the forehead.

"I knew we didn't kill that joker," Willie said. "Everybody wanted that gambler dead."

The words Willie was saying only brought more sorrow to my heart. While Willie was around, I turned off my tears, but once he'd blown out the lantern and was sound asleep and snoring, I mourned for Herman, my lover, my friend.

CHAPTER 35
CARRIE

I'd been impatient about the investigation. I was hoping and praying that my rape at the hands of Mr. Camm was not discovered and mentioned to the sheriff. I finally breathed a sigh of relief when Carl informed me that the murder investigation had been concluded.

The justice system in Jefferson County would never be fair to colored people as long as rednecks like the sheriff were in charge. I never expected the sheriff to spend a whole lot of time on it.

The townspeople were still concerned about who'd killed Mr. Camm, but not the man himself. *Was a serial murderer on the loose?*

The only person who knew the truth was me, and the rifle standing up behind the door in Momma's room.

I was learning to be a mother. I had learned without complaining how to breast-feed on a schedule, change diapers, and wash the baby's clothes. Caring for a baby had taken a toll on me. I never got enough sleep, and some days it took all of my energy to dress myself.

Ginny said, "What you doing ain't nothing. I used to have one in the stomach and one on the hip, plus I wo'ked. Y'all new-style women is too soft."

After a couple of months, I got the hang of motherhood. I had the baby on a schedule and in between times, I'd chop wood and clean house like Ginny.

One morning when I was feeding the baby, calling him *sugar pie* and *honey bunch*, Ginny said, "That chile is getting too old for those names. Don't no boy want be called by them girly names. I 'spect you's needs to come up with a name fo' the boy."

I had thought about it, and the only name that had a meaning for me was Robert. That was my papa's name. Ginny thought it was a good, solid name for a man.

It was already March and the signs of spring were blowing in with the wind. Buds were appearing on some of the trees, and the brush was sprinkled with green. Spring was coming in faster than expected.

I had been with Ginny for two months. I missed Momma, Carl, and John. Ginny and I had a wonderful relationship, but inside I yearned for my family. Ginny always had the instinctual ability to read me. "It's time ya take that baby to visit his grandma."

"She probably doesn't want to see us," I said, and sat down at the kitchen table.

"Ev'rybody wants to know their chirren, especially Mae Lou. She's a good lady, been through a lot."

"Yes, you're right. I hope she wants to see me, too."

I had prayed for Momma after Mr. Camm's death. She was all alone. I hoped that she would acknowledge what he'd done and accept both me and my baby.

The next day, just before noon, Ginny helped me hitch Ignite and Excite to the buggy. Her horses were named for her husband, who had been dead for over twenty years. "He was a young man when he left this world. Fo' a long time after he went to glory, I'd think 'bout him. He knew how to please me, so I named them ole mules Excite and Ignite." Ginny chuckled and her cheeks flushed.

The baby was wrapped tight in one of the blankets Ginny made especially for him. She'd sewn gowns and booties for Robert's feet. I held him close to my bosom and coaxed the ole mules along. The wind was stiff and chilly. The trees swayed with the breeze. The last time I'd traveled on this road was the day I'd left home.

It didn't take Momma long to open the door. A big smile rippled across her face as soon as she saw us. She reached for Robert, and I relinquished him to her. She was overcome. A tear slid down the side of her cheek. She reached in her apron pocket and pulled out a handkerchief and patted her cheek.

After all of that, she hugged me.

"I thought maybe you wanted to see the baby," I said, hesitantly.

"I'm so glad you came by. I've wondered about you, worried, too. But I knew Ginny would take care of you."

Momma went in the kitchen and sat down at the table. I followed.

"It's cold outside. Let me make you some tea, or maybe some coffee." Robert was still asleep in Momma's arms.

It was cold but the sun was shining and everything around us appeared warmer than it really was outside.

"Yes, ma'am, I'll take some. The wind is stirring today."

Momma handed me the baby. I laid him across my knee while she poured a cup of coffee.. The kitchen stove was fired up with wood and it was comfortable in the house.

"I am glad that Ginny took you in," she said, and then sipped her coffee. She looked healthy, but her eyes were still sad.

"She's been a blessing to me. How are you doing, Momma?"

"Chile, I'm still kicking." She reached over to take the baby. He woke up, but he didn't whimper. Robert was a good child. He rarely cried, only when he was wet or hungry.

"What's his name?" she asked, looking at the baby.

"I named him after Papa. He had a fine name."

She was very pleased."Yes, and he was a mighty fine man. I wish he was still living. He was one hardworking man." She paused and sipped her coffee. "It's been a little lonesome here without you."

I knew it took a great deal for her to admit that she missed me. Momma had never been good at expressing her feelings, even when Papa died.

"Carrie, I'm sorry 'bout what happened to you. I didn't understand at the time. I must've been preoccupied with my own self. I hope that one day you can forgive me for asking you to leave."

"Momma," I said, "I'm sorry, too. I wish that I'd felt better about telling you what had happened, and maybe it would not have gone as far as it did."

"Oh, chile, I have made many mistakes in my life. One was alienating my children. I carried out some of the same traditions that my momma did to me. I couldn't talk and I couldn't show emotions. I wish that I could tell you how much I care, but I don't know how." She pulled out her hanky again to catch a stray tear rolling down her cheek.

"Momma, I wish that I could have told you, too. Don't blame yourself for what happened to me. You adopted me when I was a baby and gave me a home, as much as any mother could give. I owe you the world for that. I love you, Momma."

I stayed long enough to finish my coffee. Momma still looked good in spite of the hurt she'd been exposed to in the last two months. Neither one of us mentioned Mr. Camm's name.

"You are welcome to come see me. Your room is still empty if you need a place to stay. Please let my grandchild get to know me."

As I was wrapping my head and making sure the baby was tucked in tight, she went into her room and came back with a letter.

"I know you's will want to read this," she said, smiling. "It's from Simon."

I put my arms around Momma and hugged her as tightly as I could. She needed a hug just as I did.

I put the letter inside my coat. She stood on the porch and watched us until we were out of sight. The wind calmed down a bit on the way back to Ginny's, and the old mules seemed to trot faster. I slowed them down to maintain control of the baby, who was starting to whimper.

My curiosity was getting the best of me. I had thought about Simon for most of the time I'd been at Ginny's. Inside I felt resentment toward him for his reaction. My first instinct was to throw the letter in the trash, but I loved him. Still, after I returned to Ginny's, I didn't open the letter until after I'd eaten dinner. I bathed the baby and put him to bed before I had the courage to read Simon's letter. Lying under the covers with the baby snuggled close to me, I opened the letter, dated January 25, 1921. It read:

Carrie,

Please excuse my handwriting. I'm not used to writing long letters. I'm here in Richmond waiting for the season to start again. I'm ashamed of the way I acted when you told me about what happened to you. I was hurt because I wanted to be the man for you, and I should have supported you through the hurt you were feeling. It was wrong, the way that I reacted, and I hope that you can forgive me. I want you to be my wife and would like you and the baby to join me in Richmond. You can finish school here. Think about it and let me know. Please write back.

Love always,

Simon

Tears of joy welled up in my eyes. I was speechless, holding the letter in my hand. I had never expected to hear from Simon again, even though I had said many prayers for him.

I loved him, and I needed him in my life.

I picked up my pen to write him back, yet I couldn't find the words. I decided that I wanted to go, start a new life. It was now or never. I didn't waste time writing a letter back to him. I pulled out the money I'd saved and counted it. My savings totaled twenty-six dollars. It was enough money to catch the train to Richmond, with quite a bit left over.

The train stopped in Jefferson once a week. Each time it arrived at the same time from Roanoke, Virginia, and headed to Richmond and then on to Washington, D.C. I knew its schedule, as I had hoped the day would come when I'd leave Jefferson.

I borrowed an old suitcase from Ginny and packed clothes. The night passed quickly. I spent most of it writing thank you notes to Ginny and Mrs. Gaines.

Before Ginny got up, I went into her bedroom and kissed her. It was the first time I had beat her getting up.

"Be safe, my dear," she said. "I knew this day would come." Then she smiled and kissed the baby.

I left the house with the baby on my hip. My pace was brisk, trying to get to my Momma's house before the train came. The walk to Momma's was hard. It was cold and windy. It was difficult juggling the baby and the suitcase, so I stopped at the school and left the suitcase behind the big tree, then headed on.

I stayed long enough to feed the baby and get warm, drinking a cup of coffee before I left. I did not want to miss my ride. I promised Momma that I would write and visit her. Her last words before I left were, "Promise me that you will go back to school and graduate."

On my way to the train station, I saw the sign that said the Greater Providence Baptist Church, and slowed down. I stepped softly over the new graves in the cemetery, making my way to where my father was buried. His name was engraved in large letters above his grave, *Robert Parker*. I couldn't leave without telling my papa good-bye. I kneeled down beside his burial place and told him my plans.

My last stop was at the schoolyard. By the time I got there, Hester and Anna were about to go inside. I assured them that I would write and that one day we'd all be able to get together again as friends.

When they went inside, I stood under the big tree, observing the heart that I had carved in the trunk: *Carrie loves Simon.* Then I stood there with the baby's head resting on my shoulder. I prayed for guidance in my new adventure in Richmond. I picked up my suitcase and started to leave the schoolyard. I turned and glanced back at the heart carved in the evergreen pine tree. *Even the tree knew all my secrets*, I thought.

The train stop was only a few feet from the blackberry patch where Momma and I had picked berries. As I passed it, even though they were not in bloom, I yearned for the sweet days of summer.

I made it to the depot at 1:45, just in time for the two o'clock train. I had run most of the way. After the porter took my suitcase and assisted us in finding a seat in the colored section, I smiled down at my beautiful baby.

I never looked back.

ABOUT THE AUTHOR

Ruth P. Watson has written for *Upscale*, *The Atlanta Journal-Constitution*, *Lynchburg Area News Journal* and *The Minority Business Enterprise*. She has a master's degree in business and has worked as an adjunct professor. She is the recipient of a Caversham Writers Fellowship in Kwa Zulu Natal, South Africa, and a finalist in the *Writers Digest* Mainstream Fiction Contest. She is a member of Delta Sigma Theta Sorority Inc., and attends Cascade United Methodist Church. She lives in Atlanta, GA with her husband and son. You can visit her at www.ruthpwatson.com

READER'S DISCUSSION GUIDE

1. *Blackberry Days of Summer* is the title of the book. What did the title suggest to you before reading it? It holds a great deal of meaning to Carrie in the book. What did you take away concerning the title after reading the book?

2. Were you surprised to learn about Carrie's family background? How did it help you understand her story?

3. What effect does family have on the characters in the novel? How did Mae Lou and Pearl share similar dreams? How were their dreams fulfilled? Why is the Southern setting ideal for the formation of dreams?

4. What made Mr. Camm so appealing to the ladies? How did someone with his demeanor have such a mesmerizing attraction for Mae Lou and Pearl?

5. What kind of conflicts do you think Carrie struggled with after finding her extended family? How does that affect her relationship with Mae Lou?

6. There are many strong men in the novel: Robert, Carl, Simon, Willie and John. Each of them longed for a certain type of freedom of identity, so how do they obtain it?

7. World War I is a time of The Great War, so how did the black man fit into this war and how did that experience affect him once he returned to the United States?

8. Pearl is a woman with a lot of experience with men. She has everything: the looks, profession and a man who adores her, yet something is missing. What is she really yearning for?

9. Why is Washington, D.C. so important for the time period? Why are federal jobs so hard to find for the Black Dough Boys?

10. Mrs. Ferguson is a typical Southern belle, however, for a while, she appears to be sympathetic and caring. Why do you think the author included that in the novel? Mrs. Gaines, on the other hand, is in need, and color is not really an issue. Why is she different?

11. Were you surprised when Simon left Carrie? Did you think they would get back together? Were you rooting for Carrie?

12. When Pearl leaves Willie, did you think she would take him back?

13. Why do you think Mae Lou didn't believe her own daughter? Why did she ask her to leave? Were you surprised by her actions?

14. Why is Ginny such a strong character? What is it about her that is so appealing to Carrie?

15. The church is the gathering place for the country folks, yet when Topsie is assaulted, no one would give her any help. Why do you think everyone was so judgmental? Why would she be considered edgy in the 21st century?

16. When an investigation is sparked by the murder, why is it that no one really cares?

17. Why is Ginny not considered a suspect in the investigation?

18. All of the main characters have histories that haunt them. How does the past become influential in the outcome of their futures?

19. How does *Blackberry Days of Summer* open the door to a world so mundane, yet so complicated? How do the lives of three women collide into a whirlwind of emotions? How quickly does the love turn into pain?

20. What does Simon represent in the story? How do Mae Lou and Carrie finally come together?

21. Who is the real heroine in the story? Do you feel it is Pearl, Carrie, Mae Lou? Or is it Ginny?

22. Through a keen use of dialogue, the reader is able to get into the characters' heads. What concerns does the author leave you with at the conclusion of the novel?